ELIJAH'S
Need

SHARK'S EDGE: BOOK NINE

VICTORIA BLUE

ELIJAH'S
Need

SHARK'S EDGE: BOOK NINE

VICTORIA BLUE

WATERHOUSE PRESS

For David, the only one I'll ever need.

CHAPTER ONE

ELIJAH

"It's hard. This is really hard... Okay, you remember we were friends when we were really young, and then we met again on the streets when we were, what? Fourteen? Fifteen? Something like that?"

"Yeah, something like that," Bas agreed.

"I never told you why I couldn't go home... always said family issues or some version of that."

"Right," Bas and Grant said in chorus while they waited for the bomb to drop.

"Well, the truth is..." I swallowed so hard it felt like a golf ball was moving down my throat. "I stabbed my father forty-two times, and he bled to death on the kitchen floor of my family's Bel Air mansion."

Silence.

No one said a damn word after I mortared the group with my admission. I waited for the explosion to ripple through our landscape. My life was about to change with the revelation of my darkest secret.

"Well, shiiiit..." Grant finally broke the quiet air with a response. "I've known you for most of your life, and this calm Zen thing you have going on has always been a part of your personality. There had to have been an irrefutable cause for you to do something like that."

I couldn't be sure if I felt worse or better with his unyielding support. The friendship I'd built with these two men was something I cherished as dearly as my burgeoning relationship with Hannah. I should've known in my heart that I could've told them this information years ago—then, so much of Hensley's betrayal wouldn't have mattered. Much of the devastation I'd felt when she walked out was rooted in my fear that she would reveal this secret just to hurt the people I cared about most.

Well, not anymore. And it felt so damn good to finally take that power away from her. As I nodded in agreement with Grant's assumption, I hoped like hell I wouldn't have to go into too much detail as follow-up.

But I should've known between Bas and Hannah, one of these formidably curious people would need more information before declaring all forgiven.

"In the past, you've made comments about your father that gave me the impression he wasn't a nice man," Hannah said cautiously. "Maybe abusive to you and your mother? Violent around the home at the very least? Am I on the right track?" My beautiful woman looked at me with empathy and compassion, not the accusation and distrust I had expected.

How unfair had I been to not give her the benefit of the doubt? After I'd met her parents, who seemed as perfect and wholesome as a couple could be, I thought for sure this kind of data dump would have her running for the hills. Couldn't have hurt, once again, that I had bound her to my physical body with the handcuffs. At least she couldn't take off and try to rationalize her emotions while in hiding as I'd witnessed her do before.

He was a cruel motherfucker," I replied. "He beat my mother on a weekly basis. Toward the end of his life, it was more often than that. But the night I ended him, he was on a rampage." I shuddered, remembering his booming voice as he thundered through our home.

Hannah stroked her free hand up and down my arm to ward off the memory. Not thinking, I lifted her hand to my lips and kissed her knuckles, beseeching her to understand my motive. "Please don't think less of me because of this. I know that's a lot to ask you to sidestep, but I've lived every day since that one trying to be a better man. Better than I was for losing control that night, and a better man than he ever showed me how to be."

"Elijah . . ." She sighed, and it felt like she was breathing her life-force directly into my lungs. She gave me strength and courage just by uttering my name so soothingly.

"Let's go, Twombley," Bas issued as they both stood again. "These two need privacy."

"You don't want to ask questions? Need details?" I began to ask, and Sebastian held up his hand for me to stop.

"No, I don't." He gave an exaggerated visual reference to Grant and asked, "Do you?"

"No, man, like I said before, we got you. Always."

We all shook hands and did the usual bro-hug thing we did, and Bas looked me square in the eye and spoke his mind. Exactly what I wanted and exactly what I expected.

"Go fix things with her." He pointed past me to Hannah. "That's where you need to concentrate all your effort right now."

"I don't know how to thank you guys for being so understanding about this. For years, I was convinced that this would destroy our friendship. I was a coward for not telling you and for not believing in our bonded history."

"Don't get all sappy now. We'll have a thorough interrogation up top tomorrow." Bas gave me a playful punch in the arm while Grant looked on in amazement.

"Who is this guy?" I said to our tall friend after gesturing toward Shark.

Grant shook his head from side to side as we both stared at Sebastian. "I was just thinking the same thing."

"Don't hurt yourselves trying to think too hard. Recent changes in my own life have shown me what matters and what doesn't. That's all it is."

Grant looked skeptical while answering, "All right, man. If you insist."

An echo of the front door closing broke the silence in the room. I turned to face Hannah with no idea where we would go from here. I owed her answers if she wanted them, time if she needed it, and physical space if that was what she asked for.

Okay, maybe not that last one.

She couldn't meet my entreating gaze when I turned back to her. She shuffled from foot to foot and stared at the floor like it had become the most interesting tile she'd ever seen.

"Do you want to sit down?" I asked, trying to break through the awkward silence.

"If you want to," she said in the quietest voice I had ever heard from her.

"It's not about what I want right now. If this were about what I wanted, none of that bullshit would have ever come into the light of day. Although I admit I feel like a weight has been lifted off my shoulders now that all of you know. I'm tired of having that little bitch threaten me with exposing that truth to the people I love."

"Really? She has been threatening you?" Hannah asked, finally directing her beautiful, wide blue eyes toward me.

"Yes, she has. From the day she found out that I wanted a paternity test. That was right after she walked out of my life. As recently as a few days ago, she leveled the threat again. She's been using something I confided in her in a weak moment of trust like a weapon."

We got comfortable on the sofa, but not in the usual way we used to sit, with me deep in the corner of the sectional and her in my arms. I would have given anything to hold her, but this situation was still too raw. Now it compounded the nightmare she'd endured the previous night—and all because of her association with me.

"Hannah, please know that that was the singular time in my life I ever chose violence with another human being. I'm not proud of what I did, but something in me snapped that night. I was young, raging with hormones I didn't understand, and had witnessed my father beat my mother to death." I closed my eyes and took a deep breath, trying to rid my mind's eye of the scene of that crime. It was right there in Technicolor as if it had just happened in front of us.

For years, when I heard a woman scream in distress or a man's threatening voice, I would feel the effects of that night all over again. It took a lot of personal growth and determination to get beyond that sort of reaction. I learned a lot of techniques to calm myself and avoid legitimate panic attacks, much like what I had witnessed Hannah go through. Several times now.

"Know that at any time you can ask me questions or comment on this situation, and I will not get angry. I owe you my honesty. Right now, you must be considering me the world's biggest hypocrite."

"Elijah..." Hannah sighed my name again. "Please don't beat yourself up. Especially on my behalf. It's not something I care to witness or need you to put yourself through to atone for what happened two decades ago."

"Then how do I? How can I be sure you don't think I'm a monster? I swear you are not in danger here with me. Quite the opposite. I'm trying to keep you safe. And don't think I don't see the irony in that situation too. If you weren't involved with me, you wouldn't have been in danger in the first place. I will never forgive myself for what happened to you last night and that I wasn't there to protect you. But I will do everything in my power to ensure that you are never in danger again. And if that means we go away somewhere while all this blows over, then that's what we'll do. Maybe Bas has to figure out what kind of trouble he's stirred up without me this time."

She began shaking her head before I was done with my declaration. "No. That's not the kind of friend you are. Or the kind of man you are. We will stay here and figure this out, right alongside your lifelong friends. If you feel like you owe someone some sort of penance, then help Sebastian figure out what all this is about."

While she searched my eyes, I couldn't help but think what a gift this woman was in my life. But I wasn't sure what she wanted from me now. Maybe a commitment that I wouldn't abandon my friends? Maybe a vow of complete honesty just like I had been demanding she gave me? Whatever she needed, I would give it to her. Unerringly. Unquestionably. Undeniably.

Leaning my head back on the sofa, I closed my eyes and deeply exhaled. I was exhausted, and I imagined Hannah was too.

"How does a bath sound?" I asked hopefully and kept my gaze on the ceiling.

When she held our handcuffed wrists up in answer, I tried to sweeten the deal.

"I can sit on the side. Or we can do it together." Before she could object, I held my hand up for her to pause. "I promise I'll be a gentleman." Regardless of my words, my dick kicked to life at the suggestion.

Hannah tilted her head to the side with a wordless *bullshit*, and I couldn't help the grin that spread across my lips. Some behavior was just habit, and denying the idea that getting lost in her body was exactly what I needed would just be untrue.

"Is that a yes?" I asked while standing and pulling her to stand with me. "Please let me care for you. Let me treat you like my queen."

"Oh, Mr. Banks. You and that silver tongue," she answered with a small smile, but it was a gesture I would greedily accept.

"Now why do you want to say something like that?" I asked and kissed the side of her head while we strolled toward the bedroom. "I just promised to be a gentleman, and now all I can think of is showing you just how good I can make you feel with my tongue." I felt her step falter but kept tugging her along beside me.

While we stood in the bathroom, Hannah fretted. "How are we going to get these off?" She lifted our joined hands as if I didn't know what she was talking about. "You have to have another set of keys and you're just not telling me," she accused. "And how am I going to get undressed? I can't get my shirt off with these here." Her voice gained that husky depth that shot straight to my cock.

Christ, even her frustration turned me on.

Trying not to shock her, I slowly grabbed the material of her shirt in both hands and met her stare before I tore it from her body.

"I liked that shirt!" she yelped.

"I'll buy you a new one," I answered quickly and stretched across her to turn on the faucet to fill the enormous tub. I couldn't remember the last time I'd used the thing. Women never spent more than one night in my home and never in my bed. Before Hannah, I always fooled around in one of the guest rooms, keeping this suite private and sacred. Even Shawna, the only woman since Hensley to have a repeat audience with me, never stepped foot in this space.

But like so many other things with this intoxicating, interesting, captivating woman, I wanted all our experiences to be different from my casual hookups. From day one, I knew Hannah Farsey was unique.

My shirt met the same fate as hers, and the scraps of fabric lay in a pile on the gleaming floor. I shucked my pants and boxers in one swift motion and added them to the heap. But my woman stood motionless and stared at my body. Normally, I would automatically assume it was rapt interest, but today was anything but normal. And this woman proved time and time again that she wasn't like other women.

"What is it, baby?" I asked with concern.

"I don't think I will ever get used to how stunning you are," she husked. Her quiet tone skittered up my spine and made my nerves tingle.

"Thank you." I pulled her into my chest and buried my face in her hair. "Thank you, thank you, thank you."

The woman leaned back so she could take in my expression and then asked, "What is all that for? Why are you saying thank you over and over?" She laughed a little and added, "I'm the one who should be thanking you. And I haven't done that. Not once." She looked down shyly after voicing her realization.

Where was she going with this attitude one-eighty? Before I could stifle the urge, I interrupted. "What do you have to thank me for?"

In a flash, I considered listing all the shitty things that happened in the past twenty-four hours and quickly decided against it. Why remind her of all my shortcomings, bad decisions, and moments I used questionable judgment? Instead, I waited for her to regroup and reply.

"Thank you for coming for me today when Mr. Cole called you. Thank you for inviting your friends over to shed some light on what's been going on in your lives lately. That information filled in a lot of gaps I just couldn't rationalize through. And then, why I was targeted by those creeps. And thank you"—she placed our joined hands over my heart—"Mr. Elijah Banks, for being the unbelievably good man that you are." She softly patted my chest as she finished sharing her grace.

I tilted my head and narrowed my eyes in confusion. Maybe with a touch of suspicion too. I just confessed to murdering my own father in cold blood, and this goddess was thanking me. Fortunately, though, the bath water was at the perfect level, so I busied myself with turning off the faucet while trying to work through what was happening between us. It felt like every single move was a vital step in repairing her trust, attraction, and willingness to be present in the moment with me.

I pointedly looked at her jeans. "One of us is overdressed." I took a visual stroll up and down my own body and then looked to her. "Guess who?"

She offered a coy smirk, and my heart swelled—and so did my cock—but what else was new when this one was around? Her genuine smile, offered in earnest, melted my fears from the past few hours. That one expression gave me hope that we would come out on the other side of this disastrous day. Maybe—just maybe—we would be stronger for the experience. A guy could dream, right?

Hannah and I worked together to get her jeans off. Then I had the honor of peeling her little red panties down her thighs, over her shapely calves, and off her sexy ankles. There wasn't an inch of this woman's body that didn't arouse me.

With an offered hand for stability, I wordlessly invited my beauty to climb in before me. The moment her foot touched the water, she moaned.

"This was a great idea. Thank you for being so thoughtful, Elijah."

"Scoot forward, baby, so I can get in behind you," I issued, and she followed my instruction.

After I was completely submerged, I tugged her back to lie against my body. Holding her, while simple and chaste, could ignite my blood as much as having her on her knees before me. But I promised myself to follow her lead with intimacy until she made it completely clear where her head was on the matter. I didn't want to be insensitive or too pushy, and both of those things were deeper rooted in my nature than giving her the space she might need.

Until Hannah came into my orbit. Now I would be the gentleman she deserved instead of the scoundrel I was known to be. This woman deserved my very best—of everything. If she let me, I would spend a lifetime atoning for putting her in harm's way.

Regardless of all the inner pep talks and silent promises, biology was biology. My body knew what it wanted. With her slippery and wet against my skin . . . well, what did either of us expect would happen?

"Sorry," I muttered and tried to rearrange things so she wasn't getting jabbed by my erection.

"The body knows what the body wants," she replied, and even though I just had the same thought, I couldn't make heads or tails of her tone. Was it possible she was feeling the same way in our cozy bath time arrangement? I wouldn't take it for granted, though.

"I'm not going to make a move on you until you tell me you are ready. If that takes twenty minutes or twenty days, I'll follow your lead." I couldn't help burying my nose in her hair while I spoke.

"I appreciate that. For one thing, I'm so tired."

"I imagine you are. As soon as we're done here, I'll tuck you into bed and wait on you hand and foot until you're ready to get out," I promised.

"That won't be necessary. If you would unlock these damn cuffs, I think I'd rather settle in my old room for a few days until we decide what we're going to do."

Yeah, fuck that.

"Can you elaborate on that a little more? What do you mean when you say what we're going to do?"

"I mean what we're going to do. Exactly what I said," she snapped suddenly. "Christ, it's not a complicated remark."

If she didn't have her back to me, I'd be warning her with every facial feature I had control of. But I had to remind myself that she got testy when she was tired. Patience had never been a virtue of mine either, so I hoped after a good night's sleep, she'd feel more like herself. I wouldn't push her right now. I couldn't. The bottom line was I had no right to.

I felt like a fucking fraud. And it wasn't a good sensation for a man like me. I was normally very confident—to the point of being cocky. For the better part of my life, I lived by a code I'd written for myself. My way, my rules, and I was typically satisfied with what I put back into the world. Now, a handful of hours passed, and I was questioning everything I knew about myself.

Hypocrisy was uncharted water in my world. It was that simple. Even though every time I preached to Hannah about needing complete honesty, I felt a little twinge reminding me I wasn't living by my own rules. But I was always able to rationalize the nagging feeling away by internally insisting that all was done with the purist intentions and to build a solid foundation for a future with this woman. That clarity and conviction had giant bullet holes in it now.

More like stab wounds, I supposed.

CHAPTER TWO

HANNAH

Exhausted. Shocked and exhausted didn't make the best combination for restful sleep. Fortunately, and unfortunately, I also had an appetizer of terror the night before, so the onset of sleep came easily. It was staying asleep that was proving to be difficult.

Sometime in the night, I felt the handcuff release from my wrist, and I wrapped my arms around myself. I didn't turn and ask him why he finally decided to do it, but I did catalog yet another lie. He had insisted he couldn't unlock them but apparently had a key the whole time.

My anger percolated like an old-fashioned electric coffeepot. Similarly, the longer I lay there, the stronger my anger grew. From coffee to espresso, ladies and gentlemen. Rather than get into an argument with Elijah, though, I focused on my breathing and reined in the emotion. He had to be as tired as I was at this point, and nothing would be settled overnight.

Without my permission, my thoughts started layering one on top of another.

Cut the bullshit, girl. You're already in up to your eyeballs.

Yeah, yeah. I knew what deep emotional trouble I was in without winning an argument with my own conscience about it. And what was that about? Wasn't I even on my own side? If I didn't preserve my dignity, sanity, and stability when it came to this man, he would completely bulldoze over my principles to have his way.

If I just followed my heart, I would let him. Maybe I'd resist a little, because damn it, didn't he deserve to have to work a little? Why should I make it so easy for him to sweep right in and have me back in his grasp? Every notion of self-preservation had been conquered with little effort up to this point.

I felt like a doormat. I'd been in this position in a relationship before and had sworn I wouldn't do it again. That breakup took a lot of self-help and a lot of shed tears before I reconnected with my true self. And I didn't feel half the emotional intensity for that dude as I did for Elijah.

This whole situation sucked. I'd waited years for the right guy to come along. The afternoon Elijah and Grant stormed Abstract Catering's prep kitchen, I felt the earth move beneath my feet. At the time, I didn't have a clue just how utterly captivating he was. My breath stuttered that day just from his appearance. I had no idea how sinfully skilled he was with his body, and how challenging and intriguing in mind. The sum of all his parts was an overwhelming, charming, and sophisticated package.

In my heart, I wanted to work things out between us. It was my damn brain that kept throwing up the red flags. By my age, a girl knew to listen to her head before her heart. The problem was if I let my head take the wheel, my heart would never be the same. It wouldn't be a matter of listening to it. It would be a matter of destroying it.

But the lies . . .

How could I rationalize all the lies? Especially because the bossy guy insisted on complete honesty from everyone else. It wasn't just me. He insisted on one hundred percent honesty from everyone in his life. Yet, he couldn't return that same courtesy to any of us.

Ummm ... hypocrite, is that you?

With a silent chuckle at my own sassy thought, I slithered out of bed as quietly as possible. Though I appreciated my untethered freedom, I looked back at the still-sleeping god of a man and could feel my heart actually ache. I didn't know if I could get by without him now. Even though we hadn't been together very long, he had become a vital part of my day. Of my life. My soul.

Vision blurred from unfallen tears as I slowly stepped back from the bed. I could do this. I had to do this. Another step back. Five more and I'd be out the door of the luxurious master suite. Finally standing in the doorway, I turned and hustled out of the room and down the hall.

The room I had first stayed in was on the other side of the kitchen, and the house was still dark in the early morning hours. I felt my way along familiar furniture and corners until I was there. I had to pack up my stuff as quickly and quietly as possible if I was going to get away with this escape plan. I kicked myself for having unpacked again after I thought I was going home to my parents. It would have been so much easier if it was all still in my car.

I flopped down on the bed and imagined his next flavor of the month being assigned to this room. Pictured her reaction at the grandeur of the property, the sighs on her lips when he touched her the first time.

What am I doing? Why am I torturing myself?

God, those visions stabbed me right in my already tender heart. Would he move on? Would it be that easy? I'd leave and be devastated for months, and he would probably open his little black book and get a replacement before I made it to Brentwood.

No, now I was being unfair. To him—to me—to us. I had to believe we had more than his usual romps. It was the only way I could leave—if I believed we still had a chance to work this out. These negative thoughts weren't going to keep the fire burning, though, so that shit could stay out of my head for now. I was stronger than that. Stronger than letting my own damaged self-esteem be the beacon I followed. Because I had seen that destination before, and it was a lonely, sad place.

With the most important things packed in the two suitcases I'd arrived with, I turned back to take in the room one last time. I left all the things he gave me behind with one exception—a small, beautiful lapel pin of a hot-air balloon. I would treasure it forever.

My life had changed here. There would be beautiful memories in my mind and in my heart for a long time. Maybe the rest of my life. The time I spent in this room getting to know that amazing man would always be cherished. A deep sigh and the light *snick* of the door closing played in the background as another piece of my heart fell away.

"I don't think I'm going to survive this," I whispered to the dawn's light filtering in through the blinds' slats. Once again, I battled to hold back the tears. A lump formed in my throat, making it difficult to breathe, but I couldn't have another breakdown here.

At the door between the house and the garage, I paused at the security alarm panel. The system was engaged for the overnight hours, as usual, and I realized I didn't have a code for the thing. I wasn't going to be able to get out without setting it off. If I did that, he'd be in here so fast my head would spin.

Then he would crowd me with his firm, muscular body. I would lose all coherent thoughts and have a mental reprieve from the pain. All reasonable plans of leaving would evaporate into the morning air. Of course, now my traitor body tingled at the thought of his body against mine.

Maybe if he would just talk to me and explain away all the lies, I could pretend none of this was happening. At least for a little longer. That his behavior didn't throw up major red flags. That he hadn't lost my trust.

A low groan escaped from deep in my chest, and it felt good. Exorcising these negative emotions, even if it was just one small thing at a time, might be my only chance at making it through this nightmare. Maybe he would make love to me one last time and I could hold on to that memory with fierce determination while we were apart.

Shit. What was I going to do? Oh, idea! I pulled out my phone to text Marc. He and I had formed a sort of bond that day when we drove around waiting for the police to secure Shawna at the house. The security guard was always so kind. Maybe he could give me the code. It was worth a shot.

> *Hey, Marc, it's Hannah. Sorry for the early text. I'm such a dork… can't remember the code to disarm the security system. Can you give it to me, please?*

While I waited for his reply, I debated sending another message with a string of emojis like my sister. It always made me laugh when she did it, but I decided against it. Didn't want to come off extra.

So I waited... and waited. I watched the throbbing ellipses from his end cycle on and off before a return message finally arrived.

I'm so sorry, Ms. Farsey. Mr. Banks
instructed the team not to let you leave
the property. Safety reasons.

For a few moments, I just stood in the middle of the kitchen, gaping in disbelief. I checked the message again because maybe I just read it wrong.

That high-handed motherfucker. I made a furious beeline back to the master bedroom and kicked the door so hard that it flew open and bounced off the doorstop on the baseboard.

Elijah jacked straight to sitting at the booming noise the heavy panel made and instantly looked ready to defend his home.

"What? What's going on?" he demanded, and I seethed harder.

"I swear to God, if you were standing here, I'd fucking knee you in the balls. How dare you tell your guard dogs to keep me here! Did you tell them it was against my will?"

He just stared at me for a few seconds and then eased back to his pillow. He rubbed his face with his palms, and I couldn't look away. I wasn't sure what the next move would be as I studied his features. He looked like he was having to really work at staying in control, and I realized I'd seen him do these things before and completely misinterpreted what was happening.

For the first time, I wondered if he really had a problem with his temper. How could that not be in the back of my mind after what he confessed to?

Ahhh, thoughts for another time, girl.

Right now, I was still summarily pissed off.

"What?" I snapped, and he slowly turned his face in my direction.

Uh-oh. That might have been one too many sassy demands for my formidable man. Well, used-to-be man. Again, the awful reminder that he was never totally mine danced around in my mind.

Elijah stalked to where I stood defiantly. I refused to be intimidated by his physical prowess or his intoxicating dominance. Through widened nostrils, I sucked in a breath before spewing more anger.

"You can't keep someone against their will. That's kidnapping. I should know!" He winced at my reminder, but I wasn't done. "It's the same fucking thing!" I shouted, even though he was inches from me.

"Lower your voice this instant," he growled while boring into me with his ice-green stare.

"I'll yell if I want! You aren't my keeper, Elijah."

He just tilted his head to the side in challenge but was smart enough not to say anything. When his fucking hair toppled to the side, I groaned.

I closed my eyes and muttered, "Asshole," then turned to stomp back to the door. Now that he was awake, who fucking cared if I set off the alarm?

But I misjudged his speed and agility once again. His large palm cuffed my bicep, and he spun me back to face him with very little effort.

"Take your fucking hands off me right now," I threatened and arrowed him with a lethal look.

Now he was the one inhaling sharply through flared nares. "Fuck, Hannah. I feel like you're squeezing my cock with your hand when you give me those looks. Don't fucking roll your eyes either. I never promised to be anything but a dirty man." He stepped closer. Closer. When his leading foot was between my two, he pressed me back against the wall with his chest.

I watched him from outside myself as he picked up my hands from where they hung limply by my sides. One by one, he kissed each knuckle while never breaking the magic spell of his intense stare. My turncoat libido downshifted and revved hotter.

Don't give in. Don't give in. Don't give in.

Maybe if I continued to chant those encouraging words, I would stand a chance at resisting him. Especially as he circled his hips into my body and I felt his erection heavy between us.

"Do you feel that?" he taunted and made another maddening circle with his lithe hips.

When I didn't respond, he hooked a finger under my chin and raised my face to meet his waiting green eyes.

"I asked you a question."

First, I huffed and then answered, "Yes, I feel you."

"Come back to bed. Let me have you. I need to feel you from the inside." He let his heavy lids drop to fan his dark lashes over his cheeks.

"I want you so bad, Hannah." His statement started out seductively but turned inside out by the end. The anguish in his tone cut me. But as I looked on, his demeanor transformed. I could smell the dizzying sexual need ripe on his skin, wafting off him, and a shiver racked my body.

Elijah grinned that damn wicked and sexy grin of his, and I was equally aroused and angered. Why? Why did my body sell me out this way?

No, I'm stronger than this.

"Stop. Don't get any crazy ideas." But my weak words came out with little conviction.

"Oh, baby, if you had half a clue about the ideas in my head right now..." He left the words hanging in the air like a pinata waiting to be cracked open. While most men's eyes got darker with arousal, his went the other direction. They were the lightest mint green and so piercing while he stared at me, awaiting my reaction.

"Am I supposed to be scared right now? Is that what you're trying to do here?"

"That sassy mouth is writing checks your ass doesn't want to cash. Trust me."

"I'm leaving." I wiggled from between him and the wall and made my way to the door. Damn, I'd really kicked that thing hard. There was a sizable dent in the trim where the doorstop was mounted.

Tough shit.

I shrugged with the thought before whirling around to him one last time. "Either turn the security alarm off, or I'm going to set it off when I open the garage door."

"Please, Hannah. Please don't leave." He looked utterly devastated when he issued the plea. "Don't walk out on me. On us."

I couldn't take it. I couldn't stand here and look at his face while he begged me. It was breaking me. I turned on my heel and headed down the hall. I heard his footsteps right behind me, so I picked up my pace, nearly jogging by the time I got to the door.

"Please . . ." he said again.

Facing the door, I paused, clutching the handle for support. "I need space. Time. I'm confused and, frankly, scared. I need some time in my head."

"I can't let you go. I won't do it." He moved in behind me and put his hand over mine on the door. "There's still too much danger, and I swore to protect you."

"You don't owe me your personal security, Elijah." I felt his frustrated exhale on the back of my neck.

"Baby, please. Please don't make this more difficult than it has to be." His voice modulated to his normal timbre, and in my periphery, I saw him reach out to touch me and then pull back.

I whirled around to face him and still felt so much hurt and anger that I couldn't imagine what my expression looked like.

"Make what more difficult, exactly?" Oh yeah, my voice still held a healthy amount of contempt too. With the toe of my sneaker, I tapped the floor while I waited for his answer.

"Can we sit and talk?" the man asked with the hope of a child on Christmas morning.

I could give him this. A few minutes, I promised myself. Then I would leave. My heart, while wanting so badly to reconcile with him, ran and took shelter. I felt the stutter in my chest as the pain of being without him in my life skittered through my body.

"Fine." My answer was more of a choke. The lump in my throat had gained mass, and it was hard to even breathe.

When he tried tugging me back to the bedroom, I dug my heels in to stop our movement.

"Not the bedroom. I know both of us better than to fall for

that trick right now," I said while shaking my head. "No way."

"The sofa? Please don't be afraid of me. I would never hurt you. It's tearing me apart knowing how bad I fucked this up."

"Do you really think that?" I bored my stare into him, but he looked confused. "After everything you know about me, do you really think telling me something about twenty fucking years ago would make me fear you now?" Then I was the one shaking my head, trying to call back the mounting sadness clogging my airway. "Do you know me at all?"

"I'm sorry, beauty. I'm so sorry," the handsome man said and tugged me close again to buss my forehead. While his lips were still pressed to my skin, I heard him apologize one more time.

We both took a seat, and I kept a few feet between our bodies. I angled my torso toward him and waited. And waited. It took him a few solid minutes to formulate what he wanted to say, which was encouraging. At least I knew it wasn't a practiced, unfelt speech I was about to receive. When he finally met my expectant stare, the anguish on his face once again robbed my breath.

"Hannah." He breathed my name more than spoke it, and I was captivated by his emotional state. Elijah never shied away from his feelings, and I'd seen him shed tears on several occasions in our short relationship. It gutted me that the tears welling in his eyes were because of me.

"This is exactly why I said we needed space. Needed time, Elijah. Emotions are much too raw right now. For us both." My anger ebbed with every breath he greedily took in. He was breaking me down with the oldest weapon in the book. But I knew better than to accuse him of putting on a show for me.

His reaction was as honest as he insisted I be with him.

"It will destroy me to watch you walk out. Do you understand that? Given what you know about my history, can you understand what it will do to me?"

"Right now, this isn't only about you, though. I've tried explaining to you that I just need some space. I'm not walking out on you as much as I'm putting some distance between us physically. So I can think. You bring up your history, but are you forgetting mine?" I surged to my feet, the crawling spiders of anxiety finally getting the best of me. Pacing, I finished, "I've been reprogrammed to put everyone else's needs before my own, and I don't want to make that mistake with you. I want to be with you on my terms."

"Thank you," Elijah said.

I looked at him quizzically. "What are you thanking me for?"

"Thank you for sharing that perspective with me. It makes sense when you explain it that way."

My beautiful man stood then and worked his palms down his thighs. With great caution, he walked toward me. Elijah offered his open hands for me to hold, but I paused a moment, trying to decide if I was sending him mixed signals. My heart and head were so damn confused.

When I finally took his offered fingers between mine, they were ice cold. My stare leveled to his.

"But I believe for us to work things out, distance will only make it worse," he said. "Other things will get in the way if you go live at home again. I don't want to become an afterthought. Anything other than your priority."

"Selfish much?" I muttered with my eyes down again. But he gently tugged me closer, and just like that, I could feel his breath on my cheek…then back beside my ear. He cradled my cheek in his palm, and out of habit or instinct or just plain biology, I leaned into him.

"I love you, Hannah. I'm asking you with all the sincerity I'm capable of, please don't leave me."

I pulled back from the intimacy so I could see his whole expression. For long beats, I just stared at him. This handsome, brave, and broken man was going to be the best mistake I ever made.

"Wha—" I cleared my throat of the emotional tangle stuck midway between my heart and lips. In a whisper, I asked, "What did you just say?"

"I'm begging you not to leave me."

"No." I widened my blue eyes. "The other thing." I yanked one hand free to make an up-and-over gesture as though the conversation was using an old VHS player's jerky rewind feature.

His lazy grin came out before he said, "I said I love you. I love everything about you, Ms. Farsey. I don't want to endure or even imagine enduring a moment of my life without you in it."

I started shaking my head while he spoke. That sexy grin stretched into a grim line while my gesture became more pronounced.

"You're not being very fair right now. I don't want to feel like I'm being manipulated with pretty words."

"Baby, they're not pretty words. This is me laying my heart at your feet. My fucking soul. Take it. Take it all," he implored.

"Listen. I'll stay in my old room tonight and hope to God some sort of clarity comes with some real sleep. I'll give you that much tonight, but don't ask me for more right now. Once you're not in panic mode, you'll realize what you're doing right now is terribly unfair." I dashed away the tears toppling down my cheeks.

"Han—"

But I held up a hand to stop him from saying any more. "Respect me enough to hear me right now, Elijah."

He dropped his chin to his chest and, after a long beat, dropped my hand too.

"Thank you for not leaving," he said roughly.

"Well, don't thank me yet. We'll see what tomorrow brings."

Not looking back, I walked down the hall to the very first room I slept in at this amazing house. I felt as shitty now as I did that night but for a different list of reasons entirely.

CHAPTER THREE

ELIJAH

If I had an hour's sleep that night, I was using very generous measure. I fought every urge to knock on Hannah's door more times than I could count, too. But I did what she asked and gave her space. I wasn't making promises on how much longer that would last, though.

Everything about her request went against my nature. I was a man who faced complications head-on. Always on the offensive.

I gave up defending myself about twenty years ago. Now, that godforsaken event worked its way to the forefront of my memory and was largely to blame for my sleepless night.

And I thought rehashing all that bullshit would bring me some sort of inner peace. Ha! Joke's on me, though, right? I didn't have the girl, I'd count myself completely unworthy if I still had the friends, and the one thing I didn't want—I couldn't seem to shake.

My conniving bitch of an ex. Hensley Pritchett.

Scrubbing my hand down my unshaven face reminded me I needed to get my ass in gear and get ready for work. I'd heard Hannah leave more than an hour before, and like a heartsick coward, I lay in bed and held my breath, trying to track her every move from the other side of the house.

When she closed the door on her way out, the echo bounced off the tile floors, high ceilings, and inside my hollow chest. I hadn't taken a full breath since. Too much oxygen hurt inside. Fuck…everything hurt inside, and thoughts of calling in sick taunted me.

No. That wouldn't fix anything. Much like Grant and Bas, I was a fixer. We all took matters into our own hands when things weren't going according to plan, and this bullshit? Well, this had never been the way I planned things to be. Especially with Hannah.

The woman was everything to me. My absolute. While it might seem like a heavy case of lust, or trying to fill a certain void, I knew the truth. There was something—no, so many things—so unique and amazing about my girl. And yes, she was still mine until the exact moment I said otherwise.

She made me a better man just by being near her. She made me think more tenderly, care more deeply, love more effortlessly. That was the perfection of Hannah Rochelle Farsey. She was effortless in all ways. Naturally beautiful, creatively gifted, and so fucking kind and good. If I gave a moment to honesty, I didn't deserve her.

Catching a glimpse of my reflection in the mirror, I doubled back to take a second look. Dark circles under my eyes stuck out among the wreckage. I hadn't looked so sallow in two decades. Now, panic over one secret, concern for two women—although for widely different reasons—and fear of losing my best friends had me looking the same as the night I stabbed my father.

By the time I got to the office, I had a better grip on my sanity. While showering, I decided to kick dirt over the shit pile that was my younger years and focus on what was most important. Getting Hannah to take me back with an open heart, forgiving conscience, and the devoted trust she once had would be a full-court press. If I didn't stay focused on that goal, my emotions would be back at the wheel, and I'd lose her for good. I had to come out on the other side of this with my woman and my dignity.

Since it was early, Carmen wasn't at his desk yet. I unlocked the door to my office and realized I must've left in such a hurry the last time I was here that I'd left the lights on. Weird. I was definitely distracted that afternoon. So many pieces to my careful life were falling through my fingers. I couldn't find Hannah, so I was completely rudderless.

"You're late," a female voice said from behind me while I hung my jacket on the door hook.

There was no way I'd give her the satisfaction of startling me, so on a ragged inhale, I slowly turned to face Hensley. She leaned against the window frame facing Los Angeles, acting like she had every right to be in my office.

"How the hell did you get in here?" I seethed. I could hide my surprise but not my ire.

Her coy smile stretched across her ruby lips when she faced me. As she leaned back on the window's ledge, she crossed her arms over her chest like she was settling in for a long workday.

"I'm calling security," I warned as my body temperature rose. "Leave now or be dragged out. Your choice."

"Oh, Elijah. Don't be such a drama queen all the time." She winked, and the gesture was so out of place. It should have confused me, but I had stopped trying to figure this lady out a long time ago.

I had to hand it to her. She always had brass balls. Nothing ever worried Hensley or shook her confidence. And fuck me for thinking it, but she looked good. The years had matured her features that were sharply defined now. From her nose—that had always been her best feature—to the wry arch of her brows, she was sophisticated and powerful looking. There was a time I would have found the package interesting, but that was a lifetime ago.

But her self-awareness and assuredness were a palpable presence in the room. She glided toward me, somehow making walking in four-inch heels look natural. Her cream shift dress and matching jacket were perfectly tailored and a beautiful complement to her raven hair and olive complexion. She wore her hair longer now, and the glossy mane was pulled back in a no-nonsense ponytail at her nape. She had artfully wrapped the knot with a section of hair so the whole effect was professional and somehow sexy.

Confidence always did turn me on. In a woman, a man, it didn't matter. The trait was like catnip to me.

"You look like hell, man. Following in the old man's footsteps with the booze?"

"And we're done here." I glared at her and reached for the phone at the corner of my desk.

Quicker than expected, she was right in front of me and swiped the receiver from my grasp and cradled it on the base, *tsk*ing all the while.

Her behavior had me scanning my upbringing for the reminder it was never reasonable to hit a woman. But Christ, she was trying my composure. I closed my eyes and steadied my breathing before I completely lost my temper. No one needed to witness that, especially so early in the morning. Especially because of Ms. Pritchett.

No one would blame me though, either. I spared a

moment to indulge in the fantasy of Grant and especially Bas barging into my office right about now. The sassy attitude of the woman in front of me would be sliced in half with his presence. The two shared the same opinion of each other, and to remark there was no love lost was understating at its best.

"Listen closely," I growled, and it wasn't the sexually charged version that made Hannah squirm and go all doe-eyed. My jaw strained with tension, and I had to jam my hands deep into my pockets to avoid an unplanned incident.

The woman seemed to have no sense of self-preservation, though, because her chest rose and dipped with excited— possibly aroused—breaths, and she leaned into me like I was about to share a salacious secret.

"Say what you came to say and get the fuck out of here. No, wait. The only thing I want to hear from your miserable mouth is your assent to a paternity test. Spare me the legal proceedings and do the right thing. If you're even capable of that."

Almost shocked at my own words, I reared back from her and waited for her response.

"I told you before that wasn't going to happen."

"Well, since you're not wearing another man's ring, I can only assume you didn't marry the dude you ran off with." I tilted my head slightly to cue her response, but she simply shrugged.

Shrugged? What the hell did that mean in this context? I forged on.

"You need to establish legal parentage of the child, Hensley. You know this, right? The boy deserves a father. Stop fucking around and stringing us all along because you have some scheme cooked up."

First the shrug. Now a coy smile blossomed. "Oh, there's no scheme cooking in my kitchen, dear. But it is damn hot, am I right?" She slid her fingertips down the center of her chest and dipped into her cleavage.

I snatched the phone off my desk again and hit the direct line to the security office. One ring, two, and finally after the third, the duty officer answered.

"Mr. Banks, good morning, sir. How can I help you?"

"There's an unwelcomed visitor in my office. I need the person removed. Right the fuck now." I slammed the phone down and gave Hensley the most threatening stare I could manufacture.

"You'll be hearing from my attorney," I cautioned. "I'm filing a civil suit to establish paternity before the day is over."

A sharp rap on my door was the perfect end to the altercation. Three long strides, and I whipped the thing open and stood back, pointing with a fully extended arm in my ex's direction.

"Get her out of my sight. Make sure you get a copy of her driver's license and current contact information before she leaves the building. Once we review the security footage and figure out how she got in here, we can file charges."

The officer nodded swiftly and reached for Hensley's arm.

Immediately she wrenched out of his grip. "Don't you dare touch me. Fucking rent-a-cop." She strode from the room with the man following right behind.

Less than ten minutes later, my phone vibrated with an incoming text message. Before looking at the screen, I wished it was Hannah reaching out. She had done it so many mornings since we'd met—just a quick comment to say have a great day, she missed me, or was looking forward to whatever plans we were making.

At first sight, I recognized Grant's number.

We're up top in ten.

I tossed my phone onto my desk as I slumped into the chair. Seven a.m., and I was already exhausted. There was no other choice than to put Hensley in her place, once and for all. I would not sit idly by and allow her to destroy me a second time. It was already embarrassing enough that it had happened once. There was so much more to lose now, and she wouldn't get another opportunity to manipulate me.

Sitting up, I got busy on my computer. I could log into the building's security system and watch how the devil got up to the penthouse offices with such ease. The woman was smart, but technology had never interested her beyond her cell phone. She'd either had help or talked her way into gaining access. If it was the latter, heads would roll.

The daily camera feed showed her coming in the front door of the office building about thirty minutes before I arrived this morning. From that footage, I watched her pour on the charm with the security guy on the front desk from the night before. From what I could interpret, he told her no. But the sly lady got lucky when the day watchman arrived and the men were distracted with their shift pass down. She skirted right past both men and ducked into an elevator with a few others.

With a few keystrokes, I brought up the feed from the camera in the main elevator. A simple rewind to the timestamp I just viewed on the lobby camera, and there she was. Chatting amicably with another employee of Shark Enterprises. They rode to the top floor, and the handful of people poured out into the atrium. Since Carmen wasn't out in reception at my office,

I watched her swindle the custodian to open my door.

Sure, I could turn up the volume and hear exactly what web of lies she spun to convince the guy, but what did it really matter? Hensley hadn't changed a bit since we were a couple. She had no problem lying, cheating, and manipulating whoever she had to in order to get what she wanted.

From here, I'd let the police deal with the bitch. I was done and needed to meet my best friends on the building's roof for a private chat.

As I walked across the deck, Grant spotted me first. He backhanded Bas in the abdomen to get his attention. Of course, Shark had his cell phone at one ear when he turned in my direction.

"Shit. I didn't think you could look worse than you did yesterday." He grinned at first, but I didn't share his mirth. Quickly, his features sobered, maybe getting the message that I wasn't in the mood for the usual ribbing this morning.

"Is there still Scotch up here?" I asked.

Grant's eyebrows hiked up.

Bas stabbed the end button on his mobile and slid the device into a pocket.

"Fuck me, Martha Stewart. You look like shit."

"I didn't sleep last night," I groaned and slid onto the patio furniture. "And you are never going to believe how my day started when I got here this morning."

"Well, I was just talking to the guy at the desk in the lobby," Bas said. "Explain to me how your psycho ex got into my fucking building."

I narrowed my eyes to a full glare. "How the fuck should I know? She was waiting for me in my office when I walked in."

"If you don't press charges, Banks, I'm going to," Sebastian warned.

Grant chimed in. "Has anyone pulled the tapes? It can't be too hard to spot her on the tape with so few people in the building."

"The security officer said they were working on it and will call me when they have the pieces put together," answered Bas.

"I already watched it. She'll likely be charged with trespassing and breaking and entering if you proceed." I rubbed my face with my palms while I spoke. I needed sleep in a big way.

Bas scoffed, "What do you mean *if*?"

"No shit, man," Grant said, gripping his nape with his giant hand. "If you don't do something, who knows where she'll turn up next? None of us needs extra surprises right now."

"Now that you all know about—" Shit, how could I still not say the words?

"Yeah, about that," Bas said and nearly fell into the chair at a right angle to my seat.

"Oh, thank God," Grant huffed and folded his tall body onto the cushion beside me. "I have so many questions, and I thought we'd be up here tiptoeing around the subject."

He studied me long and hard until I considered decking him. But my friend was perceptive enough to pick up the tension slogging heavy in the air between us. He finally spoke, but I noticed the way he added to the space that separated us.

"Why did you keep that shit inside all this time?" He shook his head but kept his stare pinned on me. "That couldn't have been easy all these years."

"After a while, I stuffed it all so far back in my memory, there were times I wondered if it was just some sort of fucked-up nightmare. Like maybe I could roll up to my family's home and my parents would both still be sitting there."

"So what happened to your mother? Did she split?" Bas asked with his usual cut-to-the-chase demeanor.

"That night, before I attacked him..." The memory coaxed my rough swallow, bile repeating in my throat. "He finally went too far," I rasped. Tears clouded my vision, but I could still see that fucking kitchen as clearly as if I were standing there. My two-man audience remained still, waiting for the rest of the tale.

"One of his trademark stomach kicks took her down, and she hit her head as she fell. Furniture, I think, of some sort— maybe the kitchen table? For some reason, I don't remember that. I was so focused on her face. God, I just wanted her to look in my direction and give me that assurance that she was okay, you know?" Reliving the events of that night still felt as painful as the day it had happened.

When I tried to continue, an anguished groan sneaked out. I lowered my chin and stared at the deck as a cavalcade of tears broke free. Hot and persistent, tear after tear scorched a path down the line of my nose and onto the tips of my shoes.

Eventually, I regained a bit of composure and finished the worst of it. "And the motherfucker kicked her again. She was lying there with her eyes blown wide from shock and then froze like that while her life soaked into the tile floor's grout. The coward kicked her again. Her fucking lifeless body."

"Dude," Grant said quietly and put his solid palm on my shoulder. "I'm so sorry you had to live through that shit."

"So I snapped. That's when I lost it. The knives were right there—right in the wooden block on the counter. It was the first thing my hand found for a weapon."

Sucking air in through my nose, I watched my chest rise with my inflated lungs. Then let it out slowly, trying to gain some sort of control. My emotions were cracking me wide open for everyone around me to pick at like fresh roadkill.

When I looked at my two best friends, I only saw compassion and kindness. Once again, I internally berated myself for not giving these men the benefit of the doubt. All these years I lived in fear that Hensley would expose me for the murderer I was, when in reality, if I had told Sebastian and Grant the truth, I would have had their unerring support. Exactly like they were giving me now.

"Can I ask you something, boss?" Grant busied himself with something on his trousers while he inquired.

"Yeah, sure. Shoot." After yesterday, I vowed to be an open book with these men. Always.

"What's with the number forty-two?"

"I was just wondering that too," Bas added.

With a smile, I said, "I should have known one of you would catch that."

"Well, we all know each other pretty well. I knew if you were referencing a number, there was a reason for it. Elijah Banks doesn't stumble through details."

I nodded at his assessment. "Since I was a boy, I've obsessed over the fine print. From the time I was old enough to realize what he was doing to her, I kept count of every beating. Every slap, every kick or shove. Every time he made her cry from physical abuse. The night I stabbed him, the total was forty-two." I shrugged, still believing it made sense. "I guess it was my version of an eye for an eye."

"I can only imagine," Bas said. "Pretty sure I would have done the same thing if my old man was knocking my mother around."

"Did she ever say why she stuck around?" Grant winced

and then added, "Just tell me to shut the fuck up if I am asking questions that are too personal or difficult to talk about."

"I never asked her straight out, but I think she probably felt trapped. She didn't work, and his family had the fortune, not hers. She wouldn't have been able to survive financially on her own. Plus, then she had a child to feed too. It's really sad their marriage was such a sham. They married so young, and I think she had stars in her eyes."

"Didn't you say at one point that your grandparents lived with you? In the same house in Brentwood?" Grant asked, and I nodded before he finished. "Where were they when all this happened? The routine beatings and the stabbing?"

After a couple of moments combing through my memory, I said, "I don't remember specifically where they were that night. They were busy socialites after retirement and were always doing one thing or another. I do remember my grandfather was the first to find me whimpering over my mother's corpse on the bloody kitchen floor."

While scrubbing my palms down my face, I looked up to the bright-blue sky. Such a contrast to how dark and dismal I felt inside. To my friends' ears, I must've sounded like such a monster. No wonder Hannah ran the first chance she got. I didn't even go into these kinds of details with her. But I knew I would. It was one of my favorite things about her, the way she never left a single stone unturned.

Was I setting myself up to live my days in fear? During the sun's hours, I was afraid someone would finally succeed in hurting her or kidnapping her. And during the moon's hours in the sky, I was terrified she would run away on her own. If more and more bad shit from my life kept tainting hers, I wouldn't blame her for ditching me. Because Christ knew there were still a lot of unsavory things for her to uncover.

"Banks!" Bas shouted while he paced.

With a quick shake of my head, I glared at him. "Why the fuck are you yelling?"

"I was trying to get your spaceship to land." There was a slight grin on his lips, letting me know he was just busting my balls. In truth, I had drifted off.

"What was the question? Sorry."

Grant was quick to absolve me. "You don't need to apologize, man. This is a lot of heavy shit, and you already said you didn't sleep well."

While I appreciated his understanding, I couldn't help but imagine him giving his little nut of a girlfriend the same kind of corridor. And shit, if that didn't rub me the wrong way.

Which was totally unfair. I knew that, but it didn't change how I felt. I worked so long and so hard to earn a certain reputation. I didn't want people to think less of me, especially these two men. Even though this was the safest place for me to vent, maybe it was time for me to shut up.

But both Sebastian and Grant looked like their next questions were locked and loaded. Reminding myself I owed them this truth, I inhaled slowly, let it out, and braced myself for the next round of the interrogation.

Sebastian charged ahead first. "How did you go from living in a Brentwood mansion with generations of old money to bankroll your lifestyle to living on the street?"

Grant pointed his long index finger at Shark and said, "Yeah, that."

"Are we sure the Scotch is gone? Did you look?" I volleyed my stare between the two of them.

"No, I didn't actually look," Grant answered. "But we all

know getting hammered isn't going to fix any of this. If this is too much all at one time, we can revisit this tomorrow or something."

Bas nodded along. "But the sooner we're all on the same page, the safer the women will be. This isn't the time to be playing *I've got a secret.*"

Of course he was right, but this had to be easier to be on the receiving end of this fucked-up information than it was to be the one delivering it.

"My grandfather had always been a practical man. It didn't take him long to do the math on what that would do to our family's name if the information went public. And like I just said, he and my grandmother were major socialites. I think they were more worried about being blackballed than the fact that their son and daughter-in-law were dead and I was the one holding the murder weapon."

"Did your father have a tumultuous relationship with his dad?" Grant asked.

"Man, I don't know. We were, what? Thirteen? Maybe fourteen when this all went down. I was barely aware of anything outside my own orbit at the time. The only reason I was so invested in how often he was physical with my mother was for one thing—I knew it was wrong. And more than anything, I had always been the apple of my mother's eye. There wasn't anything she wouldn't do for me. I was very protective of her. Not just with him. With everyone."

"Okay, that's all great backstory, but how did you end up on the street?" Bas repeated.

I narrowed my focus to just him. There wasn't anything more sensational about that one bit of information compared to the rest. Therefore, I couldn't work out why he was so fixated on that one answer.

Damn determined to get through this horror story one time and never look back at it again, I continued recounting the night.

"My grandfather took one look at the scene in the kitchen and told me to go wait for him in the car. At first, I didn't want to let go of my mother, but when that man shouted, it was ten times more terrifying than when my father did. The apple didn't fall far from the tree after all." I squeezed my eyes shut, willing the memory to fade to black.

My friends gave me the time I needed to find the fortitude to continue. "I only sat in the car for five or ten minutes before he strolled out like he didn't have a care in the world. When he got behind the wheel, I realized it was something I rarely saw him do. He loved indulging in the fine things our kind of money afforded, so he usually had a driver on standby. He drove downtown without a single word. Finally, he pulled over on some side street off Figueroa and told me to get out."

I watched Bas and Grant for their reactions, but they were stone-faced. I wasn't sure if that gave me courage or pissed me off. On one hand, I wanted them to be outraged on my behalf. Surely my grandfather knew the kind of monster his son was. While at the same time, their silence allowed me to feel the raw emotion of the moment and the freedom of unloading the burden.

Eventually, I spoke again to tie the story up. "The man was like a robot. He showed no emotion at all. Then while he stared straight ahead—the bastard couldn't even glance at me—he told me as long as he never saw my face again, he would make sure the police would never know what really happened."

Well, shit. Of all the reactions I could've predicted from my best friends, continued silence wasn't on the list.

Both men looked everywhere but at me. The ground, their shoes, even each other. Just not at me. Even though we were outside, the air around our trio became stifling. Was this it? Was this the point where they decided they really couldn't support me on this?

With one hand in a death grip on the back of his neck, Grant spoke first. "Dude. That is so fucked up."

"Shit. I'll say. The three of us really hit the parent lottery, didn't we?" Shark added, and we all forced a strangled laugh.

"I met you two dipshits the next night in that alley between Moe's and Madame Lanni's." Warmth finally started to circulate through my system as we all remembered the incident. No doubt we all had different memories of the exact same moment in time, and that thought made me grin—for real this time.

"Ha!" Grant barked unexpectedly. "If they could see us now, right? Madame Lanni never saw this in her crystal ball!"

"Definitely not," I said, but my thoughts skittered out of the light once again. As grateful as I was to focus on more positive memories, I craved the solace only found in the dark corners of my psyche. The mental warning signs were coming in loud and clear and pointed in one unmistakable direction. I was in for a bout of depression, and I wordlessly vowed to do everything I knew to head it off. A dark mood swing was the last thing I needed. And without a willing sub who craved pain the way I craved dishing it out, all the dark sexual energy that normally came with my emotional imbalance would remain unsatisfied.

"So where do we go from here?" Grant asked.

"With regard to what?" Maybe that snapped a little harder than I intended, but I was lost in the dread of my impending brood.

"All of this." He looked at me like I was the village idiot. "This whole shit show."

"Look, I finally told you all of this because carrying that garbage around was polluting me from the inside out. I hated not telling you that giant piece of my history."

For some reason, that was the point I needed to gulp down more oxygen. Finishing this conversation in the tidiest way possible became paramount. If I had to roll around in this mud much longer, I might have a legitimate breakdown.

"And as much as it sucks to have you both looking at me like a sideshow, I'm glad it's finally out in the open."

"You should've told us long ago, man," Grant said while standing.

"Yeah, yeah, I know. But easier said than done, you know? There were so many times it was right there in the chamber— locked and loaded and ready to fire. But something was done, or was said, and I'd click the safety back into place."

"I know you feel some relief now that we know and Hannah knows," Grant began.

"Some?" I barked. "That's an understatement."

Then Bas cut in, "As much as I hate to mention the devil woman, she's a major factor here. She has a load of dirt on you." I watched as he shuffled his feet, seeming as anxious and frustrated as I felt.

Grant interjected, "It's true it no longer matters if she tried to out you to one of us . . . but what about the police?"

Both men stared at me expectantly.

Why, of all the things that I'd worried about and planned for, had this never entered my mind as a possibility? Easy answer—my connection with my two brother-close friends meant everything to me. Without them, I wouldn't have cared if I went to prison.

Until now, of course. Until Hannah.

"Fuck me," I said under my breath and fell back down on the patio set. Just as quickly, I shot back to my feet. "No, wait a second," I said, realizing this wasn't nearly as bad as it seemed.

The guys studied me and waited for me to elaborate. "She can't go to the police. What evidence is there? She has no proof."

"Banks. People fabricate evidence all the time," Sebastian said with raised brows.

Grant picked up the thought track where Bas left off. "And she's working for the district attorney's office. She knows exactly what evidence would put you away."

Sebastian had never hid his disdain for Hensley. Proved once again when he said, "Hell, I wouldn't be surprised if she pursued a law degree simply to hang you out to dry."

Twombley added his two cents. "That would be a surefire way to keep you away from the kid. First"—the tall man held up his index finger to tick off his supporting facts—"if Daddy's in jail, Mommy doesn't have to deal with a pesky paternity test." He continued adding a finger for each thing named. "Then there's physical custody"—two fingers—"child support"—he added a third—"and visitation." He pushed four fingers toward my face and then pulled back again like he was creating some sort of special effect.

Thank fuck he cut his list there, because I was about to throat punch him.

"I still think we took the wind out of her sails. All that . . ." I circled my finger toward the two of them, as if capturing their worrisome thoughts in a finger-drawn lasso. "All of that is much more work than she's willing to do. Even if it is to burn me."

"Hell hath no fury like a woman scorned," Grant

commented and looked mighty impressed with himself.

I snapped my head toward Bas and screwed up my face while I pointed at Grant.

"Don't ask me, man." Sebastian didn't even consider coming up with an explanation.

"What?" Grant protested. "Everyone knows that quote."

I just stared at him. Pretty sure my head was going to explode into a million pieces based on the pressure building behind my eyes. No matter which problem I tried to wrap my head around dealing with first, they all seemed insurmountable.

Bas clapped his hands, and the dozen pigeons that were on standby for possible handouts took flight all at once. "Let's get back to work. We've got freight to move, gentlemen."

Grant and I stood and followed our boss to the elevator. While we waited for the car to arrive, I couldn't help but think those scavenger birds had the right idea. Maybe getting out of Dodge was exactly what my overworked brain needed.

CHAPTER FOUR

HANNAH

Around lunchtime, I finally gave in and called to ask Agatha to meet me for drinks after work. I nearly cried when she agreed, which confirmed how badly I needed to talk to someone other than my landlord.

Of course, when I texted Elijah to let him know I would be home late, my phone rang instantly.

"Beautiful, we've talked about this." His dark tone could be felt through my smartphone.

"Pardon me?" My question in lieu of an answer held much more sass than necessary. Well, it wasn't necessary for the conversation, but it fit my general mood just fine.

But the formidable man was undeterred. "You know you are supposed to check in with me before making plans," he growled from his end of the line. "Not after."

"You can't seriously think we're still keeping up that charade," I replied to his dictate. "Need I remind you who was almost gang raped by the very people you're trying to fool?" Then I huffed loud enough to cause Brinn to widen her stare.

I knew my coworker was eavesdropping while we washed tomorrow's produce, but I was done giving a fuck what anyone thought. I'd lived my whole life in that camp, and look where it got me.

When he answered, I could picture his jaw twitching in that little hollow just below his ear. Through clenched teeth, he said, "Please don't be stubborn. Let Lorenzo drive if you drink."

While I debated how to respond to that comment, he said, "I'll see you when you get home," and disconnected the call.

Couldn't say that I blamed the man. How long would he willingly be my punching bag? Did he deserve to be treated that way? Probably not.

My head was a confused jumble. My heart wasn't faring much better. One minute I was angry that he lied to me—by omission, yes, but from the man's own mouth, a lie was a lie. The next minute my heart broke when I thought of him as the young boy who endured a home where domestic violence was an everyday occurrence.

I knew he had a lot of emotional and psychological damage from being raised in that scenario. Several times he let comments slip out about failing to protect his mother. He was a boy! Children weren't supposed to be their parents' heroes. None of what happened was his fault, and the damage to my amazing man's soul would never be undone.

And there was the biggest rub of all. He wasn't my man. Not while his heart was in another woman's home.

★ ★ ★

"Soooo that's what I've been up to," I said to Agatha before taking a long drink from my glass. For the past hour or so, I had regaled my sister with the crazy events from the past few weeks.

Agatha looked at me with a sympathetic pout and

then tried to hide her expression behind the fishbowl-sized margarita. We'd both thrown caution to the wind and ordered giant drinks—to take the edge off, we agreed.

"I saw that look. What was that for?" No way was she getting off without an explanation.

"I don't envy your spot, sister. Well, except for when you get boned by that god among men. See? All those honorable deeds paid off! Karma is skipping alongside you." Then she started laughing, and I knew she would spout a one-liner next. Having learned from experience, I held off on taking another gulp of my drink in fear of spraying it out with a laugh.

"Actually," she said shrewdly, "I think you and the bitch are holding hands."

As predicted, we both threw our heads back and laughed, but then I went still with seriousness. Agatha even leaned in over the small table where we sat so she didn't miss a word I said. Happy hour was in full swing, and the place was going off.

"Girl, you don't even know."

"No, I don't. But I want to! My Gooooooodd, I want to so bad, Han. It's been so long, I think my virginity has grown back." She tilted her head and said, "Can that happen?"

And we broke out laughing again.

As I wiped the tears from the outer corners of my eyes, I studied my sister. She was beautiful and vivacious, and it didn't make sense that she didn't have a different guy for every day of the month.

"So what's the problem? Why are you having a dry spell?" From what I knew about Agatha, she wasn't the kind of girl who needed long-term promises or the guy to tick off other benchmarks to end up sleeping together.

She shrugged and moved her glass while our server put a

plate of hummus and pita bread between us. The protein would help soak up the booze. Or was that what the carbs were for?

"This is going to sound crazy, so try to temper your judgment." My sister said the last few words around a big bite.

I reached across the table and drew an imaginary circle around us. "This is a judgment-free zone. Shit, Dah, I just told you the man I love stabbed his father in cold blood." Her eyes bugged out so huge I quickly added, "And you didn't run away screaming."

My favorite sister finished chewing and dabbed her mouth with a napkin from the big stack left with our food.

"Han."

"What?" I darted my eyes back and forth and started to feel self-conscious. Then quickly swiped a napkin from the pile and wiped my mouth too. "Better?" I asked, assuming I had food on my face from the embarrassingly large bite I shoveled in.

"No, you're good. Although that was an impressive amount you fit in your mouth." As an afterthought, she asked slyly, "Been practicing?" She winked and chugged her drink.

"Oh my God, shut it. You're such a dog. Jeeessuuss." Taking a surreptitious scan of the bar, I was thankful I didn't see anyone I knew. The alto voice she and I were gifted with carried in a crowd. We were already getting fuck-me looks from the guys two tables over. If they had heard that comment, they'd be sending drinks our way.

"The reason I almost dislocated my eyeballs was what you said just before that."

My confusion must have been as obvious as the neon beer signs decorating this joint. Then she explained.

"You called Elijah Banks the man you love."

Now it was my turn with an exaggerated eye gesture. While rolling my big blues, I insisted, "No way. You must have heard me wrong. Dad was right all these years. You listen to"—I shifted my voice into the best impression of our father's—"'that crap they call music these days' way too loud. I think your hearing is damaged."

We both laughed, but my sister kept me in the hot seat and asked, "What would be the big deal if you already felt that strongly about him?"

I had no idea how to answer her. Our own parents met, fell in love, got engaged, and married all within one year of knowing each other. They would celebrate their thirty-second anniversary this year. Our mother always claimed it was love at first sight. Our dad said he knew she was the woman he would marry after their first date. We'd certainly had the perfect example of love in the fast lane right in our own home.

Finally, I decided to mention something I didn't want to voice out loud to anyone. Always afraid that putting things into the universe was a direct path to manifestation.

"What if he doesn't feel the same way about me? What if I put my heart on the line and tell him how I feel, and he just stares at me? Can you imagine what that would be like?" I tugged at the neckline of my shirt. Just thinking of that situation ramped up my anxiety.

He had told me he loved me before, but there was a part of me that thought those were desperate words in a desperate situation. Remembering the panicked look on his face during that exchange, I thought he'd be willing to say anything he had to in order to keep me there.

"No way. There is no way he doesn't feel the same way about you. I saw the way that man looks at you the night you cooked dinner for the family. I know I didn't get to spend too much time with the two of you together, but in the short time I did..."

She trailed off there, leaving her last sentence hanging in the stale air of the crowded bar.

"Okay, let's swap shoes for a minute," I said.

My sister sat up tall and rested folded hands on the table. She was always eager to give her opinion.

"What would give you pause in this situation?"

Agatha didn't consider her answer for more than one second. Breezily, she answered, "Not a damn thing. I mean, come on. He's stunning to look at. According to the way those slacks hugged his ass, I'm guessing his body is as fine as his face." She held her hand up at eye level and wiggled her little pinky. "Is he lacking in the man basket?"

Margarita went down the wrong way, and I choked while laughing. I did manage to shake my head the whole time, though. When I could finally speak again, I told her there was more than enough to keep me happy. For a few lifetimes. I had some perverse pride while watching her reaction to that comment.

"So, I've got a question for you," Agatha said and pushed the appetizer plate toward me. "You eat the rest of that. A girl can't live on dick alone."

Through clenched teeth I said, "Would you stop? I can feel my cheeks turning red."

"You make it too easy to give you shit. I can't help myself. But seriously, if I eat another bite of that"—the woman pointed at the dip like it was personally offending her now—"it will ruin hummus for me forever. I've been scarfing it down since it hit the table."

"Weren't you going to ask me something?"

Agatha's first response was a nod. She leaned across the table and gripped my hand in hers. "I think there's really only one thing you need to ask yourself, and be super honest when answering. Do you feel like you've tasted enough of the thirty-one flavors at Baskin-Robbins before you pronounce rocky road as your favorite? Because once you commit to that flavor, you only get to eat rocky road for the rest of your life." She sat back in her seat and looked pretty impressed with herself. Of course I understood the metaphor but thought it would be fun to mess with her a bit.

"Dah, everyone in the family knows my favorite is cookies and cream. Rocky road upsets my stomach every single time I eat it. I can't believe you forgot that. Sheesh, I've been out of the house like three months at the most, and you're already forgetting about me."

"Hannah," she said, serious as an unexpected pregnancy. "I wasn't actually talking about ice cream."

"Wait ... huh?"

While she had her face cradled in her open palms, I burst out laughing. And probably a little too loud, judging by the way the people at the surrounding tables all turned to look.

"And I think that's enough margarita for me," I said between leftover giggles.

"You had me worried there for a second." Agatha reached across to sock me in the arm. "You're supposed to be the smart one."

"Noooo, I think quite the opposite. I got the worst grades out of all of us." Of course, I was constantly battling an undiagnosed anxiety disorder and PTSD from an event I barely remembered. It was hard to pay attention in class when my own brain was constantly encouraging me to freak out.

The quiet stretched between us for a moment longer than I could stand. In an effort to fill the conversational void, I answered her question.

"The short answer is yes. I'd be happy to enjoy one flavor from this point on. I know I haven't tasted every flavor in the shop, but I'm not the kind of girl who needs to take advantage of all the free samples. I knew what I wanted when I walked in the door."

"I think all the questions you peppered me with when we first sat down can be answered from what you just said." My dearest sister took my hands in hers and reassured me with a squeeze. "In the end, only you can decide what the right choice is for you. You never make reckless decisions about anything. I don't expect you will on this either."

"Thank you so much, Dah. I can't tell you how much lighter I feel after this talk. I really needed it. That and some space between me and Mr. Bossypants." The smile that overtook my entire face could not be contained.

"Mmmm, I do like a bossy man, not going to lie," Agatha admitted.

I watched as she tossed the straw from her drink onto the table, tilted the massive goblet back, and finished the cocktail. With exaggerated gesticulation, she wiped her mouth with the back of her hand and gave a loud "Aaahhhh. Good old tequila truth serum strikes again."

God, the girl had me in stitches again, and I caught sight of the guys who had been making eyes at us since we sat down. *Shit!*

They were making their way through the crowd and to our table. I was in the middle of fishing out a cash tip for our waitress when one put his hand on my forearm to stop me.

I realized he was simply going to offer to buy our drinks, but a strange man just assumed he could put hands on me, and in my world that was a big, fat *No*. Annnddd—it also brought a quick halt to all my usual niceties.

Both men held their hands up, fingers spread wide like they were getting roused by law enforcement.

"Hey, hey, sorry. Sorry. I shouldn't have touched you." The guy was fumbling all over his words, and it just made the situation worse.

His buddy wasn't as cordial and grabbed his friend's wrist out of midair and dragged him away from our table.

Hands shielding my face, I rested my elbows on the cluttered table. The flat surface was at the perfect counter height for the pose. My God... how long would I have to deal with these scars? It was so fucking unfair. While the lowlife couple who tried to rob me of my youth and innocence walked free somewhere in this city, I stood trembling in fear in a bar off Melrose.

I just wanted my life back. Tears filled my eyes, and what was desperation and longing mere moments before morphed into red-hot rage and vengeance. Those fuckers didn't pay a big enough price if I were the judge. Why was the victim still being victimized? Only now, instead of the cruel, rough hands of two strangers, it was my own memories and subsequent mental illness.

So. Damn. Unfair.

A deep male voice snapped me from my dark self-absorption.

Thankfully, when I lifted my face, it wasn't Elijah. I couldn't keep falling apart in his presence. Although, Lorenzo standing in front of me was nearly the same thing. He would go home and tell my keeper what happened here tonight, how he had to escort me from the bar while half the patrons stopped to stare. And the way I slumped in the back seat and quietly cried the whole drive home.

"Lorenzo, can we give my sister a lift home?" I asked before we pulled out of the bar's parking lot. I was the absolute worst sister and friend, just leaving her back there to fend for herself. "Actually, we need to go back. We were drinking, and if something were to happen—"

"Ms. Farsey, she's already safely on her way home."

"Wait . . . what? What do you mean?" I was in no position to be so demanding, but that small shot of realization didn't thwart my self-appointed heroism. "Who is she with? Was it one of those guys from the bar? Lorenzo—" I gripped his sleeve at the elbow, the only part of him I could reach from the back seat.

"Marc is driving her to Brentwood. You know Marc. He's a good guy. He'll make sure she gets in the front door safely and be an absolute gentleman while doing so. We're professionals, Ms. Farsey."

"Thank you, and will you please call me Hannah?" I sulked and flopped back against the leather seat. As the luxury car floated through the dark night, I was lulled into a tranquil state. With the hypnotic sound of the tires on the concrete freeway and the leveled-off hum of the engine, I was moments from finding blissful peace in slumber. Until my damn cell phone rang—and still at maximum volume, as I'd had hopes of hearing it while we'd been at the bar.

"He-Hell-Hello?" I slurred. *Shit*. Was I getting drunker just riding in the car? Damn tequila. Did it every time.

I heard his laugh before anything else, and my heart picked up the pace instantly.

"I can't wait to see you. Are you on your way home? I'm tracking Lorenzo, and it looks like you're on the right trajectory at least."

How was I supposed to respond to that? Was he missing me because he enjoyed my company or because, as my sworn protector, he worried about my safety?

I just sighed and said, "You really didn't have to wait up for me. Lorenzo is making sure I get home safely. Thank you, by the way, for sending him out with me tonight."

"Beauty, you don't have to thank me. A large part of the gesture was me being selfish."

"Selfish? I'm not following you. Then again, I had a little too much to drink, so if you told me a nursery rhyme right now, I may not be able to follow along." I couldn't even force a chuckle after saying that because I hated how strained things had become between us.

How do we get back to where we were?

And was that what I really wanted? If it were, I had to make the decision with both my head and my heart. Maybe this was just the honeymoon period ending and we were having to deal with real-life issues and not always be in that magical space of new lovers.

What was I even saying? Magical space? I met the man because someone locked me in an industrial cooler and thought the entire escapade would make a great keepsake video. Hey! At least the file was already compressed for easy sharing, right?

"You still there, Han?" Elijah finally asked when I'd been inside my head too long.

Following a long sigh, I said, "Yeah, I'm here. I'm so tired, though, so I'm going to hang up. I'll maybe see you in the morning?"

And why did I phrase it like a question? It wasn't fair to string the man along with open-ended possibilities. How ridiculous to think that, though? I was certain he'd be back to his old ways before my tears even dried.

If for no other reason, a man with a sexual appetite as demanding as Elijah's wouldn't be sidelined by a frigid woman for long. Especially with so many warm, willing bodies panting in the wings.

Finally, we pulled up to the house. I considered just sleeping off those drinks here in the car, but none of the bossy men around this property would allow that to happen. I could picture at least three of them just hoisting me over their shoulder and carrying me to bed.

"Thanks for getting me home in one piece, Lorenzo," I said at the door to my bedroom. He'd insisted on walking me the entire way, and I was too tired to mount an argument. I also figured out that when the security guys acted extra protective, it was usually at Elijah's insistence.

In just my panties, I crawled under the covers. I just couldn't be bothered with more of my bedtime routine. Sleep came in no time.

Fitful and restless tossing and turning most of the night made for a difficult reveille. When I finally cracked my eyes open enough to realize where I was, Elijah was lying next to me in my bed. Of course, he looked well rested and modeling-gig ready. His warm smile made me uncomfortable. And that was before I remembered I was almost naked beneath the bedding.

Fingertips covered my lips in an effort to spare him

morning hangover breath. God, this was so embarrassing. He wore a mischievous smirk as he waited for me to pull myself together and consider getting in the shower.

"Why are you in here?" I finally asked, and continued for clarity, "In my room...my bed? And more importantly, how long have you been here?" Now that I was more alert and really thinking about it, I was kind of pissed off. He had no right to be in my personal space like this. And yes, it was his house, and yes, he was responsible for my safety at the moment, but I hadn't handed over my free will completely.

"You must have had a nightmare last night. I heard you calling out, so I came in here to check on you." He shrugged, possessing no guilt at all whatsoever. "And then I just fell asleep beside you. It's the calmest, emotionally safest space I know. I always get better quality sleep when I'm in bed with you."

The moment I stood up, I gripped my head. "Oh my God, my head. Stupid tequila," I mumbled and staggered to the bathroom to get some pain reliever. And water—I needed a gallon at least. When I came back into the room, Elijah was sprawled right where I left him.

"Aren't you working today?"

"Yeah, but I have to meet with my attorney first, so I'm getting a little later start than usual." That sexy grin of his made an appearance, and he proposed, "Want to shower together? I'll wash your back, and you can wash mine."

"No thanks. I'll pass. But I do have to go in at the regular time, so if you'll excuse me?" I walked toward the door to usher him out, but when I turned to tell him to have a nice day, he was still nestled in my bed.

"Elijah! I'm serious. Get out so I can get ready."

"What harm is there in me catching a little more sleep before I have to get up? I mean, come on. I've seen, touched, licked, and bitten your entire body at this point. Don't be shy now, girl."

His tone was playful, but I'd grown to recognize the challenging look in his eyes. He loved the push and pull when we were disputing something. He admitted it turned him on. Knowing that tidbit, I was hesitant to add more fuel to the fire burning behind those icy green eyes. I would end up beneath him again. No doubt about it.

I closed the door and decided to ignore him. I'd be in the bathroom anyway, and there was a door between the two rooms that could establish some privacy. He'd probably pick the lock or knock the thing down if he really wanted to get to me. After seeing the lengths he went to with the handcuffs, I knew Elijah Banks usually got what he wanted.

Frankly, I'd known that from the first day I met him.

My shower took longer than usual because it was a hair wash day on top of going to bed and not brushing it and putting it up. I was in for a big, tangled mess. When I came back into the bedroom, my gorgeous man was sleeping peacefully.

As if his body had a tractor beam locked on mine, I tentatively walked toward the bed. His torso was bare, and I watched his chest rise and fall with each level breath.

I wanted to touch him more than anything. God, I wanted to so badly.

No.

That would only serve to confuse us both. Him, thinking I'd leave all the events of the past couple of weeks by the side of the road somewhere.

I would be left wondering why I was denying myself this glory. My body had been treated to more physical pleasure in the few months we were together than I'd ever had in all my life. I squeezed my eyes shut tightly enough to see stars dancing behind my lids.

Christ, I was going to be late. I turned to go back to the bathroom and saw my cell phone light up among the covers. If I dug through the bedding to retrieve it, I would definitely wake him again. But if I missed a call from Rio or someone else from work, then, in their eyes, I would be unreliable. Or at least that was what I'd convinced myself of—people immediately judged me if I were anything other than perfect.

I knew it was ridiculous, and I knew it was unrealistic to expect perfection from anyone. I always had the highest expectations of myself, but living under the constant disproportionate pressure I put on myself was starting to take its toll on my body.

When I was a teenager, and even in my earlier twenties, I bounced back from mental health episodes pretty quickly. Now, when I had an instance of those overwhelming feelings, I felt off for days. Maybe I needed to start sessions with my therapist again. Couldn't hurt, especially with the added influence of Elijah in my life.

Deciding to leave my phone where it was for now, I hurried through the rest of my morning routine. Just as I was cleaning off the counter, putting everything in its place for the day, Elijah walked past me on his way to use the bathroom. The enormous erection testing the limits of his knit pajama pants caught my eye. I gave my head a little shake to clear away from that subject before we both called in sick. Back in the bedroom, I pulled the covers into place and snatched up my phone.

"I'm leaving," I called with a louder voice than normal conversation required as Elijah came out of the bathroom, so I basically yelled right in his face.

With my splayed fingers on my lips, I tried to hold in my laugh.

"Oh, shit. I'm so sorry. I didn't expect you to be there." I wrinkled my brow and bit my bottom lip, anticipating his reaction.

"Sorry, hon—" I spluttered, but this time he covered my mouth with his own, and it was heavenly. I'd been missing him so sincerely, and his kisses were drugging on a good day. Fine, they were on bad days too.

I pulled back from his body, or I would never leave the house.

"What was that for? And seriously, I need to leave, so I'll see you later."

Not wanting to stand around while he concocted pretty lines about that kiss, I bustled out to the kitchen. Two water bottles in hand, I went to the garage to hop in my car and go. Elijah took up the entire doorway and watched every move I made. He looked as feral as a hungry animal.

Well, this day was off to a great start.

CHAPTER FIVE

ELIJAH

That blond chef was going to drive me crazy until I locked her down. If that meant literally locking her in a cage somewhere, I would do it. More figuratively speaking, I could marry her. Then every other asshole on the planet would know she was taken.

My dick was rock hard when I woke up in her bed. Being surrounded by all the different smells that made up her unique scent pushed my physical need for her into a primal situation. I stalked after her from the guest wing and into the kitchen. She was so worried about being late, she didn't even know I was hot on her trail.

We'd had conversations about this exact habit, but I hadn't seen improvement since the last time we talked about it. To be frank, she wasn't doing anything that looked like work toward making it better, either. At times, her anxiety got her so spun up she lost focus on what was actually happening right in front of her. It was a dangerous symptom of her anxiety disorder, and I meant it when I challenged her to get on top of the problem. We were all going to regret it one day if she didn't take the situation seriously.

Burns or cuts from careless accidents in the kitchen to a fatal car accident flashed through my mind on a regular loop. All things that could be avoided if she learned some mindfulness or did a few quick and easy concentration exercises. I made a mental note to bring it up again. There was also a random thought skipping around in my mind about couple's therapy.

Everyone knew I was a therapy junky. I was one of those people who looked forward to his sessions and practiced the exercises and techniques my doctor suggested. If I hadn't, I didn't think I'd still be alive. Dark, dark days consumed me when I was first living on the streets. Going from completely ostentatious living to taking handouts from strangers really fucked my teenage-boy psyche. And pride. And self-worth. Oh, and self-esteem, too.

No use beating that dead horse, though. I needed to get showered and dressed for work, or I would be rushing around too. Hannah and I shared an opinion on being late to anything. My motto had always been if you were on time, you were already late. I preferred to get to an engagement a little early and assess the whole scene. Maybe it was one of my control issues. Or maybe I just tried to pay the person I was meeting a little respect by being mindful of their time.

When I arrived at the office, Carmen was already at his desk.

"Good morning," I said to my assistant.

"Hey. Morning. How's your day going so far?"

I paused for a moment in front of his desk and considered my answer. There wasn't a singular emotion I could settle on because the morning had been a feelings circus already.

Sticking with the safe answer, I replied, "Good, good. You?"

"So far, so good. But it's early, you know? Scales could be tipped in either direction."

I gave the man a good-natured chuckle and went into my office. It already felt like concentrating today was going to take real effort. If I were lucky, I would have a jammed-packed schedule and no time in between appointments to worry about my home life.

The usual text came from Grant to meet him and Bas on the roof in ten minutes. I hadn't even looked at my email yet, so I pulled the app up on my phone and closed my office door behind me.

To Carmen, I said, "Meeting with the boss. You can text me if anything urgent comes up."

"All right. Sounds like a plan. I see you have a nine o'clock appointment here. Is there anything you need me to prepare?"

"No, I don't think so. That's a team meeting with the security staff, so I have some notes but nothing to be distributed. But thank you for offering."

"Of course. That's what I'm here for."

"You're too good to me, man," I said with a friendly smile.

"I keep telling you that," he said as I turned the corner and headed to the elevator bank with the first genuine smile of the day.

When I reached the rooftop, I saw I was the first to arrive. No doubt the other two would be along soon, so I strode across the wide-open roof and looked down over the city. Being up so high immediately triggered a memory of Hannah's hot-air balloon ride. My smile spread wider and wider as I thought of how much I loved that woman. She had so many facets to fall for, and hidden traits too. Only I got to see those. I wondered if she would say yes if I asked her to marry me. I didn't think I could handle the rejection if she said no, and I didn't want to test it. So I'd wait until I was absolutely sure.

Probably should warm up to the idea by telling her I loved her more often. She already knew I did by that point. I'd said versions of the sentiment to her a few times, but she still looked surprised to hear it.

The metal door from the elevator shaft clanged open, and my two best friends stepped out, deep in conversation. Immediately, I noticed Grant's body language. He wasn't the usual open, gregarious, playful man he normally was. Whatever they were talking about had his complete attention.

"Morning, boys," I said and greeted Sebastian with a quick thump on the back. "Feels like it's going to be a scorcher today."

Grant and I went through the steps of our handshake, and Bas just shook his head like he did every other time.

"I swear the two of you stopped maturing in fifth grade," he groused.

"We've offered to teach you countless times, Shark," I teased. "You really can't complain."

"We need a coffee machine up here," Grant bemoaned. "I keep forgetting to bring a cup with me from downstairs."

"Tell Pia about it," I suggested. "She'll figure out a solution, I'm sure."

"I haven't seen her around much," Grant said. "Do you have her chained to her desk working on the Edge interior?"

"Please." Bas actually rolled his eyes—such an unexpected gesture from the stern man. "She's had a mood board or whatever the hell it's called in the middle of her office for months. She's been steadily plugging away on the project."

Grant and I both nodded with smiles for the woman. She was like a little sister to all of us, and we all wanted the very best in life for her.

Bas pinched the bridge of his nose, and we knew something

was coming that he didn't want to admit or discuss.

"I heard through my niece—who can't keep a secret to save her life—that her mother has been dating someone."

"Vela told you that?" I asked in surprise. "How the hell did that come up? How does an eight-year-old even know what dating is?"

"The child doesn't miss much, trust me," Bas said. "And holy hell, she talks nonstop. I thought it was intense when she was little, but now? Good Christ, she makes me want to invest in noise-canceling ear buds every time she comes over. It's just so . . . overstimulating."

"It has to be better than a crying baby, though," Grant offered. "At least you can communicate with her. Babies? Not so much."

"That reminds me," Bas interrupted. "I'm going to be a father again."

He said it with such smug pride, I could feel the emotions rolling off my friend. Grant and I gathered closer to congratulate Shark on the new bun in the oven.

"Hannah mentioned Abby was sick the day of the wedding," I said as I sat down on the sofa. "I think we've all been expecting this news to some degree."

"Now, will she be as sick as she was the first time?" Grant asked innocently. "Like . . . does a woman go through that every time if they already did once?"

The man was the most clueless male when it came to pregnancy. But really, where would he have been exposed to the event? At least I had been through the first and second trimester with Hensley. Before she left me.

"Abbigail keeps saying it's not that bad, but I think she's full of shit. I think she's afraid of me laying down the law again and insisting she rest. But God"—he cradled his face in his palms and leaned back to let the morning sun fortify him—"I won't live through another scare like we had with Kaisan. I seriously won't," the man pledged. "I will not let that headstrong woman run herself into the ground again like she did the last time."

After a beat or two, Sebastian focused his attention on Grant. "Has Rio given you any idea on which way she's leaning with the settlement offer?"

"Honestly, I'm just trying to stand back and let her work through it on her own. I know she was blown out of the water initially—the amount of money is shocking. I also think there's an internal battle about taking it as a trade-off for her husband's life."

Grant held his large hand up to stop Bas from responding because the man was already poised with a comeback.

"I know that's not what it is, and in her heart she knows it too. I'm just trying to be supportive however she needs because I'm completely out of my wheelhouse with the whole situation."

"Catch me up. What happened? When did this happen?" I asked, hating feeling left out of something that had both of my best friends so tied up in knots. Anxiety was rolling off the pair of them while talking about this subject.

Sebastian answered first. "Remember the other day when I mentioned my attorneys wanted to make a settlement offer to Rio?"

I nodded along while he spoke.

"Well, the four of us got together a couple of nights ago, and I presented an offer to Rio. She asked for some time to think about it."

"I think we would all like to put the incident behind us,"

Grant added. "Or maybe I should speak for myself. I would like to put this all to rest so we can move forward with our lives. I really think this will put a lid on that box once and for all for Rio."

"Yeah," Bas sighed. "I think we could all use some closure on this."

"This is really big news, Bas," I said. "What was it like for you to make that offer?"

"What do you mean?" He screwed up his face in confusion.

"I mean, was it hard for you? We all know you are not normally a sentimental guy. I'm just checking in with you. I would think the emotions were running pretty high in that room."

Bas narrowed his gaze. "Dude, you spend too much time at that shrink's office. You're starting to sound like one."

Grant chuckled and nervously picked at his trousers. "I don't think she will keep you waiting too long for an answer. I mean, she hasn't once mentioned anything about pursuing a lawsuit, so I actually think this came as a surprise to her. It's just not the way the woman's mind works."

Our buddy nodded a few times and said, "All right, all right. I just thought I'd ask. So let's talk some business, yes?"

I leaned forward and rested folded hands atop my knees. "I have some news. My team finally got a bite on the phone number where Hannah's hang-up calls were coming from. They were using pretty sophisticated technology to stay hidden."

Grant chimed in, "That doesn't really make much sense to me."

"What doesn't?"

"Wouldn't you think they would want us to know who it

is? Really, how long is this going to go on? This cat-and-mouse game they are playing. If there's an actual agenda, why aren't they making a bigger move? Since my situation"—he winced after using such an obvious euphemism for his kidnapping— "we haven't heard a word. Not really, I mean."

I reared back and looked at him like he was an idiot. "Hello? Hannah at the Edge construction site? That wasn't enough of a word for you? She could've been fucking gang raped and left to die."

Grant held up his hands in instant apology. "You're right. You're right. I'm an idiot. I'm so focused on my own shit with all of this. Dude, I'm so sorry." He looked at me, and I saw that young guy I first met in a dirty alley on the east side of town. I knew deep down he didn't mean to be so thoughtless.

"There could be one hundred reasons why they've been quiet," Bas said. "I don't like sitting and waiting for the next move, though. I prefer offense to defense any day of the week."

"Maybe we need to make a move," I suggested. "Force their hand, you know?"

"I was thinking that too," Bas said with frustration. "But we need to come up with something solid. It's hard to know what will flush them out when we can't figure out what they want."

Grant shot to his feet. "You know, I've been thinking about something, and I can't get it to add up no matter which angle I come at it from."

Whatever he was talking about had him riled up, so I encouraged him to go on.

"Talk to us, brother. What is it?"

"Okay, so hear me out." He bounced his stare from me to Sebastian, and we both gave quick nods of assent.

"When I chartered that yacht for Rio and me? I only made the arrangements like, what...?" He looked to me since I'd been instrumental in helping him with those plans. "Maybe twenty-four hours on a fast clock?"

"Right," I added, trying to lead him to his point.

"So how did word get to these bastards that I was on that yacht? Even you didn't know where we were. No one did." My tall friend gripped his nape and stared at me to enlighten him somehow.

Why would I have an answer? I wanted to spout but knew my role in our crew. I was the guy who figured shit out. Suddenly it dawned on me that maybe I was letting them down. Maybe my mind had been too focused on Hannah and her issues that I hadn't been giving this topic right here my all.

I felt like shit because of it. I prided myself on being a more loyal friend than I was currently acting.

"I'm so sorry, you guys." I knew they wouldn't know what I was apologizing for until I explained further.

"For what?" the two men said in tandem.

"I don't think I've been one hundred percent dialed in on this like I need to be. There's been so much going on in my personal life, I just..."

"Oh, for fuck's sake, Banks," Bas shot back. "Be serious."

"Elijah, come on." Grant gave a slight left-to-right head gesture.

"I'm totally serious. These women in my life are sucking my soul dry."

"I'm sure something is being sucked, but I wouldn't say it was your soul," Grant said and bumped me with a shoulder.

"We all have lives outside of this one problem, man. I don't want to hear shit like that again. Not to mention, it's been good to see you lighter than you've been in years. I can only assume it's the blond chef's magical touch doing it."

"Regardless, I'm going to do better. I'm going to make this my number one priority until this is behind us. Hell! I have more men on my security team than ever. It would be nice to relieve some of them too."

Mentioning the security team immediately reminded me of my nine o'clock meeting. I checked my watch and still had about five minutes before I had to head back inside. I didn't want to leave Grant hanging on the point he made, because it was a solid one.

"Let me think about this a little while, big guy. I think you're bringing up a good point, but I need to let it bounce around in here for a while," I said, tapping on my temple.

"Fair enough," he said, and we all started walking toward the elevator.

Sebastian asked, "Are either of you sitting in the meeting with Cole?"

Grant straightened his tie as the doors slid open. "What time is that?"

"First thing after lunch," Shark said. "I believe it's one o'clock, but check in with Craig to be sure."

"What's on the agenda?" I asked. "I'll try to get there. I'm not sure what I have going on later. Although, I would like to chat with him again about the morning he found Hannah. Some of those details aren't adding up for me."

We got in the elevator and descended back down to the penthouse. Before the doors opened, I asked Sebastian, "What are your thoughts on me doing a more intense background check on him?"

"On Cole?" he asked with raised brows.

"Yeah. Just to be absolutely sure, you know?"

"I'm not going to stop you," Bas answered. "Let me know if anything comes up."

We all went our separate ways for the rest of the morning and agreed to try to be back for the meeting with the young architect. The guy just seemed too squeaky clean for my liking. Nobody was ever as innocent as that guy seemed.

But maybe my overactive imagination was getting the best of me. I wasn't as jaded as Sebastian, but I wasn't as naturally trusting as Grant. I guess I balanced the two of them out by coming right down the middle. Oftentimes, that was how our relationship went, and it was why it was so good. There was always someone there to be your check and balance.

Later that afternoon, Hannah called.

"Hello, beautiful," I purred down the line. When I heard her little stuttered inhale, my grin got that much wider. I loved hearing, seeing, and feeling the effect I had on this woman. Because she wasn't full of artifice, I got pure reaction mainlined right to my heart. And to my dick, but what else was new with this one?

"Hi, you. How's your day going? I hope I'm not interrupting." Her joyous voice came through the line and was as good as holding her in my arms. Well, almost as good.

"Nope, I'm in between things. Just trying to clear some email. What's going on, babe?"

"I wanted to ask you if I could invite my sisters over? Maybe to swim and just hang out. My guess is two of the four will actually show, but I didn't want to invite people over without checking with you first."

"Hannah." I had to stop her rambling, albeit adorable.

"Yes? Oh, sorry," she apologized quietly. "Nervous rambling. Sorry."

"For one thing, you have nothing to apologize for. Do you understand?" I waited for her reply before continuing.

"Yes, I understand," she huffed. I knew this habit of mine irritated her, but I wasn't considering changing.

"Secondly, beautiful, I want my home to be your home. You can have visitors anytime you'd like."

"Oh . . . okay. Thank you."

There were a few moments of quiet before I spoke again.

"Is there something else, love?" My voice had dipped into the lower register I used to get my way with women.

"Umm, well, yes," Hannah flustered. "I wanted to tell you some great news I heard today. Well, I think it's great news."

"I can't wait to hear it!" I said, trying to be more excited than seductive.

"Abbi's pregnant. Confirmed at the doctor and everything! Isn't that great?"

"It is," I said. "Bas actually told us this morning."

"Awww, bummer," she playfully whined. "He beat me to it."

"The man's already stressing about her well-being." I laughed.

"But there's more . . ."

"What do you mean?" I pursued.

"Well, I overheard Abbigail talking to Rio, and they were talking quietly, so you can't say anything about this."

"Tell me." I issued sternly, but I was getting a kick out of her secret-stealing side.

"I heard Abbi ask Rio if she wanted to buy her out," Hannah whispered.

"Of Abstract?"

"Mmm-hmm," my girl answered proudly.

"How interesting. What did Rio say?" Now I had to know the whole story.

"I couldn't stay to hear that part because someone came around the corner where I was posted eavesdropping," she said in a giddy voice but at once switched tones. "Oh, yuck. That makes me awful, doesn't it?"

I could picture her sagging shoulders while she berated herself, and I wasn't going to stand for it.

"Stop."

"Huh?"

"Stop beating yourself up like that right now. I'm serious. You didn't do anything wrong. You're not spreading the information around to hurt anyone, right?"

"Of course not," she agreed.

"Then stop being so hard on yourself. So what time is the sister squad coming over? It's pretty hot today, isn't it?" I asked in an effort to steer her away from the self-examination.

"Definitely. I was so glad it wasn't my day to do the lunch run. It pays not to be the new girl anymore," Hannah answered in a voice sounding much more like her normal upbeat, cheerful self.

"Do you mind if I'm home when they come over? I'll definitely stay out of your way. Or I can find something to do away from the house if you'd rather be alone. Of course, the security team will still be there. That's nonnegotiable."

"No, don't be silly. I'm not going to chase you from your own home."

"I just want you to be comfortable, beauty. I know women need alone time too."

"You can be the most thoughtful man at times." She sighed dreamily.

"And what about the other times?" I teased.

"Well, we don't need to get into that right now, do we?" She laughed in response. "All right, so I'll see you at home after work today, and you won't be surprised if there is a gaggle of girls in your backyard. Although, I don't suppose it would be the first time."

Whoa. What the hell was that sniper fire? That was totally out of nowhere. I thought she was over my sordid past. Rarely did she show signs of insecurity like that. Maybe it was the thought of her sisters being around? I decided to let it lie there and walk away rather than start an argument. That was definitely unfair, though.

"Talk to you later, Hannah." I disconnected the call. Probably a little abruptly, but I really didn't want to get into it with her right now, plus I needed to be down to the boss's office if I was going to be in on the meeting with him and Jacob Cole.

About fifteen minutes later, I knocked while opening the door to Bas's office. Craig had already announced my arrival, so I didn't bother waiting for his permission to enter. Unfortunately, I was the last to arrive, and Jacob Cole was already midstride with his update.

"Once the amenity deck is completed on level seven, we will hit the tower hard. From there, it will seem like a blink of an eye and your building structure will be done."

"This is really great news, Jake. At the risk of inflating your ego . . ." Bas chuckled. "You continue to impress me. Now what did we decide on the amenity deck exactly? And where are you with liaising with the interior decorator? I know she has big ideas for that space." Bas rolled his eyes. "It's all I've been hearing about for the past month."

"We've been communicating via email up to this point

but have our first person-to-person meeting scheduled for this afternoon. I look forward to meeting her, though. I really admire her design ideas," the young architect said while examining the prints.

Finally, when no one said anything, he looked up from the drawings in front of us.

Bas was giving the guy a strange look I couldn't interpret. For the past couple of weeks, I was sure he was trying to play matchmaker between Jake and Pia, but now, judging by the look on his face, he was ready to give the man a brotherly warning.

Grant noticed the shift in Sebastian's demeanor as well and shot me a sideways glance.

I gave a subtle shrug because I couldn't figure out what was happening either.

As usual, Cole seemed oblivious to the disturbance in the air around Bas and segued into his next talking point. He pulled out another blueprint and unrolled it on top of the others.

"This is a blown-up detail of the amenity deck. The main feature here is the pool of course," he explained while pointing to the pool on the blueprint. "There are changing rooms—or locker rooms—whatever you want to call them—on the north and south ends of the pool. Those have already been roughed in with plumbing and electricity of course."

"Of course," Grant added with a hint of sarcasm, and Jake looked up.

"Do we have a change here?" the architect asked, bouncing his eyes from Bas to me and Grant. "I mean, now is the time to speak up if you don't like this layout. It's possible we can move some things around, but this is how it was designed initially." He sounded a little stressed after making the offer to make amendments.

"No, Jacob. Grant is just being a smartass," Bas said while giving Grant a death stare. "It's part of his charm."

Grant just gave his lazy grin and slid his hands into his pockets. "Please, go on."

And without missing a beat, Jacob did. He picked up right where he'd left off describing the plans. He paused for a moment while something caught his attention. We'd all seen the man's mind in action enough at this point to wait out the silence while he worked something out.

"This here"—he tapped on the drawing with his pen—"this may need to be changed slightly. It can be tricky having foliage planted directly into the ground like this. I see what she was going for as far as the aesthetic, but the water intrusion possibilities just aren't worth the design element." He scribbled a few notes on his smart pad and once again looked up to our silent faces.

"Does that make sense?" he asked sheepishly.

"Yes, perfectly," Bas remarked. "But I'll let you and Pia hash out those details."

"Very good. I think we'll come to an easy alternative," he said assuredly.

The rest of us cracked wide grins.

"What?" Jake asked.

"You just don't know who you're dealing with yet," Bas said. "My sister can be even stronger willed than I am."

"Ahh, noted. I appreciate the insider intel."

"On that positive note," I said. "Jake, always a pleasure. Please let me know if you need anything security or IT wise." I offered my hand in salutation.

"Thank you, Elijah," Jacob said while we shook hands. "I appreciate it. Your men run a really tight ship around the jobsite."

"That's what I like to hear." I smiled and then directed my attention to Bas and Grant. "Gentleman, I will see you tomorrow."

"Wait up. I'm dipping too," Grant said while gathering his belongings. "I've got one last meeting and then home. I think we might go down to the beach. It's so damn hot out there today."

Out in the hall, our conversation continued. "What do you have going on tonight?" my friend asked.

"Not much. I think Hannah is having her sisters over to swim and visit. I'll probably just lie low," I answered with a shrug. "You know, I've been thinking about what you brought up this morning, and I think it really deserves some more focus."

"About the yacht?" Grant clarified.

"Yeah. No one knew you were on that boat except the company you leased it from, the crew on board, and me." I thought about it for a few moments. "So how did those bastards get that intel?"

"That's what I've been trying to figure out. Maybe my phone was tapped? You and I had a lot of back-and-forth before we actually cast off."

We walked in silence until we reached his office.

"Maybe I was being followed, and then they got the information they needed from the leasing office at the marina?"

I tilted my head in thought but realized the gesture looked like I was being skeptical instead. "That's a possibility too. But that one is a little less likely. From what you and Hannah have both said about the men you actually interacted with, they aren't the sharpest tools in the shed."

I watched my lifelong friend for a bit before he realized I was observing him.

"What?" he barked shortly.

With exaggerated movement, I reared back from his reaction. I didn't have a chance to say anything before he apologized.

"Dude . . . sorry." Grant gripped the back of his neck for dear life and groaned. "I just want to fit some pieces of this nightmare puzzle together and clear it off my desk, you know? I'm so fucking tired of feeling like this."

"Like what?"

He gave me a look.

"No, seriously, tell me what you mean."

"I feel fucking violated!" he shouted, even though we were still in the middle of the corridor. "What do you think?"

"All right, I'm sorry that upset you. It wasn't my intention. I'm trying to empathize with you, brother. I don't know what you're dealing with because I don't have the same experience under my belt, you know?" My watchful eyes stayed focused on him while he worked through what he wanted to say.

"Those motherfuckers are in here," he said, thumping his head with his index finger. "They're in here, and I can't get them out. The shit they did to me. I feel like it's going to haunt me for the rest of my life."

"Look, man . . ." I reached out to touch his forearm, and he winced away from the gesture. I waited until his blue eyes lifted to mine but then kind of wished I hadn't. The anguish I saw in my friend's expression gutted me.

"Grant. Listen to me. I would give anything to be able to take this memory from you. Period. To hold the burden myself, because I can't stand watching you like this. Please tell me you are keeping your appointments."

"Yeah, yeah, I am. For the most part it's helping, but there are still some dark times, man. I'm not gonna lie, I've had some dark moments."

"Can I ask you something?" I waited for him to assent in some way. When he gave a quick nod, I asked, "How has Rio been?"

I could feel his hackles rise the moment her name came out of my mouth. I wished she and I hadn't gotten off on such a rocky footing. I hated there was this taboo subject between my best friend and me.

"What do you mean?" he snapped.

I held my flat palms up to him in surrender. "Just what I'm asking. How is she doing, and why is your fuse so short today?"

The tall man looked up and down the hall—I supposed to make sure we still had privacy—and then let his head fall forward until his chin bumped his chest.

"Doctor Mindfuck put me on some kind of *mood stabilizer*," he said with air quotes around the final two words. The added eye roll was just in case I didn't pick up his opinion on the new medication from his tone alone.

With a chuckle, I said, "And you are not a fan?"

"You know I'm not a fan of drugs. Imagine that," he added sarcastically.

"Prescribed medication is a completely different thing than using street drugs to get high. You know that."

"Well, anything that is going to alter my state of mind and cause side effects probably doesn't belong in my body."

"Whatever side effects you're having will likely level out once you adjust to taking the medication. Be patient, all right? In the meantime, if you think of anything I can do to help, please let me know. Day or night. I only want to see you come out on top of this, my friend." This time, when I reached out to touch him, he didn't pull back. Landing a few quick thumps on his back, I said goodbye in front of his door and continued on to my own office.

The three of us had offices on the top floor. Sebastian's was immediately when you stepped off the elevator. Of course, that made the most sense as the CEO and the person most people would be looking for on this level. My office was at the far end, and Grant's was right in the middle. A separate elevator—for staff members only—ran along the end of the building where my office sat, so I used that more often than the one that led to the public lobby.

As one thought led to another, I remembered with disdain that I still needed to check in with LAPD regarding Hensley's break-in. That bitch would not get away with that stunt if I could help it. My days of cowing to her had long since passed. Now that I'd exposed my biggest weakness to the ones I loved the most, there was nothing stopping me from going for her throat.

CHAPTER SIX

HANNAH

I drove home from work with the top down because it was a glorious day in Southern California. My sisters were coming over to Elijah's house for a swim, and I planned on cooking dinner for them.

As expected, Agatha and Clemson immediately responded to my group text and said they'd be there. Maye said she would try but had an assignment due and needed to make headway on it or it would never be done on time. In other words, she wouldn't be coming but was too nice to outright decline my invitation.

Sheppard just didn't answer at all. I wasn't surprised, but I was disheartened. I maintained hope that one day she would get past whatever issue or issues she had with me and it would be the five of us again. Like it used to be. In the meantime, she was the one missing out. I had to stick to that attitude, or my heart would be too heavy to enjoy the company that was coming over.

Clemson came right from school, so she was the first to arrive. I answered the door with my bikini already on and bare feet. The cool tile floor felt good beneath my overheated body.

"Hey, beautiful," I said and pulled her in for a long hug. "I'm glad you found the place okay."

"Holy shit, Hannibal. This place looks like a fortress from the street. What did you say this guy does for a living?" She peppered me with questions while she turned in circles in the foyer. Poor thing was going to blow a gasket when she saw the pool in the middle of the house.

It had been my favorite feature of this home from day one. Having an inground lap pool was a luxury on its own. Having an inground lap pool in the center courtyard of your home was next level.

"Am I the first one here?" my youngest sister asked with exuberance.

"So far, yep." I answered with a big grin. Inviting my sisters over was the best idea. I really needed a familial recharge. "You know what that means, though." I gave her a sideways glance while we walked toward the kitchen.

"Yeah, you're going to put me to work."

"You got it," I said and pinched her little nose. I always liked her nose better than my own. We all looked very similar. There was no doubt we were sisters, but each of us favored one parent more than the other. I looked just like my mom did when she was my age, while Clemson was a physical echo of our dad.

I loaded her arms with drinks and slung a tablecloth over her shoulder too. Elijah had plenty of service people come in and out on a daily basis but didn't employ staff around the clock. Luckily, I remembered where I saw the things I needed to entertain while routinely using the kitchen. Whatever I couldn't find we would just improvise or make do without.

"So . . . tell me, little sister, what's new with you?" I asked while I followed Clemson out into the courtyard. Then I laughed and asked her, "Are you still dragging that poor boy around by his tongue?"

She looked at me with genuine confusion. "What do you mean?" Something clicked, and she said, "Oh, you mean Jeff, right?"

"Is he the one who was at dinner the night I brought Elijah over to Mom and Dad's?"

"Yeah, that's him. He's fine." She shrugged and added, "I think he wants more out of our relationship than I do. I'll probably have to cut him loose soon."

Together we stretched the tablecloth above the table and let it settle onto the surface. It definitely could have used an ironing, but this was a spur-of-the-moment party, so too bad. Plus, these were my sisters. We could eat off paper plates balanced on our laps, and no one would mind.

"What has he done to give you that impression?"

"What's with all the questions, Hannibal?"

"I just miss you. I miss being involved in your everyday life." I shrugged. "So I want you to catch me up." I wrapped my arm around her shoulders and squeezed her close to my side. "Don't give me any crap about it, either."

"I see the bossy thing is contagious in this place," she remarked offhandedly.

"What's that supposed to mean?" I giggled but honestly was a bit surprised she would've picked up on that vibe.

"Hannah," Clemson said, deadpan. "I'm young. Not blind or dumb. Jeez." She rolled her eyes for good measure.

"Oh, baby sister of mine." I paused until she looked directly at me. "The entire world knows you're neither of those things. Trust me." I squeezed her again because I just couldn't help it. I loved this girl and her big heart and her mighty personality and all the things that came with it.

"Your new lord and master seems very . . . ummm . . .

instructional?" She ended the comment like she searched deep and wide mentally for the word.

Before answering, a sly grin spread across my lips. She had no idea just how domineering my man could be. My lower abdomen flexed instinctually, and I sucked in more air.

"Yeah, he definitely gives a good lecture."

Clemson and I both burst into a fit of laughter, and it felt so good. I heard the intercom buzz that someone was at the front gate, so I went to check the monitor and hopefully let Agatha in too.

With the iPad on the kitchen counter, I pulled up the video feed from the security system like Elijah and Marc both showed me.

Only, it wasn't my sister. It was Hensley Pritchett.

What the hell is she doing here?

I quickly texted the security team the emergency code they'd given me and clicked on the intercom.

"Can I help you?" I asked and was impressed how strong and clear my voice rang out.

"Hello, dear," the bitch purred in a sultry voice. "Is your daddy home?" Maybe she didn't know there was a camera capturing her bullshit for posterity, because she actually giggled at her own stupid comment.

"I'm sorry, you must have the wrong address. Please leave. Good day." I sat and watched her process being dismissed so succinctly before she rang the call button again.

"Can I help you?" I said for a second time. Marc had already texted back that they were approaching from the front and back. I needed to tell Clemson so she wasn't scared by their arrival.

"Clemmy?" I shouted out into the courtyard.

"Yeah?"

"Can you come here and help me, please?" I knew it was the quickest way to get her inside because the girl never turned down someone who asked for her help.

Promptly, she hustled into the kitchen and gave me a mock salute.

"At your service, ma'am." Her grin was wide and playful.

I lowered my voice so she understood the moment was serious.

"Listen to me. There is someone at the gate who is not supposed to be on this property. I've already alerted security, and they are coming to take care of the situation."

At her alarmed expression, I grabbed her forearm and bored my stare into her. My little sister had already tasted the anxiety disorder that was genetic-deep in our brains, and I didn't want her to freak out.

"Darling, nod if you're okay," I said gently and waited for her to follow my instruction. Finally, she dipped her chin quickly, and I continued. "Good. That's good. We are not in danger here, but we need to stay inside until the guys take care of this."

Clemson widened her eyes and whispered, "Hannah, what have you gotten yourself into here? I don't think you've been telling the truth." She turned her head slightly and looked at me sideways. "You're not really house-sitting here, are you?"

Well, no one could ever say that this girl wasn't bright. A proud smile stretched across my lips, and she looked more alarmed.

"Why are you smiling?" Then she snapped up tall and looked shrewdly down her nose at me. "Oh, I get it. You're just fucking with me. It's Agatha, right?" She actually tried to shove past me and go to the front door and see for herself. I reached out to stop her and the material of her shirt slid right through my fingertips.

"Clemmy, no! Stop!"

"Yeah, sure, you're so funny," she called over her shoulder while reaching for the door.

I froze in time. It was that awful moment when you knew something bad was about to happen and everything shifted into slow motion. If we were filming a movie, my voice would be slow and distorted while I shook my head and mouthed *Noooooo*.

My sister swung the door open wide while still looking back to me. My eyes went saucer wide, and we both shifted our stares to Agatha standing on the front stoop.

"You've become quite the jokester lately, Hannibal," Clemson chirped and stood back to let our other sister come inside. "I like this lighter side of you. Must be the hot, bossy dude's influence."

My oldest sister flung herself into my arms with her usual gusto and squeezed me hello. When we parted, she hugged the youngest of our brood too. Quickly, she thumbed over her shoulder toward the front gate and bugged out her eyes.

"I don't know what the hell I just passed on your front sidewalk, but do you have a male harem now? Who the hell's the muscle?" With hands planted on her hips, she tapped her toe and waited for my response. The whole situation made me burst into a fit of laughter.

Whose life am I living?

"Uhhhh, no, not quite," I stammered.

The girls both stared at me and waited for me to continue. Having no idea what more to say, I offered, "Who wants to drink?"

"Christ, with the day I just had? Make it a double." Agatha slung her arm around my waist, and I did the same to Clemson on the other side, and we moved into the kitchen as a trio.

"Maybe you need to quit that job," I offered in suggestion. I hated seeing my sister so unhappy and stressed.

"Well, we all can't be as fortunate to have a sugar daddy paying our rent like you, princess," she teased in response.

I scrunched up my nose. "Ha. Very funny. I don't pay rent." I bugged out my eyes and stuck out my tongue. After a few beats, I said seriously, "You never say anything good about that job. Why bother? You're not even using your degree."

"Oh, don't you start too," Agatha warned. "You sound like Mom and Dad."

A subject change seemed to be the best choice, so I asked my guests, "How do margaritas sound?" I poked my finger into Clemmy's shoulder and said, "Yours can be virgin."

Immediately she whined, "No. Come on! I can handle one drink."

I pursed my lips. "Okay. One. Just one, though. And don't you dare tell the units."

My tall sister signed an X over her heart and vowed, "Promise."

They kept me company in the kitchen while I made our drinks, and then we all moved out to the pool.

Agatha looked around the courtyard and whistled long and low. "Damn, Hannah. He's that hot and has this sweet place? Girl, spill it. He must have a hideous flaw somewhere."

Like he murdered his father in cold blood? That probably counts as hideous, right?

Instead, I grinned like a cat that swallowed the canary and said, "If he has one, I haven't found it. And trust me"—I leaned closer, as if to impart a secret—"I've been looking."

Agatha hooted and leaned way back on her butt and kicked her legs up in front of her. My God, this girl was such a riot.

"You dirty bitch! I knew you had to be shagging that man!"

"Whoa, wait a minute!" I laughed. "Who said that? You have an overactive imagination, lady."

Noticing Clemson's obvious unease with the shift in subject matter, I tried to get my other sister to rein in her boisterous enthusiasm with my best death stare.

"Oh, don't give me that innocent bullshit, Clemson! I know you and that boy of yours are hittin' it too," Agatha goaded. "Just stop with the theatrics."

"We are not!" Clemson said through giggles.

"That look on your face says otherwise, young lady," I piled on. "Sooooo, how long has this been going on?" I bumped my shoulder into hers, nearly knocking her off her seat.

"I'm not telling either of you anything."

"What? Why not? How else will we blackmail you in the future? Spill all the tea right now!" Agatha demanded.

Pointing, Clemson said, "That, that right there."

I was laughing so hard I snorted—which, of course, made us all laugh harder.

When we calmed down a little, Agatha said to our youngest sister, "Seriously, though, tell the truth. You peg that boy, don't you?"

"Dah!" I said, exasperated and so thankful I hadn't taken a sip of my drink. I definitely would have either choked or sprayed it all over the two of them after that comment.

Clemmy's face morphed into a confused expression. "I what?"

"Cut the shit, girl."

Immediately I scolded, "That's fucked up, Dah. Leave her alone."

"It's not fucked up. It's hot. Are you saying you've never done it?" my sister challenged.

"Have you?" I fired back.

She quirked a brow. "I asked you first."

"Well, I'm the oldest. So you have to answer first."

She burst out laughing. "That doesn't even make sense."

Clemson scrunched up her face. "What are you even talking about?"

Together, we both said, "Google it."

We sat in silence while Clemson pulled out her phone and Googled pegging. I had to put my hand over my mouth to stifle my laughter, watching her eyes dart back and forth, back and forth, as she read what I guessed was the Wikipedia entry on the subject since that was usually what popped up first.

With a heavy arm, she dropped her phone into her lap and looked up. "Yeah, no. Definitely not happening." Then she mumbled, "Deviants." But after a few beats, she cocked her head, reminding me instantly of Elijah. "But wait a second. You guys are doing this to your boyfriends?" she asked with a combination of curiosity and confusion.

I took a long, slow drink from my cocktail and let Agatha give her answer first. Only seemed fair since she was the one who started this dumpster fire.

"Well, I don't have a boyfriend as you both know, so no, I'm not," she answered matter-of-factly.

Clemson nodded as she listened intently and followed up with another question.

"Have you ever...done...that?" she asked shyly. And

honestly, it might have been one of the few times I'd ever seen my baby sister wear that particular expression. It was endearing at the very least and reminded me just how young she was.

"Are you thinking about doing it to Jeff?" Agatha teased.

"I don't know. I think I'm just curious. I like trying new things. I seriously never knew this was a thing, though, you know?"

Agatha looked at me pointedly and said, "Excuse me, Miss Hannah Banana. Don't think we haven't noticed you haven't answered yet."

I shot to my feet with a burst that nearly toppled my chair over. "Who needs a refill?" I asked in a manic tone.

Agatha threw her head back and cackled. "Oh, dear sister! Guilty minds need no accusers!"

"That's not what this is!" I protested immediately. "I'm just...just so thirsty! And I'm trying to be a good hostess."

Both sisters were laughing now, and I couldn't help but laugh too. The whole scene was so ridiculous. Picturing Elijah submitting to anyone was what had me entertained, but I wasn't about to explain that dynamic to my siblings.

Time to reroute the conversation for good this time.

"What sounds good for dinner? The freezer and pantry are completely stocked, so just give me some ideas, and I'm at your service. And seriously, do either of you want another drink while I'm up?"

"Yes please." Agatha held her glass aloft, and I snatched it as I passed by.

"I better not." Clemson frowned. "I have to drive home."

"You're more than welcome to spend the night, darling," I offered. "We have plenty of room."

"Oh, it's *we* now, is it?" Then she switched to a terrible British accent and said, "Have you become the lady of the manor?"

I flopped down on the end of the nearest lounge chair and let my shoulders slump forward over my knees. "Why are you two busting my balls so bad today?" I whined.

"Because it's so much fun." Agatha shrugged. But when I didn't lift my face from my palms, she pushed at my knees. "Hey . . . you know I'm just messing with you, right?"

Finally, when I looked up and she saw the tears in my eyes, hers widened with instant regret.

"Hannah! What's wrong? I was totally joking around. Oh my God, now I feel like an ass. I'm so sorry. What's going on? You knew I was playing—I mean, I thought you did." My sister stumbled and stammered through her apology.

I wanted to alleviate her guilt by accepting her apology, but the tears seemed to come on with renewed purpose. I had no idea what the hell was happening.

"I don't even know why I'm crying!" I said while wiping my cheeks. "I'm so sorry." This was completely ridiculous.

"Only you, Hannah," Clemson said, shaking her head.

"What?" I warbled.

"Only you would apologize for someone making you cry," she explained. "That's so ass-backward."

"What can I say? I'm a hot mess," I tried to tease while wiping my cheeks again.

With perfect timing, I heard Elijah's voice from inside the house.

"Hey, beautiful, I'm home."

"Shit," I muttered and took a deep breath and tried to calm down. My sisters both watched me closely.

Agatha leaned close and quietly asked, "Are you not allowed to show emotion?"

I mouthed the word *stop* and widened my eyes, silently pleading with her to ease up. My gorgeous landlord stepped out into the courtyard and greeted my sisters while I looked on. It was almost comical watching the effect this man had on the opposite sex.

"Oh, good. You ladies were able to make it."

He approached Agatha first with open arms, and she hugged him hello. If I were more the jealous type, I might have thought she indulged in the embrace a bit longer than necessary. Instead, a grin spread across my face as I watched her drink him in. Next, he went for Clemson, and she stiffened as he approached her. It was subtle, but I knew her well enough to see the slight change in her body language. I quickly covered my lips with my fingertips to stifle the giggle.

"Clemson," Elijah greeted happily. "It's good to see you again."

"Hi. Same. You have a lovely home. Thanks for letting us crash the place for the afternoon." My baby sister smiled at my boyfriend, and all felt right with the world. The number of happy vibes floating around the backyard recalibrated all my internal scales back to zero once more. A girl needed that sort of readjustment every now and then.

I really didn't want to be the party pooper, but I had to speak to Elijah about Hensley showing up at the front door earlier.

"Hey, babe? Can we have a quick chat in the kitchen?" I asked with my eyebrows hiked all the way up to my hairline.

Hopefully he picked up on the sign that it wasn't really a question but more of a demand for his audience.

"Of course, Hannah. You know I'm all yours anytime you need me," he said with that sexy wink, and I heard one of my sisters audibly gasp.

Great. Another female down in the wake of Elijah Banks.

Inside the house, I turned to face him, and he immediately pulled me against his body. God, how I had been missing this. The safe and secure feeling that blanketed my entire body from contacting his at one physical point. It didn't have to be sexual in nature or direct skin on skin. The man was always like a furnace. Wherever he touched me, I could feel the heat and vitality of his existence.

We stood quietly for several minutes, neither one of us wanting to ruin the magic of the moment. Both of us starving for how good we had been just a few days before. Before I was attacked. Before his ex-girlfriend reappeared in our lives. Before he exposed his darkest secret. Before he showed me his deepest vulnerability.

Something happened in this quiet moment. Somehow things became clear to me—things I was having so much trouble seeing before. I was elated and felt like shit at the same time. I pulled back so I could see his face, but he just held me tighter.

"Elijah," I whispered.

"Please don't give up on us," he whispered into my hair.

"Never, baby. Listen to me. I owe you an apology." That caught his attention, and finally he loosened his hold. Although it was just enough so we could look at each other while I spoke, it would have to do. "I've been a terrible partner. I've completely let you down, and I have to pray that you will forgive me now." I could feel the tears welling up from the heavy emotion strangling me.

He was already shaking his head before I even finished what I needed to say. "No, Hannah, you don't owe me anything. Why would you think that? You have been so amazing and understanding. I don't know what I would do without you. I can only beg you to be patient with me while we work through this. While I work through this." He lifted my hand to his lips and reverently kissed my knuckles.

"I hope with all that I am that you see something in me that is worth staying by my side while I get my shit together and be the man you deserve."

I smiled through blurry tears. "Beautiful man, I'm not going anywhere. I am so sorry that you opened yourself up to me finally, made yourself vulnerable by sharing a very dark and personal story from your past, and I abandoned you when you needed support the most. That was terrible of me to react that way. I have to reassure you that that is not the kind of partner I intend on being in the future. All I can do is ask you to trust my words, because my actions thus far have told an opposite story. And I regret that so deeply. I am so sorry. I am so sorry I let you down. Please say you can forgive me."

I squeezed his hands so tightly in mine and stared up at him. Hot tears tracked down my cheeks one after another. I could not imagine my life without this man in it. It would be utter devastation if he sent me away now.

Now the shitty part of this conversation. "Did the security guys tell you that Hensley stopped by today?"

Elijah grimaced and said, "Yes. I watched the security footage, and the guys handled it with the police department already. I am so sorry you had to deal with that situation. Especially on the day you just wanted to visit with your sisters. It makes me sick that my past keeps affecting your present life."

"What do you think she wants? She won't let you see the child. She won't voluntarily do a paternity test. If she wants you back and is still in love with you, wouldn't she know how much you wanted a child? I would think she would be doing everything in her power to make you believe that child is yours, not the opposite. It doesn't make sense to me. So what does she really want? Could this be about money?"

He shrugged and said, "I can't pretend to know that woman. The only thing I do know was how much I never knew her at all. One thing that hasn't changed, though—she always liked to be the one calling the shots."

"You're right." I rolled my eyes. "That certainly hasn't changed, then."

"Enough about that bitch. Go enjoy the time with your sisters. Do you want me to make you guys some dinner? Or have something delivered?"

"You don't have to do that." I smiled up at him. Stepping closer, I wrapped my arms around his waist and said, "It's very nice of you to offer, though. Maybe I shouldn't offer them dinner so they leave sooner and you and I can be alone." I waggled my eyebrows in suggestion.

"Mmmm," he hummed against my lips. "I like this line of thinking, Miss Farsey."

"Well, we were having a very interesting conversation before you came home, and it has my engine running a little hot." I gave him a sly grin. "Know what I mean?"

"Is that right?" He tilted his head, and his hair flopped over to the side. "As much as I would like to usher them out the front door right now, that would be very selfish of me." He grinned and kissed me swiftly. "Go enjoy the pool and sunshine with your sisters. You and I will have the whole night to ourselves after they leave." With his large hands at my waist, he turned me and shoved me toward the French doors that opened onto the courtyard. My sisters had been watching our entire exchange, and their grins were as wide as mine.

"Last one in does the dishes!" I called and dashed across the deck and performed my best cannonball into the pool, ensuring my splash soaked them while they hurried to join me.

CHAPTER SEVEN

ELIJAH

For the first time in weeks, it felt like things in my life were heading in the right direction. Hannah lay in my arms, and the sound of her soft, steady breathing soothed my heart and soul. If I still had a soul, because I always thought teenage me gave that up when I took my father's life. Or maybe over the past few years, when I spent debauched nights disrespecting women and their bodies.

But here I lay with this angel, surrounded by magic and bliss. That was what this woman was to me. Or maybe the words *purity* and *love* described her better.

Yeah, those work too.

She was as close to perfect as a human could be. And she was mine. There was no going back for either one of us now. Let anyone try to come between us and see what happened. Very few people understood what I was capable of.

I stretched my neck so I could see the clock on the nightstand. I only had five more minutes before I had to get up and get ready for work. I was really starting to resent that place when I could think of so many better ways to spend the day. I'd much rather spend the day in bed with this woman, showing her how much I adored her and how much I appreciated her perfection.

She had no idea how good I could make her feel. We really had only explored the tip of that iceberg so far. But her sexual appetite was growing by the day. I really had awakened a beast in this fine female, and I had no interest in taming her. Quite the opposite, actually. I loved the naughtiness buried right under the shell of her insecure femininity.

Now there were two words you wouldn't catch me saying out loud in front of Hannah or any of her sisters or friends, thank you very much. I liked my balls exactly where they were. Why didn't women understand men liked the fragile, insecure feminine side of them as much as we enjoyed the fierce, strong warrior side of them? The former allowed our protective, dominant, manly characteristics to shine while the latter gave us comfort knowing our women could handle themselves when we weren't around.

It was literally the best of both worlds. Having our cake and eating it too.

I turned off the alarm and got in the shower while trying to remember what I had on my calendar for the day. Something was in the back of my mind, but I couldn't remember what it was. I went through my normal routine, and when I got out of the bathroom, I made a beeline for my closet to grab my phone to check my calendar app and see what I had planned for the day.

Holy fuck.

It was Hannah's birthday, and I'd completely forgotten. How did I become such a fuckup in so little time? Last week I kept telling myself I had tons of time. Don't sweat it. I'd think of a killer present and blow her mind, and she'd love me for all time.

And promptly forgot about it. Until right now. For Christ's

sake. I deserved to be broken up with. Well, I guess I knew how I was spending my lunch hour. But this morning—I needed a grand gesture for this morning when she woke up. It was too late to make breakfast in bed. I needed to be at the office in thirty minutes, and with traffic in this hellhole town, I wouldn't even make it driving straight there. Fuck!

Okay. Okay. I could still pull off a great birthday and not look like a total ass. I finished knotting my tie—I made sure to pick her favorite one—and came out of my closet to find the bed empty. I strode through to the bathroom and found my beautiful birthday goddess under the shower spray. I leaned against the counter and took her in. It didn't take long for her to feel my presence in the room, and she wiped the steam off the glass enclosure to see me watching her.

"Happy birthday, my love." I gave her the best fuck-me grin I could muster.

She narrowed her eyes, and I smirked because she was even more adorable when she was trying to seem angry.

"How did you know today is my birthday? Oh, never mind." She waved her hands through the air. "Silly question, right?"

I just kept watching her and grinning. I was so into this woman it made my chest ache. Finally, when she stepped out of the shower, I said, "Don't make plans for tonight. You're all mine."

"Elijah—" she began to protest, but I covered her mouth with mine and ended the debate in the most efficient way I knew.

"If I didn't have a vital meeting with my attorney this morning, I would take you back to our bed and lick every one of these warm drops of water from your skin." I swept my fingertips from the hollow at the base of her throat out across her collarbones to her delicate shoulders and then down her arms to cup her elbows in my palms. I repeated the same path several times. If I weren't careful, I would never leave the house. I'd be a total no-show for my attorney.

"Have a great day, baby, and I'll see you back here this evening and we'll celebrate." I gave her one last deep kiss and then backed away with deliberate steps.

A rosy flush had crept across her chest and up her neck, betraying her arousal. I blew her one last kiss and winked before I spun on my heel and left for work. I heard her whimper as I walked down the hall toward the kitchen. A grin tugged at my lips, knowing I had her right where I wanted her. She'd be thinking about the ways I could bring her pleasure clear into the lunch hour if she was half as obsessed with me as I was with her.

Since I had to run so many errands to get ready for this impromptu birthday celebration, I drove myself to work so I would have a car at my disposal. If I needed an extra set of hands to accomplish all the tasks that needed to be done, I could send Carmen out to help. The dude loved this kind of shit anyway—and let's be honest, so did I. If it was something to make Hannah happy, I was all about it.

With the Bluetooth activated in my car, I dialed Grant. "Hey, big man. How are you this morning?" I asked my best friend.

"Not bad, not bad. You're at it early."

"Yeah, I got a lot going on today," I said, getting right to the point. "Any chance Rio is still with you?" I let out a soft chuckle at the absurdity of the question. Under any other circumstance, the thought of me calling for his woman was ridiculous. He and I both knew that I'd rather have fire ants crawling around my balls than need her for something.

Which was the likely explanation for his laugh too. "Nah, man, she left for the kitchen hours ago."

I palmed my forehead. "Oh, that's right. I wasn't thinking. Shit, this whole morning..." Damn it. I needed to get a plan together.

Grant's deep voice broke me out of my pity party. "She said she told Hannah she could come in late this morning since it's her birthday and all. Rio went in early to help pick up the slack."

"Yeah, that's what I wanted to talk to her about. Hannah's birthday, I mean. I'm such a shitty boyfriend." I mumbled the last part.

"Oh no, you didn't! Say you didn't..."

"Nope, I most definitely did. I forgot my woman's birthday. But in my own defense"—I hurried to follow my admission with an excuse—"we've been dating for what? Like three days?"

I could hear the frustration and hint of anger in my own voice, and I needed to pull that shit up right here and now. It wasn't Grant's fault that I was a dipshit, and it certainly wasn't Hannah's. But it wasn't my fault either. Not really.

The day we talked about her attempted childhood abduction, Hannah mentioned it was the day before her birthday. But the date got overshadowed by the horror of the event itself. I never thought to add it to my calendar after that because our conversation was focused on the events and aftereffects of that experience. It would make sense that her birthday might have become a reminder of something horrible instead of a celebration of her life and all the things she had achieved.

"You still there, man?" Grant asked impatiently. Judging by the tone of his voice, he might have asked more than once.

"Yeah, sorry. I was just thinking. I hope I'm not fucking up here."

Grant sighed. "I can only guess what you're talking about if you don't give me something to work with."

"You know I told you about that attempted abduction when Han was little?"

"Mmm-hmm," Grant mumbled around what sounded like a mouthful of food.

"That happened on her birthday. Well, the day before her birthday. Lisa, her mom, had all the girls at Target shopping for things for a family party." One beat of silence expanded into a few more while I gave my thought more consideration.

Grant broke the spell of quietude when his curiosity got the best of him. "What is it, my brother?"

I rubbed my cleanly shaven jaw. "Well, now I'm wondering if her birthday has become a negative memory instead of a positive reason to celebrate, you know? I wanted to get everyone together tonight and have a nice dinner to honor her, but I don't want it to be one giant trigger. I'm totally confused what I should do." Through the windshield, I watched the traffic ahead slow down and then grind to a full stop.

"Fucking perfect," I groaned.

"Wha?" he asked, still chewing.

"Traffic," I complained. "What the hell are you eating?"

"Burrito from this rat trap down the block," he explained once he swallowed. "I'm totally hooked on their carne asada."

"Shit, that does sound good right about now," I said at the same time my stomach grumbled so loudly I thought Grant might have heard it over the phone line.

"Think about it, man. What's going to trigger her about getting together with her friends for dinner? Rio loves her, and I'm pretty sure Abbi does too. They'll have a great time. I never told Rio about the incident when Hannah was young. It's not like I've been hiding it from her, but it's just never come up in conversation, you know?"

Grant quickly absolved his own guilty conscience about possibly being evasive with Rio, and I couldn't help my wide grin as I listened to him bluster. Dude had it bad for that woman, and I couldn't be happier for him.

"Yeah, I guess you're right," I finally agreed when the silence had gone on too long. Then my brain took a sharp left, and I realized Grant should've been on his way to work by now, but it sounded like he didn't have a care in the world lounging around at home.

"You're not working today, tall man?" I asked with our usual brotherly jest.

"I'll be in a little later this morning," he said. But he didn't say more than that, and my suspicious mind downshifted to gain the momentum I would need to launch an interrogation.

"Everything okay?" I asked.

"Oh yeah," he said in his easy tone.

"Did you have another PTSD episode? A flashback or whatever?" I pressed on, even though he clearly didn't want to talk about it. I couldn't stand not knowing what was going on. He knew this about me, so he had to be toying with me on purpose. And like the rat I was, I stole the cheese he set out and tried to take off before I got my ass snapped by his trap.

The bastard chuckled before answering, "No, man, I'm solid. Haven't had one of those in weeks. Hell, what's the date today? It may be over a month now."

"That's great. I'm glad they're getting further and further apart."

"Yeah, so am I. They fuck me up for days. I think the meds are finally doing their thing, and Dr. Shomberg has really helped by teaching us ways to deal with the scorched earth I leave behind afterward and stuff to do before bed to reduce the chances of having them in the first place."

"That's so interesting to me . . ." I drifted off with my reply, not wanting to wade through my best friend's murky mire if he wasn't in the mood.

"What's that?" he asked, encouraging me in knee-deep.

"I never thought much about it. That your state of mind as you enter the sleep cycle can actually affect your dreamscape," I explained for starters. Still, I felt compelled to summarize. "I guess I always thought of dreams as completely random snippets that popped into your resting mind."

"I'm just telling you what the man told me," Grant replied so nonchalantly I could picture the carefree shrug and friendly grin that would accompany his response.

"Well, my brother, I'm finally pulling into the parking garage. Thanks for keeping me company on the commute. Guess I'll see you later this morning. By then, I should have more solid plans regarding tonight," I promised Grant as I climbed out of my car.

"All right. Talk later." And with that, he was gone.

Carmen was already at his desk when I walked down the hall from the elevator. The guy was never late, and just as reliable, his genuine smile stretched from one side of his chiseled face to the other when he saw me approaching.

"Good morning, Mr. Banks."

"Morning, Carmen. You're especially chipper this

morning. Is there a particular reason why?" I slowed my pace until I came to a complete halt in front of his desk.

He gave me a sly grin and a shrug and answered, "I don't think so."

"That was a total yes," I ribbed.

While I was talking to my assistant, I noticed a framed picture toward the back of his desk that I'd never seen there before. The young woman in the photo was simply stunning. The type of beautiful you'd remember seeing before.

Following my line of sight, Carmen zeroed in on where I was staring. His smile changed from one of mischief to one of pride.

"She's a real beauty, isn't she?"

"Stunning."

Nothing more needed to be said. The woman was that naturally breathtaking. Her tan skin was a similar shade as Carmen's, while her eyes were icy like mine, but the blue version instead of green. In the picture, long brown hair hung in a loose braid down the center of her back, and shorter pieces blew in the breeze and framed her face.

"So, is this the future Mrs.?" I asked my assistant and gestured with my chin toward the frame on the desktop. "It makes perfect sense why you're always smiling now."

"Ummm, no. That's my sister. My baby sister."

I tilted my head to the side, and my hair followed suit. I could hear Hannah's hiss in the back of my mind and chuckled.

"I don't know, man... Doesn't look like much of a baby to me." I hiked my eyebrows as high as I could and gave my assistant a crooked grin.

Carmen shooed me with his hand. "All right, you can go now. You will never even be in the same room with her if it's up to me."

Pretending to clutch my heart, I stumbled toward my office door with grand flair. "Carmen, the pain. Your words … they stab me." I fell to the ground in front of the entryway.

"Oh my God. You big fool," he said while laughing.

I rolled to my back and stared up at the grid of fluorescent lights and T-bar ceiling tiles while considering how good it felt to just laugh. Laugh and act up for a change.

Then I heard Carmen say, "Oh, hey, Ms. Farsey, what brings you by so early?"

How I didn't either split my pants or throw out my back from the combination of moves I executed to get up off the floor as fast as I did was a wonder of physics and the human body. Quickly, I looked left, which was ridiculous because the closed door to my office was right there. I whipped my head to the right to see no one in that direction either. Carmen, however, was laughing like he'd just heard the best joke ever.

Or played the best joke ever.

I narrowed my eyes and leveled my best threatening stare straight at him.

"Ohhhh …" I drew out, trying to sound menacing. "It. Is. On." I pointed at him with my index finger. Even shook the thing a bit to seem more threatening. "You're going to regret that, junior."

And while he gave his best effort at schooling his features, the moment I turned my back to go into my office, I heard the man let out a quiet snicker. And then another. Just as I closed myself off from the rest of the comings and goings out in the corridor, I heard Carmen laugh fully.

I sat at my desk grinning like a kid for at least five minutes after that episode. The only task I was good for was deleting junk email, so I spent some time doing that until I was ready to be serious again. I really had to enlist Carmen's help with Hannah's birthday celebration. We probably needed as much time as possible, too, so I called his desk phone directly from mine and waited for him to pick up.

"Yes, Mr. Banks?"

"Can you come in here, please? Bring something to take notes on."

"You got it," my easygoing assistant said.

A few minutes passed, and there was a quick knock at the door and Carmen strode in and crossed the room with his smart pad tucked under his arm.

"How can I help?" he asked, and that was one of my favorite things about this guy. Always willing to help first, ask pointless questions later.

"Well, I kind of fucked up." I gave him my best *who, me?* look that I'd perfected when I was a boy and charming my mother and the house staff was my full-time job. I shirked responsibility for more broken windows and antiques with the look I was giving Carmen than I could count with both hands and feet.

He narrowed his eyes and drew his head back a bit before saying, "You don't have to do that charming stuff with me. You pay me a salary. That's enough. Plus, I'm straight. So . . . yeah, no. What can I help you with?" He sat down in the chair across from my desk and opened the device's cover and waited.

"Today's Hannah's birthday, and I had no idea." I stared at him while, mentally, my words tumbled around with the consequences a statement like that might bring in a relationship as young as ours.

Carmen's hand hovered over the pad on his lap while he slowly raised his eyes to meet mine. That was all it took for panic to surge through my body.

"What is it?" I demanded and heard the strangeness of my own speech and the way it climbed at least two octaves in reaction to his expression. "You need to get that look off your face right now. We can't be looking like that," I ordered the man while shaking my head.

Again, I paused to digest the absurdity of my own voice. Out from behind the desk, I set across my office to pace back and forth. I was speaking so fast, it was a wonder he could understand what I was saying. After a deep, steadying breath, I leaned against one of the office's floor-to-ceiling windows and faced my assistant.

"Okay. Okay. I'm sure you're right," Carmen said when I stopped rambling long enough for him to get a word in. "Actually, I have one simple question that will tell me everything I need to know."

"Shoot," I invited and raked my hand back through my hair. Christ, I hadn't even looked at my calendar to see if I had an appointment this morning other than with my attorney. "Wait, do I have anywhere I need to be after my lawyer?"

Carmen shook his head efficiently. "Not until a lunch meeting along with Mr. Shark." He snapped his fingers twice. "I'm sorry I can't remember who you're meeting with, though."

"No worries... Okay, go ahead. What were you going to ask?"

"Is Hannah more like Miss Abbigail or Miss Rio in temperament?"

I thought about that for a few moments. My gut reaction would be Rio, but Hannah had a lot of control issues like she mumbled about Abbigail having too.

"You're already overthinking it," Carmen encouraged.

"What was your first instinctual answer?"

"Rio." I grinned at the irony of admitting that. "They're actually really close friends," I added.

I watched as Carmen jotted a few things down and then asked, "Is she her best friend?"

"No, I'd say one of her sisters probably is. Agatha."

He took a few more notes before looking up to meet my eyes. "How many sisters does she have?"

I kept eye contact with the man for a moment longer than necessary to try to read his intention in the moment. Was this part of his research for Hannah's birthday party, or did we just shift into personal intel? Honestly, I'd have no problem vouching for the guy if he wanted to be set up with one of Hannah's sisters.

"She has four sisters." I grinned when his eyes widened. "So, including Hannah, who is the oldest, there are five of them. And yes"—I held my hands out in front of me pretending to hold back an advancing throng of people—"they're all knockouts. Different in their own way, you know? But very much the same. It's quite the gene pool."

"Interesting," he muttered. "Do you have"—he scrolled up on the screen a bit, clearly looking for something he'd written down—"Agatha's phone number? I think she'd probably be very helpful."

"I'm sure I can get it. But listen, I don't want this to be like the Olympics' opening ceremony. I was just thinking a nice dinner with our friends and some family because they're very important to her. There's just no way I can get all of it done myself," I explained.

"I hear you, boss." He nodded. "First, I'm going to go out to my desk and come up with a menu for you to approve, and then I will call the caterer. You work on the guest list while I'm doing that, and then together we will try to contact everyone you want to invite since there isn't enough time for anything other than a direct phone call."

I nodded along like I was keeping time with a pop song.

"Sounds like a plan," I said excitedly. "I can't thank you enough, man."

"Well, don't thank me yet. I'm sure fifteen things will go wrong between now and party time," Carmen said, and we both laughed and then abruptly stopped because we knew he spoke the truth.

"I just want her to have a great night," I confessed. "Something she'll always remember."

"We'll make it the best ever," my assistant vowed.

A spark of an idea caught on a memory or recollection of something Hannah shared with me one time while we walked along the water's edge.

Bless the man's soul, Carmen stayed motionless while I let the entire idea flare to life so I could relay the details to him.

"Someone just had a major brainstorm," he said, grinning. "That or he finally remembered where he left his spare house key."

"I think we should have the party on the beach. We can make a bonfire and have a volleyball net set up. Oh, and horseshoes. Line up some tables and chairs." The more I spoke, the more I loved the idea.

Carmen was smiling—just not as big is mine.

I continued to pitch the idea. "Hannah will love it. She loves the beach. She loves the kicked-back vibe instead of the fancy, stuffy indoor cocktail party shit." By the time I finished regaling him with my idea, all the way down to the table decor, his smile was even bigger than mine. Dusting my hands together as if to say *my work here is done*, I looked to my aide for his input.

"That's not a bad idea. It's still warm enough, and it won't be as crowded because it's midweek. Is there a particular beach she favors?" he asked, fingers poised above the Bluetooth keyboard he was using with his smart pad.

"Dude," I replied flatly, but he just stared at me. I guess there was a possibility he didn't know I lived on some of the most desired beachfront property in the country.

"Why do I feel like I missed something?" Carmen asked. "Or do I have something on my face? My nose?"

He frantically wiped at his nose, then his mouth, and just as quickly had the camera on his phone turned around as if to take a selfie but was using the lens as a mirror to make sure he wasn't committing a sinus or, more accurately, a nares faux pas.

"I don't see anything," he nearly hissed, looking from me to his phone screen and back again, working up to a spectacular meltdown.

"Settle down, man. There's nothing on your face. Anywhere. I never said there was." I added that last bit when he aimed death rays at me from his normally friendly eyes. "You were the one who said that and then went DEFCON over it. I was an innocent bystander," I added, to ensure he knew where the blame belonged.

My assistant fixed his glare to my face after giving me the head-to-toe sweep I'd only seen women do to each other before.

"Somehow I find it difficult to reconcile those words"—he used jazz hands to accentuate an imagined theater marquee above our heads—"innocent victim and Elijah Banks."

I squinted and said, "Very funny. The point I've been trying to make this whole time is I live in Malibu. Residents on the west side of the street have a private beach from the back of the house toward the water. I don't know . . . maybe one hundred yards?"

Now he got the picture I was painting.

"Do you mind having the party at your home?" Carmen questioned.

"Not at all. I think Hannah would actually prefer it. That way she can move around leisurely and visit with everyone. You know, instead of sitting in one place at a table the whole time like it would be at a restaurant?"

The younger guy nodded. "I'm totally with you on this plan. You still want to have it catered, though, right? I know she's a chef, but you can't expect her to work in the kitchen all night and ignore her guests. And still be talking to you the next day."

"Absolutely. It will probably be like pulling teeth—keeping the Abstract team out of the kitchen—but I can have my brothers level some threats to their women on the way over, and that should help with at least two of the girls. And those are the two that I suspect would be the biggest problems." I was laughing by the time I finished the comment, if for no other reason than the expression on my assistant's face.

"Do I even want to know what you're talking about?" Carmen squeaked his question, and I chuckled when I noticed the hue of his ears and cheeks matched the pink stripes on his green tie.

My grin got wider with my answer. "Not if that simple comment made you blush like it was your first summer at band camp."

He brushed my comment off with his own cheeky grin and then executed a sharp change of topic, so I decided to let it all blow over too. We really had fallen into a nice, simple working relationship, and I wanted to keep it that way. There was nothing worse than an assistant who didn't know his place.

Bas's former executive assistant, Terryn, had been the perfect example. The woman had always been two beats out of step from everyone else. For the most part, she'd gotten her job done, so Shark let the weird stuff slide without paying her too much mind.

When my best friend had asked odd things of her, she never complained. She had been loyal and trustworthy to a fault. In the end, the same characteristics that had given her the dedication to outlast most of his other assistants had also made her the perfect Trojan horse for his enemies.

Had she been playing along with the enemy to double-cross Sebastian? Or was she just a simple girl with an innocent crush on a powerful man who on most days seemed larger than life?

The most frustrating part of that whole shit show? We'd never know the truth.

CHAPTER EIGHT

HANNAH

I watched Elijah from across the firepit as he talked with his best friends. One hand slung casually in the pocket of his shorts, the other clutching the long neck of a beer bottle.

When my dad approached the guy gang, they easily worked him into the conversation. In no time, my dad was laughing and ribbing the others like he'd known them for years. But that was so typical of the man, and Elijah too. So why would I even be surprised that putting them together in a crowd would net that result?

Agatha and my mom plopped down across the table from me and stole my attention from the boys. My sister pushed an unopened hard seltzer my way, while I tried to give her my best glare. Those damn drinks were starting to sneak up on me the longer I sat still.

"Come on, sister. It's your birthday. Live a little. Look! Your boss is right over there."

We all shifted our stares to where Rio stood with Grant. It looked like she was trying to get her way and failing miserably. We all winced in unison when she tripped over her own feet and then exhaled together too when he easily caught her before she took a spill. Our audible reaction embarrassed her equally if not more than if she'd actually hit the deck.

When we all refocused on our little group, my sister continued as if none of that just happened. "I think she'll understand if you tell her you won't be at work tomorrow."

My mom chimed in then too. "She may be calling out herself from the look of things."

We all looked back over to Rio and Grant just in time to see the tall guy bend forward and plant his shoulder into her midsection and hoist her up using no effort at all. While laughing might have been a normal reaction to what we were watching, we all had the same starry-eyed expression when we turned back to our own conversation. This study showed that three out of six Farsey women liked a dominant man based on our reactions to that caveman display.

On a heavy sigh, Agatha finally lamented, "Well, then."

"Hannah." My mom issued my name, and for whatever reason, either the tone of her voice or the way her eyes were assessing me while she did so, I felt like I just got caught doing something I shouldn't have.

"Yes, Mommy?" I made every facial feature as childlike as possible until Agatha started gagging over the side of the table. I pushed her hip with the sole of my entire foot, and she followed the gravitational pull on the lowest body part to the ground—her head—and fell face-first into the sand.

"Hannah!" she and my mom both shouted in unison as I cackled.

"Serves you right." I giggled as my sister stood up and brushed sand off her face and forehead.

"I'm going to track sand into your mansion. How does that sound? I'll bet Mr. Hottie over there"—she motioned to Elijah with her chin and went on—"won't appreciate that very much." She said it all so smugly, and I widened my eyes, immediately realizing what she had done.

Fucking alcohol and loose lips. Internally I begged every name for God I could think of with a buzzed brain to allow my sister's comment to go right over my mom's head.

"Mom, what were you about to say before Dah fell off the bench?" I laughed at the look my sister shot me but turned my full attention to my mom and waited for her answer.

"Hmmm…" She giggled too. "I can't really remember now. My God, what's in these things?" She picked up the hard seltzer can and held it at a straight-armed distance and squinted. "Shit, I still can't read that. It looks like there are two of everything. I think I've been rubied."

"What did you just say?" I asked my mother, tilting my head like my sexy landlord and boyfriend had the habit of doing, as I tried to make sense of what she said.

"Rubied," my mom said impatiently. "Hannah, come on. You can't keep living such a sheltered life, dear. Everyone knows about rubies. I just saw a story about it on *48 Hours*."

Agatha looked at me and then to our mother. Through sporadic fits of giggling, she asked, "Mom, do you mean roofies?"

"I don't know." Mom looked bewildered. "Do I? I thought they were saying rubies, not roofies." She leaned in and put a flat hand up to shield her mouth from anyone seeing. The universal signal she was about to dish out some top-secret dirt. If you wanted in on the scoop, now was the time to lean in.

Of course, my sister and I both did the natural thing and bent closer to our mother to hear her say at a totally normal, conversational volume, "I think they even said Bill Cosby gave unsuspecting women rubies and then took advantage of them."

My sister sank to the bench beside me, and somehow, through uncontrolled laughing, we tried to convince our more-than-buzzed mother that one of the date rape drug Rohypnol's many nicknames was roofies, not rubies.

Seriously, it was the funniest thing I'd heard in a long time.

"I think we're going to be telling this story at every holiday meal until we have great-grandchildren," Agatha said to me, still snickering between gulps of her drink.

"You're probably right," I agreed. Then I motioned to the bottle she just set down. "You're also not driving home. You're not going to give me a hard time about that, are you?"

She thumbed back to herself and mouthed the word *me* with an accompanying overexaggerated facial expression. As if she were ever innocent a day in her life.

Bumping into her with my shoulder, I said, "Yes, you. Cut the shit. No one here is buying it. Unless you ask the people over there." I pointed out the table filled mostly with my coworkers. "Because they don't know you." I laughed at her overdramatized sad face and dug my sandy feet on top of hers beneath the table.

My gorgeous man checked in to see if we needed refills, and while I declined, my sister said she was ready for another. Elijah looked at me and raised a brow.

I just shook my head and said, "She's a big girl. She knows what a hangover feels like." But there was no missing the fact that my sister had crossed over that line where one minute you were fine and the next—you were completely shitfaced.

"Yeah, listen to her," Agatha said in an obnoxious, too-loud, slurring drunk voice. "It's her birthday." She stabbed a finger into the side of my head.

"Shit, Dah. Stop it," I whined and tried to bob and weave away from her pokey finger.

She took both of my hands in hers, and I could barely keep

a straight face while she implored me to hear her out. "No, Han. I'm saying it's your birthday. You get to do and say what you want on your birthday because you're the queen." She gave an exaggerated wink and nodded until I gave in and nodded along with her.

"Excellent!" she shouted and clapped her hands together in delight. It must have required too much hand-eye coordination, because she nearly toppled backward off the bench. By then I was laughing so hard, if she had fallen, I would not have been able to save her.

Carmen and my man returned and joined us at the table. Elijah set a bottle of water in front of me, and I smiled and leaned closer to thank him with a kiss.

"You're always so thoughtful." I faced his assistant across the table and said, "Thank you for whatever hand you had in all of this." I motioned to our surroundings. There was no way Elijah came up with and executed this entire production on his own. Especially since, just this morning, he was in a full panic when he left for work because he'd forgotten it was my birthday. He could deny it until pigs grew wings and flew, but I knew what panic looked like on my guy's face. And this morning? One hundred and ten percent panic.

Carmen's smile was warm and genuine. "I only did a little bit. You know, just tied up some loose ends. Mr. Banks had most of the heavy lifting done already."

"You're a good man." I reached across the table and patted his hand, and we all knew it was a condescending gesture. But my intention was lighthearted, and hopefully everyone knew that too.

"So, I'm pretty sure my parents have worked out who lives here and who is not really house-sitting," I said for Elijah's ears only. While I spoke quietly near his ear, my guy used the opportunity to wrap me in his embrace. His strong chest was the perfect place to settle against as the night started to really cool down.

"Are you warm enough? It's dropped a few more degrees, but I don't want to keep feeding the fire because we should probably wrap it up soon. People have to work tomorrow."

I had to look up to answer him, but he met me in motion, and I was instantly swept away by the magic of his kiss. I could kiss Elijah for hours, until both our mouths were swollen and tender from the press of hungry lips and the stab of willing tongues.

There were hours of sensual enjoyment just waiting to be experienced in his full pucker. I wanted to be the woman who claimed every single kiss good night and each good morning peck from this moment until forever. I wanted his mouth to be the only one touching mine until the end of time.

Could I make that my birthday wish?

It couldn't hurt to try, right? It was my birthday, after all. I should be able to do whatever I wanted to do.

"Hannibal! Where's the fucking cake?" my sister bellowed so everyone from Port Hueneme to Point Loma could hear.

Elijah and I had just stood, so I planted my face directly against his chest to hide my mortification. Thank God my parents had already said good night, or they would be dragging my sister out with them.

"What was she drinking?" he asked. "I didn't really see her getting that many from the bar."

"Hard seltzer. Those things sneak up on you. I've been telling her all night, and she kept saying"—I imitated my sister's voice, which in truth sounded very much like my own, so my impression of her sounded nothing like she actually did—"*I drink them all the time. Stop nagging me.* I told her she had to spend the night, no arguing, so at least that part is covered." Then I realized I never checked with him if it was okay and shot my eyes up to his. "I mean, you don't mind, do you? I'm sorry. I should've asked you first."

"Beauty, this is your home as much as it is mine. I want you to think of it that way. Okay?" He kissed me again so I couldn't get in a single word to the contrary.

My oldest sister stood just as we broke from our kiss and just as quickly tumbled right back down onto a bench alongside one of the tables. She put her head down on her stacked forearms, and by the way her legs were akimbo beneath the bench, she must have felt like the entire planet was tipping on its axis in hopes of tossing her off.

"Carmen," Elijah called to his assistant to get him back to where we stood.

I felt so bad for the guy because he had just walked away a minute before. He probably wanted to meet some new people tonight.

"What's up?" he chirped, not seeming bothered at all.

Okay, never mind, then. Showed how much I knew.

"Can you see if Hannah's sister—right there…" He put one hand on his assistant's shoulder and leaned closer while pointing with the other. Carmen must have said something I didn't catch because my guy gave him a quick grin and continued.

"Her name is Agatha. Will you take a little walk with her down the beach and back? She needs to walk off some of the alcohol she pickled herself in this evening. At the very least, she needs the opportunity to vomit somewhere other than inside my house." Elijah bounced his stare between Carmen and me.

It was a tight race which one of us objected quicker. The two of us could just take turns convincing Elijah his idea was a bad one—more of a tag-team approach.

Immediately, I started talking. "I don't know, babe."

"What? It works, trust me. The fresh ocean air will make her feel better."

"I just feel uncomfortable with this," I replied.

"Yeah, what she said," Carmen added while thumbing his bent arm toward me.

"No offense, Carmen," I said and put my hand on his forearm. "I'm sure you're a super nice guy and all. But between recent experiences of my own"—I touched my sternum for visual reference—"and my mom talking about rubies half the night." That absurd tangent totally distracted me from the serious point I was trying to make.

With faces screwed up in confusion, Elijah and Carmen said in chorus, "About *what*?"

The uncoordinated way Agatha lifted her head to join the conversation reminded me of a marionette being yanked upright by its tethers.

"Rubies!" she shouted and dropped her face back into her folded arms as gracelessly as she had raised it.

I covered my face with my hands. "Oh my freaking God," escaped through spread fingers while so many thoughts were careening from one side of my brain to the other. Like county fair bumper cars with twelve-year-old boys behind the wheels, the scene felt chaotic and uncertain. It was equal parts funny and terrifying not knowing what was going to hit you next.

I should've captured her antics on video. Undoubtedly,

she would want to kill me, but I'd love to have the footage for future blackmail currency. Internally I was warring with myself, knowing I should probably get her inside and tucked into bed. But I kept thinking maybe Elijah was on to something that a walk would do her some good. As far as experience in this arena went, he surely had more to go by than I did.

She would definitely puke before the sun came up again. I'd partied often enough with the woman to know her pattern. It always included a trip to Pukcville. With the way my head was already pounding, I could predict with incredible accuracy that I was not going to work in the morning, so there was no way in hell she was either.

"Shit," I muttered. When did Rio and Grant leave? I should've told her while she was here, just like my mom and sister encouraged.

Finally, all my jumbled thoughts and half-mumbled ideas centered when I locked eyes with the most handsome man I'd ever known. Elijah had walked across the party zone to say good night to some of the neighbors who stopped by while on a walk. They were folded into the fray on the fly, but now the woman gave me a friendly wave good night as they headed off down the sand toward their house.

My devious man made his way back to me and looked so predatory, oxygen stuttered in my airway on its way to my lungs. Instead of breathing deeper, I froze. Dark curtains began to close on my vision, and my eyelids grew heavy. As my grin became seductive and playful, my man reached for me and banded his strong arm around my waist and yanked my body to his.

Against my lips, he said quietly, "Breathe, beautiful." I felt his command more than heard it.

With the buzz I had from the alcohol, his breath fanned over me hotter than it normally felt. His words sounded dirtier than they usually did, and his lips pressed to mine with more suggestion than ever.

I wanted to kick everyone out and take him up on the birthday present he offered earlier. While our guests had sung happy birthday, my sexy man had whispered filthy promises low in my ear. By the time I'd blown out the candles, I'd been burning as hot as those little flames atop my cake. And those candles hadn't been—and weren't—the only things I wanted to blow.

"What are you thinking about?" Elijah asked with a dark rasp to his voice. Just his sound made me shiver. "Are you cold, baby?" He pulled me even closer without waiting for my answer, and I didn't protest.

Being wrapped in this man's arms was one of the highlights of my day. Every single time I found myself there, I took a moment to marvel at my fortune.

My grin grew wider, and I leaned back in the circle of his embrace so I could see his expression while I told him, "I was thinking about the things you whispered to me earlier, and now I'm wondering how much longer these people are going to stay."

Of all the times for my bashfulness to kick in, while I was trying to be a seductress was most inconvenient. I let my eyes drop to the base of his throat so I could finish admitting my desire. Given the intimate time we'd shared, I was being absurd. Elijah Banks had explored more of my body than any other person ever had. As far as I was concerned, more than anyone ever would.

"Good Christ, woman." He groaned. "What are you doing to my body?"

"I think it might be the other way around," I said with my eyes riveted to his Adam's apple as it bobbed beneath the tan skin of his corded neck. The liquid courage of those damn hard seltzers fortified me, and I leaned close and took a slow, barely there lick across the protrusion.

"Mmmm," we hummed together, and the salty taste of his skin exploded on my tongue. Just as I was moving in for another lick, Elijah grabbed a fistful of my hair, low at my nape where the pull felt perfectly painful.

A soundless *Aahhh* came out on my exhalation, and we both grinned. Mine was the mirror image of his cocky half grin, which made us both smile that much more. I'd always heard that couples started acting and looking like each other the longer they stayed together.

Well, that didn't take long, did it?

"What?" I asked through my smile, but then he tightened his grip, and I hissed softly. "Eli—"

"What is it, beauty? I wish you could see your face right now. Completely stunning. Your eyes are the darkest blue. Reminds me of the ocean at night. And your pupils are big and curious." He leaned closer and kissed me just below my ear, and I exhaled a shudder.

"More," I gasped.

"More what, my love?"

"More . . . everything."

Elijah chuckled. "Greedy girl." He kissed a trail that started near my ear and moved forward along my jaw, then down my neck. Sharp bites were mixed with tender kisses and arousing licks.

Finally, someone noticed the hot scene the birthday girl and her man were creating and got the hint it was time to call it a night.

When I looked over to the table where Agatha was sacked out, she was gone. Gone! Alarms went off in my brain, and the surge of adrenaline destroyed any happy, aroused vibe I had brewing.

"Whoa, whoa, Han." Elijah stepped in front of me and gripped both shoulders. "What's going on? You're pale as a sheet, and I can see that in the dark. Talk to me."

"Where's my sister? She was sitting right there, and now..." I dug in my pocket for my cell phone and looked at the screen for missed calls. "She's gone. Where the hell could she have gone?"

"She and Carmen went for a walk. Remember? To see if she could sober up a bit before going to sleep. We were hoping she wouldn't puke inside the house." Elijah gave me a sideways look as he reminded me.

I smacked my palm to my forehead, and my hand hit just as there was a lull in conversation, so the echo of flesh on flesh sounded disproportionately louder than it hurt.

But then the second round of panic barged in. "Elijah!" I shouted to his back as he said goodbye to a few guests.

He turned to see what all the commotion was about, and if I hadn't been the one freaking out, the look on his face would've been comical.

What? What is it? he mouthed.

My voice, however, was at mid volume, which was equivalent to most people's shout. "I thought we decided it was a bad idea for her to go with him. We don't know him and all that—"

Two lengthy strides and he was back in front of me and speaking quietly to ease my building hysteria, probably hoping I would subconsciously mirror his tone and volume.

"No, *you* thought it was a bad idea. I know him quite well, beautiful. I work with the man every day. I'm sure your sister is in perfectly fine hands."

"I don't think she's in any condition to be in anyone's hands, you know? Good, bad, or otherwise. Which way did they go? I'm going to go look for her."

As I took off, the bossy bastard snaked his strong arm around my waist and pulled me right back to the spot where I had been standing. My footprints in the nighttime sand still held my body heat that I could feel when I filled them again.

"It's too cold out here for her to be roaming around alone. I don't even know if she had shoes on. I need to go find them and bring her a pair of shoes. She's going to catch a cold—or worse!"

"She's not alone," he reminded me, and while that was meant to comfort me, it just added to my stress.

"Please, can you please call him? Please?" I begged while gripping on to his arm. Unknowingly, I dug my fingernails into his forearm like I did to myself when I was in the throes of an anxiety attack.

It wasn't until he lifted his phone to his ear and waited for the call to connect that he pointedly looked down to where I was abusing him. I followed his gaze to where I was clawing into his skin and was horrified. Four little crescent marks damaged his forearm.

He anticipated my reaction and was ready to respond. With the phone cradled between his chin and shoulder, he was free to grasp and hold on to my hand so I couldn't pull away. But could he anticipate how badly I wanted to not just run away but sprint away and hide in mortification?

There was a good chance he had worked all that out too,

because next, he folded me into his safe, comforting embrace while he left a message for his assistant. I just wanted to melt into his chest and become part of him.

No one would notice, right?

What would life be like to go through each day with such confidence? To be so sure of every idea you had and every move you executed? To never fear looking silly or being wrong? To never think your ideas were dumb or might cause someone to hurt themselves or someone they loved?

What would that be like?

On days when I felt really anxious and uncertain, I worried that if I didn't do something perfectly or wasn't able to finish something I was working on, I might cause another person who also suffered from anxiety to feel the way I was feeling. It was a continuous loop of anxiety, and there was no way to stop it. Actually, it got worse exponentially because it was affecting more people. The circle grew and ensnared more and more innocent friends and family.

"Han? You okay?"

By the time Elijah's voice made it through the mental chaos, I was breathing rapidly and clammy beads of sweat dotted my brow and top lip.

"I'm fi-fi-fine. He didn't answer?" I asked but stopped myself just before sliding the fake cheerleader facade into place.

"No. But breathe, please. Breathe with me? I'm so proud of you." My beautiful man kissed the top of my head and took an exaggerated breath in so I could follow his lead.

Together we inhaled to a count of five and exhaled to the same. I wasn't in a calm enough place yet where I could hold it for any period of time.

Jesus Christ, how did I find this man? More accurately, how did he find me? Thank God he did—and thank God I wasn't scaring him off.

"Good job, beauty. That's better. Again?" he asked, keeping his eyes glued on mine.

I nodded, but what came out of my mouth was something altogether unplanned.

"I love you," I said. And then froze. No counting—no breathing either, to be fair.

Until the broadest smile split his face, and he took mine between his caring, capable palms. "I love you, Hannah. Damn, that feels so good to finally hear you say that out loud. I love you so damn much." He mashed his lips to mine and breathed in and out for us both.

We broke apart from the kiss when we heard Agatha and Carmen meandering up the path from the public area of the beach to the private section right behind Elijah's home. Only a handful of guests remained, and I wrapped an arm around my sister.

"You feeling okay?"

"Yeah. Still hammered, but that ocean air did wonders. That was a great idea, but I think I should sack out here if you don't mind?" she asked sheepishly.

"Oh my God, I wouldn't let you drive no matter what you said." I laughed and squeezed her closer to me. "Come on. Let's get you set up in one of the guest rooms."

An awkward moment passed between Agatha and Carmen as they exchanged quick glances with each other and then with me. I forgot how uncomfortable it felt to be the fifth wheel.

"I'll see you inside," I said and thumbed over my shoulder toward the house.

I didn't know if Elijah invited his assistant to stay the night, and I didn't want to overstep a professional boundary if he hadn't. I caught up to my sexy man in the kitchen, where he was grabbing a few bottles of water from the fridge.

"There's my birthday girl," he said and set down the water. I stepped into his open embrace, laid my cheek against his chest, and smiled.

"Thank you for a lovely evening, Elijah. Seriously." I leaned back to study his breathtaking face while I spoke from my heart. The heart I had willingly and completely handed him with my declaration this evening.

Of course, the nag that was my self-conscience reminded me that I should've done things differently. I should've had an eloquent mood set up beforehand. Maybe romantic ambiance with dim lights—or even better, candles. Some sort of sexy music or time-tested love songs should've been playing softly in the background while we ate his favorite meal I labored over the better part of a day. And instead of windblown and tousled, my hair and makeup would be sleek and sexy. I would be wearing sexy lingerie and a robe that gave him little peekaboo views while he ate his dinner. By the time I made my proclamation, he wouldn't be able to keep his hands off me.

But life rarely played along when I tried to execute perfect plans or set up some sort of scrapbook-worthy moment like that. I ended up getting more frustrated and anxious over the little details coming together according to my big vision than simply enjoying the reason at the heart of the hoopla.

"Are you ready for bed?" he asked.

"Shouldn't we wait until everyone is gone? There's still a lot of stuff out there to bring in." I motioned out the back slider, where the last guests were still lingering on the beach.

"Lorenzo and the rest of his team will close everything up. What they don't get to tonight, they will finish in the morning."

While he was talking, I put a few dishes in the dishwasher and Elijah wiped down the countertop.

"Did you invite Carmen to spend the night? My sister looks much better after that walk, but . . ."

"But what?" He grinned like a troublemaker. Cavernous dimples were carved into his cheeks from his mischievous smile, and I guessed he knew where I was trying to lead the conversation but in no way would alleviate me from the discomfort of saying all that needed to be said. Especially since he saw how embarrassed I was at the notion.

After rolling my eyes and huffing out a breath strong enough to blow the wispy hair around my face straight up into the air, I leaned closer and said in a conspiratorial whisper, "I was definitely getting a hookup vibe from them when they got back. They must've really hit it off on that walk."

"I told him earlier he's welcome to stay, so that will be his call."

"I'm going to get her set up in the room I used to stay in—before you robbed me of my virtue, that is." I barely finished the comment before a giggle erupted. Thinking back just a few months, and I remembered I'd never been so ready to give a man what he wanted.

After we walked down the same memory path, we locked stares. If mine was half as hungry as his, we were going to burn the house down with our passion. With the possessive swipe of one large hand, he hooked me around the waist and yanked my body to his.

I stood on my tiptoes and threaded my fingers through one another at his nape.

"Now, about that bedroom suggestion…" he growled against my lips, but we both pulled back when we heard the slider open behind us.

"S-Sorry. Sorry, Han," Agatha spluttered before she gained her footing. "But shit, get a room." She playfully bumped her shoulder into mine, but because she was still drunk, whether it was less than before the walk or not, she was still a bad judge of her own strength. She knocked me so hard I barreled into Elijah on my other side, catching him by surprise too.

"All right, let's get you to bed before you break something. Or someone," I said to my sister and pulled her toward the guest suite. She was giggling about something while I called back over my shoulder to Elijah, "I'll see you in our room?"

"Yes, my queen." He executed a gallant bow, and my smile felt like it might split my face into two equal halves.

My sister whisper-shouted as only drunk people could manage, "Hannibal, that boy is so in love with you!"

We both giggled, and I tried to get her behind the closed door of the bedroom before addressing her comment.

"I think so too."

"Do you love him?" she asked, beginning to strip her clothes off.

"Hey, hey. Slow down." I tried to get her to stop undressing before I found her something to wear. As far as I knew, she didn't bring a bag, and if I had to give her something from my closet, I'd have to go clear across to the master.

"I want to sleeeeeep," she whined and flopped back on the bed.

"I know you do, but you might be doing it in the clothes you have on if you didn't bring a bag." I looked at her expectantly.

"Don't you have something I can wear?" She made a ridiculous sad pout, and I burst out laughing.

"Don't laugh at me," my sister whined again and pushed me. Damn the girl was strong, because she nearly knocked me off my feet again.

"Okay, no more pushing. When did you get so strong? Maybe this is why you don't keep a guy around? You're getting too physical with them." We both were laughing by the time I finished my thought, but it was worth exploring when she was sober. I was pretty sure guys didn't enjoy being man-handled by their woman. At least for the most part.

"You lie down while I go get some pajamas you can borrow," I instructed while I pulled the covers down on the bed.

"I'll come with you, and then you can just stay in your room."

"No. You'll never find your way back here. Dah, this house is huge. Trust me, you'll get lost."

"I can walk her back," said a male voice from the doorway, and we both looked up. Carmen looked very handsome in the low light where he leaned against the doorjamb.

Trying to be covert, I gave my sister a questioning glance, and thankfully she gave me a quick nod.

"All right, let's go get some pj's."

I quickly shot a text to Elijah that we were coming his way, because the last thing we needed was to find him naked on the bed or something equally embarrassing.

Finally, about ten minutes later, I was alone with my man. I decided to take a quick shower so we wouldn't end up with sand in our bed, but when I was taking too long combing through my hair, he appeared behind me in the mirror.

I watched him take the brush from my hand and set it down on the countertop. He twisted my wet hair into a long rope and fastened it atop my head with two claw type barrettes he produced from thin air. They were mine, but I didn't see him pick them up, so it truly looked like a magic trick.

"I have something for you," he said while keeping my stare captive in our reflection. "I bought this for you a while ago," he went on, his voice getting darker and more seductive, things I didn't think were possible. My gorgeous lover kissed my shoulder and then started a path up toward my ear. When he was about halfway and my breathing and heart rates had doubled, he said, "But I was waiting for the perfect moment to give it to you."

Elijah slowly ran the tip of his nose up and down my neck where he had just kissed. His warm breath fanned across my skin and skittered goose bumps over my entire body. We both noticed the blond hair on my arms standing on end, and he danced his fingertips up and down my forearms to heighten the pleasure.

I leaned back into him with my entire body, and he groaned into my neck. "I love you, birthday girl. I hope this is the first of one hundred more birthdays we spend together. Now, close your eyes and don't open until I say."

"Elijah," I whimpered. I wanted to see him. I wanted to see every part of this moment.

"Do as you're told, girl."

I huffed and squeezed my eyes shut really tight.

"Such a brat," he said behind me, but I felt something very heavy around my neck and then him working on something at the back. He was fastening something there. I held my breath because he brought up the collar subject once, and I'd made it pretty clear how I felt about the idea, but whatever he was clasping on my throat felt more like jewelry, not what I'd been picturing during that conversation.

"Okay, beautiful. Face me."

"I want to see," I complained.

"And you will. My God, Hannah. You are perfection. Absolute perfection. Open your eyes."

When I did, the first thing I saw, of course, was him. But the way he was looking at me with so much love and adoration, it filled every single cup I had and could ever dream of needing to be filled. He gave me all he had in that moment with that one look and the promise of all I would need for the rest of my life.

"I love you, Elijah Banks. With everything I am, everything I ever will be."

"And I love you. With everything I am, everything I will ever be. And I will always strive to be everything you need. And if ever I'm not, you say the word and I will do my very best to be what you need."

"Can I look now?" I asked, not being able to stand the suspense any longer.

With his large hands on my hips, he turned me to face the mirror, and I was completely speechless. The necklace was beyond words. My hands fluttered to my neck to touch it, and then my brain kicked in. I silently chastised myself and quickly dropped them to my sides again but leaned in closer to the mirror.

"Elijah..." I turned to look at him standing behind me, then quickly turned back to look in the mirror again. "This is breathtaking." I covered my mouth with both hands then, emotion threatening to completely overtake me.

"I can't." I shook my head from side to side and turned

around to face my man. "I can't accept this." One more look couldn't hurt, though, so I turned back to the mirror and, that time, carefully let my fingers glance over the stones. "Oh my God, I've never seen anything so stunning in my life."

"I have," Elijah said, with his eyes fixed on mine.

That was the final hit to my heart's armor. I broke down in messy sobs. He had to expect it would come eventually. You couldn't just give a woman a gift like this, shower her with undying love and attention, put her up in your castle-sized home, and throw her a surprise birthday party with all her family and friends and then not expect waterworks at some point.

"I can't... I don't... It's not..." I couldn't complete a damn thought or even collect myself enough to express one or two of the things I was feeling.

So I held on tighter. I burrowed into his chest deeper and cried a little more. Through it all, he stroked my hair and swayed back and forth like he was rocking an infant in his arms. My God, how did I get so lucky to have this man cross my path that day at the prep kitchen in Inglewood?

Finally, when I felt a little calmer, I leaned back so I could see his face. He stroked my hair away from my eyes, and I smiled shyly.

"I must look a fright," I chuckled.

"You've never looked more beautiful," he said adoringly. And I thought he really meant it. He fingered the necklace where it rested on my chest. "This really is a stunning piece. It looks perfect on you. Just like I imagined."

"It is beautiful. You know I can't keep this, though. It's just too much. I do have to ask—do the emeralds have significance?"

"Firstly," he said as he led me to sit on the bed, "you most certainly will keep it." When I attempted a protest, he gave me that stern look he had perfected, and I pressed my lips into a pout.

"When will you learn what that sexy mouth does to me?" With his thumbs hooked into the neck of his shirt, he whipped the thing over his head, and I was treated to his bare torso.

My pout instantly became a sultry smile even though I tried my best to remain serious.

"No fair," I muttered.

Elijah ignored my comment, but I was pretty sure he heard me based on the grin he tried to hide. He climbed onto the bed and moved my legs so he perched on his heels between them.

"The emeralds have two meanings. One, they're my birthstone." He leaned in and gave me a slow, delicious kiss. When he pulled back, I followed him, not wanting it to end yet.

"Emerald? That's May, right?"

"Hmmm?" he hummed distractedly while he tugged at the belt on my robe.

I tried to cover the knot he was having trouble with so he would answer me. "Your birthday's in May?"

"Put your hands down." His voice shifted to that *don't fuck with me* tone that went hand in hand with his dominant persona.

Mmmm, I like this side of my man very much.

Well, it was my birthday, after all. I should have a little room to play, right? My blue stare met his icy green one while I covered the knot with both hands and repeated my question.

"Your birthday's in May?" I even gave the head tilt a little try on for size.

"Are you looking to redefine *birthday spanking*?" He grinned mischievously.

I crossed my arms over my chest and *hmphed*. "No. I just wanted to know when your birthday is. Why is that such a big deal? You said there were two meanings, like you wanted me to figure it out." I was totally whining. Even I could hear how obnoxious it sounded.

"Reach over your head, birthday girl, and grab on to the headboard."

With one arm, I began following his dictate, and a growl came from somewhere so low in his throat it was hard to believe he actually made the sound.

"Both hands, beauty. Mmm, nice."

Once I was in the requested pose, he climbed over me to stand beside the bed and undress. I would be a satisfied birthday girl if just looking at his glory was my gift. His muscled frame and virile cock were primed to treat me right. I met his stare and waited for his next instruction.

"Do you know what the second thing the emeralds symbolize? Have you worked it out yet?"

Left to right, I indicated *no* with a slight roll of my head back and forth on the pillow.

Elijah bent at the waist and kissed my abdomen. Just one, slow, soft butterfly kiss right above the place where one day, I would carry his child. At least, I hoped I would.

My beautiful man climbed over my body, this time straddling my hips with his powerful thighs, and before he let his weight touch down, he parted my robe in its two halves so we were skin to skin.

Eyes slowly drifted closed—his, then mine—and we both let out sighs of contentment. I sensed him getting closer, so I sneaked a peek just in time to see him approaching for a hungry kiss.

We started slow and built to a fevered desperation for each other so quickly it was difficult to catch my breath between collisions of lips on lips, lips on necks, teeth on skin, and everything in between. I was panting and writhing beneath my lover and grinding my clit along any firm part of him I could make contact with.

"Jesus, girl, you're so fucking hot. I need to be inside you. I need to fuck you more than I need to breathe."

"Yes." I nodded crazily. "Yes, please. Fill me, Elijah. Please, fuck me."

With each plea, his eyes grew wilder.

"Please, can I let go? I want to touch you."

"No. You stay right there." But suddenly he reared back from my body completely, and the loss was unbearable.

"What? What's wrong? What happened?" My breath caught in my throat while I waited for his answer.

But then I saw his entire face shift. Uh-oh. The devil was back and was making mischief just beneath his regular features.

"I have an offer. A trade, of sorts." He smiled wickedly.

Shit, I'd seen that smile before, but still, I just stared— drank him in, all wild hair and flexed muscles. His tan skin looked like bronze in the sultry light of the bedroom.

"Let's hear it, Banks," I said, trying my best to sound laissez-faire.

His growing grin told me he wasn't buying my bit for a second, but he said, "I'll trade you holding on to the headboard for a spreader bar at your ankles."

Damn it, where was a camera when a girl needed one? The mix of hopeful teen boy and really dirty, dominant man kneeling between my parted thighs was a sight to behold. I took extra seconds to answer because I really needed to commit everything about him to memory.

The truth was still the truth, though. "I—I don't know. I've never used that. Umm . . . one of those." I made a nondescript sound in the back of my throat, and all my cool-girl vibe vanished with one silly noise.

"You trust me?"

"Of course I do."

"It's not something that hurts. At all. It's just a restraint that I'll cuff around these sexy ankles." He slid his palm down my leg from my knee to where the cuff would attach, then lifted my limb to his lips for a seductive kiss. He spent a few moments licking and nipping the thin skin around my ankle until I was moaning and dropped my other leg open wider.

"Is this sexy invitation your consent, beauty? My God, your cunt is so creamy, baby. Just feel how slick you are here." With two fingers, he circled the opening to my channel, and again, we moaned in chorus.

I shook my head, though he spoke the truth. This man gave his all in the bedroom, and I knew the experience would be unforgettable. It was the consent part I was unsure about. Anxiety got in the way anytime the word *restrained* entered the conversation.

"Oh, shit, that feels so good." I moaned. "I need you so badly, please," I begged again while chasing his fingers with my pelvis.

"Just my fingers?"

"If that's what you want. Whatever you want. Just make me feel good."

"What about my mouth?"

After that teasing question, he leaned closer and flicked

my swollen bud with the tip of his tongue, and I froze to feel every bit of the pleasure. Until he stopped.

My cry was much louder than I planned, but he deserved the alarm it caused. "Noooo. Stop teasing. You're the worst tease."

"Just tell me what you want, beauty. Tell me, and it's yours. Talk dirty to me, love," he taunted. "Look how hard I am for you." He kneeled up tall again and stroked his cock. My pulse throbbed between my legs with every pull he took.

"Elijah…" His name came out on a croak, and I watched him drop his head back in ecstasy while he handled himself.

I knew I'd probably get in trouble—but I let go of the headboard and reached out to scratch my nails up his thighs. He usually loved when I did that, but he brought his head level so quickly I would've thought he'd be dizzy. But no, he shot his stare down to mine that looked so fierce, I should've been afraid. Instead, I felt even more turned on.

Christ, we were all over the place tonight. Nothing was predictable.

"You like that?" I taunted. Interesting. Maybe this was the gray area where my inner vixen was hiding. I pushed up to my bent elbows and said, "You want it harder?"

Elijah leaned down so our eyes were on the same plane and hissed, "What's this, birthday girl? Are we playing something new?"

I gave a careless shrug. "You think you can keep up?" I ended the question with a sassy head tilt and had no idea what possessed me, but the chemicals coursing through my blood stream were buzzing like a swarm of hornets.

My favorite grin of all the ones he cycled through in the course of a day made an appearance, and I knew he was on board regardless of what he answered next. We'd talked about this a while back and agreed neither of us smiled in any way, shape, or form if we weren't fully game for what was happening. We weren't the type who smiled when we were nervous or sad. And Elijah had broken my bad cheerleader smile habit soon after I moved in.

I sat up and, with both hands, pushed his shoulders as hard as I could. The only reason he lost his balance, I was sure of it, was because he wasn't expecting me to make that move. From that point forward, I wouldn't get the best of him physically because he'd be on the defensive. In fact, as I was making that observation, I watched his entire demeanor change again.

In my busy mind, a conversation replayed that we once had. I had told Elijah that the icy color of his eyes made them so expressive. The man's face was a captivating movie screen, and his emotions were the star of every show. Lucky for the world, he did nothing to hide how he was feeling. The audience was treated to a mesmerizing feature with every interaction.

Elijah chuckled as he righted himself on the bed—well, the best he could, because I was already straddled across his lap, trying to take him inside my body. Just as I predicted, though, he easily overpowered me by bucking his hips just one time, and I toppled off to the side. Luckily, I got my arms out in front of my body to brace my face-first fall into the mattress, but I still hit with an *umph*.

"Asshole," I said into the sheets but loud enough for my opponent to hear.

"Are you offering?" he asked with a silky taunt. "It wouldn't take much effort right here," he went on while he spread my ass for better access.

"No!" Now I shouted for real and squirmed with enough

force to get out from under him to about my calves. But the bastard caught me by the ankles before I could escape completely. In some crazy maneuver, he crossed his hold on my ankles and flipped me over so I was on my back, staring at the moonlit night through the skylight cut in the ceiling.

My chest heaved in and out with my wild panting, and I burst into a ridiculous cackle. What the hell had come over us?

My gorgeous landlord covered my entire body with his, ensuring none of my limbs could break free and strike him in a weak zone when he least expected it. I couldn't help but feel his chest pumping as hard as mine was or the steely cock stabbing my abdomen. And definitely couldn't miss how it all made me want him that much more.

"Is it a full moon tonight? I've heard when you have your birthday under a full moon, it's magnetic pandemonium."

"Are you fucking Sylvia Browne now?" I sniped.

"Ummm...isn't she dead?" he asked with a cocky grin. Damn this man and his grin.

I just burst out laughing, because firstly, he actually knew who I was talking about, and secondly, he was totally right. The famous astrologer and medium died years ago.

"Give me your fucking dick and stop talking. Or get off me. You're not exactly light, you know?"

"I told you before to ask for it. And make it dirty. Go, girl."

"Yeah, no. I'm not in the mood anymore." It was a total lie, and we both knew it when he reached between my legs end unceremoniously fingered me. We both felt how wet I still was, and he looked back to me and raised one eyebrow, challenging my last declaration.

"Asshole."

"Do you remember what I told you about calling me

names when I was standing over you in the kitchen? Just about to mark you for the first time with my come?"

"Blah blah mouth full of soap... Is that what you're talking about?" I bucked my torso, hoping to get him to move. But it was useless. He was much too heavy, and I was running out of steam.

"I said soap or come. And you have definitely graduated from soap, my love. But if I come in your foul mouth, we can't make the second part of this beautiful necklace come true, can we?" He tilted his head and waited for my response.

"What?" I spluttered because I couldn't jump from subject to subject the way he was. My brain was in an incredible sex fog at the moment.

"From right now until it works, every time I come, it's inside you. I'm planting my child inside you. Then our child's birthstone will be emerald, too. Now, be good and spread your legs for me."

"Elijah..."

"Open."

"But..."

"Your."

"Don't you think..."

"Legs."

"Oh my God, yes. God, yes. Ooohh, that's what I need, right there, baby. Fuck, yes. So good. Aaaahh—"

He moved inside me with a slow, casual rhythm for long minutes. It felt so good I wanted to cry. Fucking was seriously one of the best things in life. It was a shame people didn't do it more or settled for mediocre or plain bad sex when there was the potential for it to feel this good. But not everyone cared about the experience as much as my guy did. Thank God he did.

"Beauty? Are you going to come for me? Better yet, with me?"

"Yes. Yes, I'm right there, Elijah. Right there. Please don't stop."

"No, baby, I'm not stopping. Give it to me, girl. Come on my cock. Squeeze me with that hot cunt. Fuck yes, just like that." He was panting so roughly, no more than two or three words were coming out with each lunge.

"I'm... I'm... I... I... Elijah, yes."

Elijah thrust so deep a few more times. With the last stroke, he stilled inside my pussy so deeply that I felt his dick twitching in my belly as he climaxed. I didn't know if either one of us was really ready to be a parent, but the odds were low that it would actually happen anyway. We'd had unprotected sex a few times before and had gotten away with it, so maybe this would be the time our number was up. Or maybe this would be another time we got away with tempting fate. I could worry about not overanalyzing it beforehand when we woke up in the morning.

Because right now, I was completely spent.

Elijah rolled off to my one side and pulled me into the protection of his embrace. His strong chest cocooned me from behind, and we fell into a coordinated breathing pattern. Soon after, we were both sleeping soundly.

It was the best birthday ever.

CHAPTER NINE

ELIJAH

"I see how it is. You want something, and boom, she makes it happen. I ask, and she makes me ask three times before she even considers it," Shark bitched while Grant made a cup of coffee at the new coffee bar on our downtown rooftop oasis.

"It's a sibling thing." I tried to ease his ire, but he gave me a skeptical look.

"And you're basing that on what?"

He had a point, so I just shrugged. Plus, I was nursing a bit of a hangover and couldn't muster a quick comeback.

Grant came to my defense. "Don't be a dick over it."

"It's cool," I said. "I liked being an only child when I was really young, and later I would've hated to see another human subjected to the bullshit I went through." And that was the honest to God's truth. Seeing my mother suffer at that monster's hands was what finally drove me to end him. He was such a cruel bastard. No one deserved his abuse.

We all took seats, and a strange quiet settled over the group. Almost like we all had so many personal things swirling in our heads but no room for group problems at the moment. The problem was, we still had a major group situation front and center.

Grant broke the silence. No surprise there. "Great shindig

last night. You pulled that one out of your ass at the last minute." He took a sip from his steaming cup, but his giant grin never fully disappeared.

"No kidding, right?" I adjusted my watch for something to fiddle with. "Carmen was clinch on all the planning. That dude is invaluable. Can I get the guy a raise or a bonus or something?" I directed that last part to Bas.

"For planning your girlfriend's birthday party? Nah, man, I don't think that would fly with payroll, you know?" Bas replied with way more attitude than I was in the mood for.

"No, dipshit, in general." I scowled at the guy. "He totally deserves it."

"So go through the normal process. You know what to do. Give him a performance review and recommend him for a pay increase. They'll either approve it or they won't." Bas shrugged, and I looked at Grant, but he just shrugged too.

Maybe I just needed to go down to my office. Maybe it was my mood that was sour and I was projecting on my two friends.

But then Bas dropped a bomb I definitely wanted to stay around for.

"So, Grant, what are Rio's thoughts about buying out Abbigail?"

There was a part of me—and fine, it was a bigger part than I wanted to cop to—that wasn't liking how much time the four of them seemed to be spending together lately and not including Hannah and me. I didn't think it was necessarily intentional, but if it was, I had no one to blame but myself. The women all got along famously. Hell, if Abbi and Rio could recover their relationship from the shit show it was not even a year ago, any relationship had hopes of mending.

No, this was all on me. I was terribly rough on Rio Gibson

from day one. I had grown so protective of Grant over the years that the moment someone came into his life and seemed less than perfect for him, I bared my teeth. And it wasn't fair. He loved that woman, and now that all the dust had settled, she seemed damn good for my best friend. I owed her an apology, and probably—no, *definitely*—owed him one as well.

But that would have to wait, because right now I needed to get this news hot off the presses. Especially so I could scoop Hannah when I talked to her next.

Grant laughed in reply, but Bas sat forward on the cushion of the outdoor sofa. "No, I'm totally serious. Where do you think her head's at?"

Grant looked at me and raised a finger in warning. "Not a word."

I held my pleading hands up in front of me. Yeah, totally needed to apologize to my brother. Sooner rather than later.

He angled his tall frame more toward Sebastian. Shit, even sitting down, you got a good sense of how tall Grant was. His fucking legs were so long they made obtuse angles instead of right angles when they bent.

"I think she's still trying to reason with the new balance in her bank account." A huge grin split his boyish face. "I've caught her a few times just staring at her bank's website, looking at her balance like it's going to disappear if she takes her eyes off it. The woman is so kind, and honest, and pure through to her heart. I seriously don't know how I got so lucky."

Christ, by the time I had the courage to look at his face again, he was so emotional I immediately teared up too.

Instinct drove me then. I stood, and so did he, and we did the bro-hug thing. Bas stood but to back away as quickly as possible. Grant and I both chuckled when we looked at him, and he just shook his head.

"I mean, I'm happy for you and all, but yeah...no." He kicked at the ground uncomfortably a few times, probably hoping we'd be averting our eyes by the time he looked up again.

"When are you guys going to get hitched? Any solid plans?" I asked, both out of curiosity and also to let Shark off the hot seat.

Grant couldn't hide his smile. "We've been kicking around hopping over to Vegas some weekend and just making it official. She's been married before..." He inserted an exaggerated eye roll. "No shit, right?"

We all laughed and all also knew there was nothing remotely funny about the information other than the awkwardness of it.

"And since neither of us have family..." He shrugged, but Bas and I looked at each other, then both quickly fixed our glares on him.

"Excuse me?"

"Heellloo?"

"Well, you know what I mean," Grant said in defense.

"Yeah, we're coming along. I'm sure that's what you meant. So you better get to it, because this one"—I backhanded Bas in the abs—"can't stop making babies, and she won't want to fly or make a long drive soon. Shit, dude, remember that drive from Twenty-Nine Palms?"

"Don't." Bas held up a hand. "Don't remind me." We could all agree those were some bad weeks. Well, maybe not for Grant, because that's when things got hot between Rio and him.

"You know, my brothers, we've lived crazy lives. Haven't we?" I said.

"Hell yes, we have. As crazy as it's been, I wouldn't change a thing." Grant nodded along while he spoke but then abruptly stopped. "Okay, those pirates can go fuck each other, but yeah, other than that."

"Do you think any of those Elvis chapels have a two-for-one special?" I asked Grant.

Now two inquisitive *What the hells?* were fixed on me.

"What? We're totally ready. Plus, I think she's knocked up. Don't tell her, though. She doesn't know it yet." I could feel my proud chest inflate on my next breath.

"Dude," Bas said and tilted his head. "That's not how it works."

Grant slung his long arm across my shoulder as we headed toward the elevator. "See, from what I understand, first she figures it out, and then she tells you. Not the other way around."

Bas thumbed sideways toward Grant. "What he said."

"Mark my words," I said with smug confidence. "I was in there last night. Things are different."

They both looked at me like I'd lost my damn mind, and I laughed.

"It's not the Men's Department at Saks, asshole. 'I was in there last night.' Who says shit like that about a pussy?" Grant said and burst out laughing as we stepped into the elevator.

I turned to face the door and pushed the button for the penthouse. In the reflection of the shiny stainless doors, I watched my smile stretch from one side of my face to the other.

"Talk to me in a few weeks," I said. "But seriously, let's go out to the desert this weekend. Talk to Rio, see if she's game."

"She'll be game if I tell her she's game."

"Oh, that's right, big boss man," I taunted, and he pushed the back of my shoulder so hard I flew forward exactly as the elevator doors opened and I jettisoned out into the corridor, nearly knocking a woman to the ground.

"Twombley," I growled while righting myself and the woman I didn't fully see as I tried to step around her. It wasn't until I heard the chorus of growls coming from behind me that I took another look at the female.

"What the hell are you doing here?" Sebastian seethed.

"Sebastian, so nice to see you too. Pleasant as always, I see." Hensley Pritchett looked down to brush at her fitted pencil skirt while she issued the insult.

"I'll call security," Grant said and strode down the hall toward Craig's desk.

"You know damn well that you and your client have restraining orders in place. The judge won't look kindly on this choice you've made," I threatened quietly. No use causing a scene for the gossip mill.

"I thought you'd want to talk about your son." She dangled the offer smugly, like she had the winning hand in some creepy poker game we were playing.

"Oh, *now* the kid is his. How convenient for you. You're a fucking piece of work, lady. Get the fuck out of my building on your own or be thrown out with the rest of the trash." Bas advanced on her, and I stopped him with a straight arm across his midsection. The look he shot me was lethal, and I was reminded why few people crossed the man.

"Meet me down at my office," I issued to the woman and waited until she was well past Sebastian's office before I turned to him.

"You can't be fucking serious right now," he blurted and pinched the bridge of his nose. "Why does that woman lead you around by your balls?"

"It's not like th—"

"Cut the crap, Banks," he said through clenched teeth.

"It's not!" Immediately, I schooled my tone, my volume, my very being. This was not the place nor the time to lose my shit. It definitely wasn't the person to aim it at either.

"Sorry. But seriously, it's not like that. I'm in love with Hannah. That woman is everything to me." I pointed toward the roof. "You just heard me say I want to marry her."

"Then why the hell would you fuck it up by going near that viper? She's so fucking toxic, but for some reason, you've had blinders on from day one when it comes to her."

And then I almost fell over . . . because Sebastian Albert Shark reached out . . . and touched me. The man put his meaty hand on my shoulder and leaned in until our foreheads *thunked* together in a friendly head butt. It was the closest thing I would probably ever see in the way of affection from the man. Ever.

I reached up and gripped his wrist, not to move it away, but to hold on for dear life. This was such a powerful moment, he didn't have to say words. With a gesture so outside the man's comfort zone, he spoke volumes. He cared about me that much.

A million things I wanted to say were running through my head, but they became a jumbled clog in the back of my throat. I couldn't speak or even swallow, so I just gripped his wrist tighter. He bumped my head with his once more and then pulled away.

"Get her out of here. Now. Don't fuck up what you have going on with the chef."

He turned on his heel and strode into his office. The heavy door slammed so hard behind him, poor Craig jumped in his seat just outside the thing.

"Mr. Twombley called from his office and said security has removed the problem outside your office door," Craig spoke quietly when I was right in front of his desk.

I rapped my knuckles on the surface and nodded, then strode down the hall.

For the first time in as long as I could remember, Carmen didn't have an affable smile for me when I approached his desk. He watched me like a circus sideshow. As I walked past his desk, and when I stopped in front of my locked door, I could feel his eyes burning a hole into my back.

"Say what's on your mind, man," I finally said and rested my head against the lacquered wood door.

For Christ's sake, the man spent the night at my house, slept in one of my beds, banged my future sister-in-law for all I knew. Did things have to be this awkward now because of Hensley? Damn, I despised that woman.

"Great party last night," he chirped in his usual upbeat tone.

Immediately, I relaxed my stiff posture but still debated facing him.

Luckily, he plowed right through any remaining discomfort. "Poor Agatha won't be feeling so great this morning. What the hell was she drinking?" He chuckled after making the comment.

Finally, I turned to look at my assistant. "Please tell me she made it to the toilet. I hate cleaning up vomit." I noticeably shivered and said, "God, especially someone else's."

He grinned, and it quickly passed to me as well because these Farsey girls had a way of getting under a dude's skin pretty fast.

"Soooooo..." I dragged the one syllable out across a few

beats with my eyebrows raised as far as they could go. When my assistant didn't pick up the ball and run with it, I fed him a few prompts. "Is there a spark there? Are you and Agatha going to see each other again?"

Trying to play it cool, he shrugged and sat back in his chair. He swiveled toward me and said, "I'd like to see her again. You know, when she's sober." As if a particular memory popped into his mind, he laughed spontaneously and shook his head. "She's very funny, and I like that in a girl, you know?"

I was already nodding before I spoke. "Yeah, Hannah is really funny too. She and Agatha are the closest from what I can tell. She's told me they clown around a lot together."

"What do you know about the family?" Carmen asked.

"What do you mean?" I asked him, not really sure what information he was trying to find out. And there was a part of me that thought *hell no*, he should go through that misery himself like I had to. Fuck that.

"I don't know. Are they all close? How many sisters are there? Quite a few, right?"

"Dave and Lisa were busy." I laughed. "Hannah is the oldest, then Agatha, then the twins, Sheppard and Maye, and the youngest is Clemson. All girls, and all blond bombshells. Dad has had two heart attacks." I scrunched up my face, wondering if I had that detail correct. "Yeah, I'm pretty sure it was two."

"Shit, with that many daughters who look like those girls do, is it any wonder?" Carmen asked with a wince. "And wait, did you say twins?"

"Dude, you're not asking anything I haven't already thought." I chuckled. "And unless you have some kind of weird fetish for having your balls handed to you physically and verbally at every turn, stay away from Sheppard. She's hostile and has a chip on her shoulder the size of Vermont."

"Vermont?" He laughed. "That's not random or anything."

A quiet alarm sounded from Carmen's computer, and he shifted his gaze to his monitor. "You have an appointment in thirty at the Edge. I'm sure you knew that, but just a reminder. Do you need a car?" He swung his gaze back to me and waited for the answer.

"Can you contact Lorenzo and see if he's in the area? It'll give me some time to chat with him about that shit show this morning. I'm going try to get through some email until it's time to leave," I said while opening my door.

But instead of sitting down at my desk and immediately getting lost in the sea of email I knew was waiting for me, I crossed to the windows that looked out over the city. So many things had happened already today that my mind was swirling with so many different thoughts. Of course the things that stood out among the others were the ones about Hannah.

I wasn't just bullshitting my best friends when I said I thought she was pregnant. I did have experience on the subject—something they tended to forget. There was a difference in a woman's body when she was preparing to carry a child. But only time would tell, so there was no use getting my hopes up before we knew.

I wouldn't even mention it to Hannah. She deserved to discover the exciting news herself for the first time. I mean, shit, I hoped she would be excited.

Then there was the idea of marrying her. That just felt exciting too. I didn't think it would take much convincing to get her to agree to it, but really, was that something I wanted to have to convince her to do? All right, so this snippet deserved more thought—but not right now. I needed to pull this idea out and put it to the side for later.

The bullshit with Hensley deserved no more time. At all. She could deal with my attorney now. That woman needed to understand there was nothing she could say to me that would take me off my game. Especially if my behavior toward her was giving others the impression Sebastian accused me of. That she was leading me around by my balls. Maybe there was a time that was true, but not anymore. I was so done with her.

Thinking of Sebastian brought up what we shared today. A huge smile took over my entire face. The three of us had been friends for a really long time and never had that man initiated a physical exchange like that. And yes, we'd had moments during sexual escapades while we shared a woman, but those were always much different than what happened today. That was something I would cherish for the rest of my life.

My desk phone rang, and I strode across the room to pick the thing up.

"Banks."

"Lorenzo is waiting downstairs for you," said Carmen.

"All right. I'm on my way." I grabbed my bag since I hadn't unpacked it from this morning and headed out the door. I was already talking to Carmen as I was going through the doorway.

"What do I have after this?"

"Come on, I'll walk with you," the man said as he sprang to his feet and grabbed his smart pad. We kept a good pace on our way to the service elevator at the end of the hall.

"Looks like your lunch is open today, but I checked this morning, and Hannah is doing deliveries. Did you want me to schedule a lunch for you with Abstract? I'm assuming you took a stalker break last night?" He looked up from his device with a mischievous grin and waited for my answer.

"Can you request that our building is last and that I am the last in the building? Then order two lunches, and maybe I can talk her into staying with me for a while."

"You got it." He quickly scribbled some notes. "And you have an early afternoon Zoom meeting with your therapist. That's at one thirty, and to wrap up the day, it is Public Works and security here in your office at three."

I did some quick figuring in my head and asked Carmen, "Can you see if my attorney will speak to me at two forty-five regarding this morning? It has to be prompt at two forty-five because I will only have that fifteen-minute window. If he can't give me a full fifteen minutes, reschedule it for another slot that I have open. I don't want to get billed for a fifteen-minute block and get eleven minutes of his time. Bastard's a criminal with that hourly rate."

"I'm on it," he responded, but I held the door open with my foot because I could tell he was going to say something more.

"I'll share a calendar event if it works out... That's it! Have a good meeting." My helper bid me farewell with a salute.

As the doors were closing, I shouted my usual, "You're the best!"

I heard his typical reply, "I keep telling you!"

Dude was totally getting a raise whether accounting and HR approved it or not.

* * *

I could barely concentrate on that damn meeting at the jobsite knowing I was going to see Hannah when I got back. I felt like a teenager when it came to this girl. I never wanted these feelings to end. I never wanted to do anything to make her stop feeling this way about me too. When the soft knock came at my door, I almost broke my leg rushing to answer it. Carmen had stepped away to take his lunch, and I recognized the sound of her timid announcement.

I swung the heavy door open and sucked in a breath. Every time I saw her, she was more beautiful than the time before. It was hot out today, so she had a fitted T-shirt on with her clown pants. Her tits were stretching the limits of the cotton so deliciously, the moment we were behind a closed door, my hands were all over her.

"Elijah . . ." she said breathlessly.

"Hi, baby." I grinned. "Christ, your tits in this T-shirt. I can't take it." I stepped back to drink her in again. "I can't believe you looked like this in front of every dickhead you served lunch to today." An involuntary growl escaped my throat on the tail of that sentence.

She tilted her head and said, "You're in a mood today."

"I can't help it. I'm possessed."

"More like possessive." She widened her eyes and giggled.

"Well, yeah, that too." I pulled her into me and ground my half-hard cock into her belly. "Mmmm, let's fuck on my desk. Forget about the food. I want to eat you for lunch."

"Oh my God, you're crazy! What's gotten into you today?"

"Crazy for you. I can't get enough of you. Is that a bad thing?" I leaned in and bit the side of her neck. Really hard.

Hannah moaned, deep and sexy, and my dick responded with the rest of my body.

"Oh, shit. Ooohh, that feels so good. My God, man, you're turning me into a sex maniac. Stop." She pushed at my chest and got nowhere. "Let's eat."

"I already proposed a plan for that," I reminded. While wrapping my arms around her waist, I lifted her off the ground and held her against me.

"My sister was in baaaad shape this morning. I can't wait to harass her about it the next time we talk," Hannah supplied while I let her slide down my body. She went to her cart and got our lunches and continued prattling on about Agatha. "She was still sleeping when I left for the kitchen, but I told the guys to make sure she got off okay. Wait . . ." She held up a flat palm so I didn't add some fourth-grade humor to her blunder. "Not like that. I meant make sure she got out to her car and everything," she finished with an eye roll.

"Let's sit over here," I offered and grabbed one of the trays from her. We set everything up on the coffee table in the sunny sitting area and continued to talk about the previous night.

I connected the only dots I could for her. "Carmen said she got sick about four times throughout the night. So, while I don't think he got lucky, he did his best to take care of her."

"He seems like a really nice guy. I wonder if they'll try to see each other again?" Hannah looked to me before digging into her meal. She must have suspected I had the answer.

"I have no idea. I already got the pick of the litter." I shrugged. "So too bad for him." I winked, and she smacked my bicep.

"Ow," she whimpered and shook out her fingers. "You're so hard everywhere." And then she turned beet red when she realized what she had said.

My brow was up in my hairline while I gave her a playfully skeptical look. How was she maintaining this innocent bit even after I continuously did so many dirty, dirty things to her?

I never wanted her to change.

"Will you marry me?" I blurted out and then quickly took a bite so I wouldn't have to say anything else. Half brave, half chickenshit. It was the best I could do.

Hannah looked like she'd swallowed what she was chewing whole. When she spoke, it sounded like it was still stuck in her throat.

"Like...right now? Or in a year or something?" She screwed up her face and added, "You're acting so strange today. Seriously, what has gotten into you?"

I figured being honest was the best approach. I always demanded the truth from her. I should give the same in return.

"We were talking this morning—me and the guys, Grant and Bas." I made some dumb gesture with my hand, like, *you know who I mean*, and realized how stupid I must have looked and dropped my hand back to my lap.

"Ohhhkaaaay." She waited patiently for me to go on.

"Grant and Rio are going to get hitched in Vegas, and obviously, we're all going." I rolled my eyes at *obviously* and realized I was really fucking this whole thing up.

"Obviously," she repeated, including the eye roll.

Yep, fucking it up hard, indeed.

"But I thought, why not do it?"

"Umm, my family will slaughter us? I mean, there's that."

"What if we just kept it to ourselves? We can do another ceremony after the—" Whooooaaa there, cowboy. Holy shit, I almost blew the whole baby thing in one idiotic sentence. See? This was why I should've just fucked her instead of this chitchatty bullshit. Stick to what I was good at.

"After the what?" Hannah asked.

"What?" I tried for confused and knew it was a long shot.

"What were you going to say?"

"When?"

She tilted her head. Damn, the woman had picked up so many of my habits and now was using them against me. I couldn't decide if it was adorable or infuriating.

"Stop bullshitting me, Elijah Banks. What were you just going to say? After the what?"

"After everyone warms up to the idea. I just want to marry you. Is that a bad thing?" I leaned across the small table and planted a searing kiss on her lips. The kind I knew scrambled her brain and left her with only one thing on her mind.

We straightened back to our seats, and I was ready to swipe all the food off the surface in a clatter and feast on her the way I'd wanted since she came through my door.

Instead, she gave her head a little shake and said, "But why the rush? I mean, I definitely want to be with you. That's the easiest part of this conversation. I'm just trying to figure out what's gotten into you today."

Slowly, she regarded me from another angle and then, very carefully, set her fork down. "Elijah Banks, you tell me the truth this instant. Were one of those two hellcats from your past here to see you? Are they threatening you again?"

Holy. Shit.

How the hell had she put those pieces together? The problem was the two facts were true individually but existed separately. One was not connected to the other. Yes, I wanted to marry her sooner rather than later. Yes, one of my exes had stopped by my office just hours before she did. But the two had nothing to do with one another.

And now I was in the same motherfucking spot I was in before. I was going to have to call Bas and Grant in here to get me out of the hot seat. Again. Just like the night Hannah took off in Rio's car and was nearly killed on the Edge's jobsite.

Fuck this bullshit! If I ever considered murdering another human, it would be Hensley fucking Pritchett. One well-thought-out plan, and she could be eliminated.

"Elijah!"

Hannah's sharp tone cut straight through my fantasy, and I snapped my head to focus on her.

"Huh?"

She stood and came to my seat and crawled right into my lap. Of course, I made room for my beautiful girl and wrapped my arms around her to band her close to my body. I'd hold her here for the rest of the day if I could. Tell Carmen to just cancel my appointments, and I'd sit and hold my pretty kitty until it was time to go home.

"Please tell me what's going on in this complicated, beautiful mind." She kissed my temple, my brow, my eyelid, and the bridge of my nose.

I met her lips with my own and sucked in her perfection with the breath I stole with my kiss.

"Nothing's going on, beauty. I want to marry you. You would make me the proudest, happiest man if you agreed to be my wife. That's all. I want it more than I want my next breath."

There. That was better than the last clusterfuck that came out of my mouth.

"I would be proud to be your wife. To make a home, a family, a life with you." She kissed me again but pulled back too soon for my preference. She looked down at me from her perch like she was trying to decipher some complicated code.

"What is it?" I asked and then thought better of it. The less I dug into her head, the better.

"Is this really your proposal? Like, this is it? Right here?

No ring, nothing to ... I don't know ... commemorate it by? Just a spur-of-the-moment panicked blurting?"

"That's not what it was."

She did that damn head tilt again, and I was starting to get a very clear idea why it pissed some people off—namely her— when I did it.

"And who said I don't have a ring?"

She pointedly looked at her empty left ring finger, then looked at me, made the visual rounds a second time, now with brows raised high, and then huffed a loud sigh.

"You see, there are certain things girls dream about all their lives. This here"—she tapped her ring finger with her right index finger—"is one of the biggies. Maybe the biggest."

"Yeah?"

"Yeah. That's the one you don't want to mess up." She kept her eyes trained on me, cataloging every move—damn, every twitch I made.

"Noted. Damn, who would've predicted how bossy you really were under all this sugary sweetness?" I teased and pinched her fine ass so hard that she squealed.

After Hannah left, the rest of the day flew by. Before I knew it, Carmen was poking his head around the doorframe of my open office door to let me know it was his quitting time.

"Hey, boss, do you need anything before I go?"

"Nope, I'm getting ready to shut down. Hey, actually, can you give me five minutes? Sorry ... If you need to be somewhere, it can wait. It's personal." I finally looked up from the email I was finishing to get a read on the young guy's face.

Carmen Sandoval was a good-looking guy. Tall, good physical shape, slender build, might be a runner if I had to guess. He didn't have his sister's mystical blue eyes, but with that surname, naturally tan skin, and her incredible blues led me to believe the family was of Spanish descent.

"Close the door, will you?"

"Oh, yeah, sure. What's going on?" he asked as he came and stood in front of my desk.

"It's nothing bad, man. Calm down. You look like you're standing in front of the principal." I chuckled.

"Sorry." He gave a deprecating laugh. "I have very strict parents. Hate getting in trouble, so I immediately shift into panic mode when someone wants to talk to me. It's an old, bad habit I'm trying to get better at."

"Ahhh, another thing we have in common. My dad was a certifiable asshole." An icy chill ran up my spine, like talking about the man invited his ghost into the room. "Abusive bastard when he got angry. Didn't matter who was around or who got in his way." After a whole-body shiver, I changed topics. "But no use dragging that shit up when what I wanted to talk to you about is good news. Happy news."

"Yeah?" Carmen perked up. "What's going on?"

I knew the guy loved office gossip as much as the other assistants in the building. I'd seen them all sitting together on their lunch breaks, clucking like a bunch of hens.

"I'm hoping to be away for a few days, probably a long weekend."

"This coming weekend? Like two days from now?" he asked in surprise.

I didn't take much time away from the office, especially if it didn't have to do with security in one way or another. Maybe with Hannah in my life, that would change too.

"Yes. So I just wanted to let you know ahead of time so you could try to not book appointments for Monday and maybe

Tuesday if it can be helped." I slid my suit jacket on and closed the lid on my laptop.

"All right, no worries." Carmen followed me out into the hall, and I locked my office door.

"If the plans don't come together for this weekend, then we will probably go next weekend. I'm waiting on word from the tall guy."

"Oh great, some guy time. You all deserve it. You work too much."

I grinned. "Nah, that's not it."

He looked across his shoulder and waited for me to go on. When I just kept smiling, he widened his eyes and said, "Are you going to leave me hanging here?"

"No, but this is why I said it's personal. And if you gain an audience with Ms. Farsey again, you cannot say a word to her." I gave the guy a threatening glare. "I'm serious, man."

"I've already asked her out." His wide smile gave away her reply.

"Good for you, dude." I smacked him on the back in friendly congratulations. "What are you guys doing?"

"Oh, no you don't." He watched his feet as we stepped onto the main elevator.

"What? Don't what?" I asked innocently. Seriously, I had so much on my mind, the last thing I was doing was playing word games.

"Don't change the subject," he joked.

"No, I'm genuinely happy for you."

"Thanks, Elijah. I'm pretty excited. We really hit it off, so hopefully it wasn't just the alcohol, you know?"

"From the little time I've spent with her, she seems really great."

"Come on, though. What is this news you were going to tell me?"

After a deep breath to center myself—because shit, this was a big deal—I rushed out, "The four of us, Grant and his woman, Rio . . . she was at Hannah's party"—he nodded, so I kept going—"and Hannah and I are getting married in Vegas."

Carmen stopped dead in his tracks in the middle of the main lobby of Shark Enterprises with both hands crossed over his open mouth. Enough people were still in the process of leaving for the day that he caused a bit of a scene.

Briskly, I grabbed his elbow and ushered him out of the quitting-time pedestrian flow.

Through gritted teeth, I said, "People are staring. Pull your shit together, man."

Carmen dropped his hands and inhaled deeply through his nose.

I craned my neck to the side as far as humanly possible to get a really good look at the guy. I mean, this was the same guy I spoke to every weekday for the past four years, right?

"What the hell has gotten into you?" I seethed. "Why are you acting so crazy?"

"Sorry." He put his flat palm up and rolled his eyes. "Sorry."

But then like lighting a string of firecrackers, he shot one question off after another after another.

"Does Hannah know? Are you surprising her? I mean—I didn't see a rock on her finger. What do you think the parents will say? Are they going? Are you sure you're not going to get off on the wrong foot there? We didn't talk about a lot of meaningful things, but I definitely got the vibe that those Farseys have a super tight family bond. What can I do to help? This is like the party of all parties, you know? And now that you know I love to plan parties, just give me a list, and I'll get it done like *that*."

With the last word *that*, he snapped his fingers directly in front of my eyes, and I was thankful he had, because that one long run-on sentence he just spewed out without taking one single breath sent me into a catatonic state. Every question he asked—that I caught, at least—planted another seed of doubt.

Was this a selfish mistake? Would Hannah resent me for the rest of our lives for rushing her into a drive-thru wedding?

No. I couldn't think like that. I lived without apologies. Damn, it was all but tattooed across my forehead. That was how strongly I believed the mantra. No regrets. No looking back.

Hannah had a very strong will of her own. If she didn't want to do this, she wouldn't do it. We would stand beside our best friends and share in their happiness as spectators, and that was it. We'd have a great time no matter what part we were playing.

Yep! That was my story, and I was sticking to it.

CHAPTER TEN

HANNAH

How was this my life? I was on a private jet, surrounded by every luxury money could buy. On our way to Las Vegas.

To get married.

My parents were going to disown me. That same thought was playing on a continuous loop in my mind like a bad orchestral rendition of a favorite pop song.

In a haunted grocery store.

That only had one register open and a line wrapping around the store.

I slammed back the champagne in my glass and nudged Elijah's arm with the empty. I couldn't make eye contact with him; I just needed another drink.

"Please," I finally said when it seemed like it was taking too long for him to take the empty glass from me. If he wouldn't get it for me, one of the flight attendants would. They were very helpful on this small plane. But really, what else did they have to do?

The flight from Los Angeles to Las Vegas was very quick, and there were only eight passengers on the plane. If I wanted a drink, damn it, I'd get up and get it myself.

Finally, the empty glass was replaced by a full one, and I lifted it to my lips. Then immediately looked at the glass.

"What? Why?" I looked up to the man towering over me where I slouched in the ridiculously comfortable seat. He had given me a champagne flute filled with club soda.

"Because I don't want to carry you off this plane, my love, or nurse your hangover all day tomorrow." Then, with a very boyish smile that was hard to do anything but smile at in return, he said, "Plus, we have a wedding to attend. You don't want to miss that, do you?"

"No, you're right." I pouted and then mumbled, "What else is new?"

He flopped down in the seat beside me. Each couple was huddled together as far away from one another for our outbound trip. Maybe everyone was having last-minute jitters. Not just me.

"You feel okay, beautiful?" Elijah asked for at least the sixth time.

"Yes, please stop asking me that. I'm nervous, and my stomach isn't super happy with this smaller plane. But every time you ask me, it just makes me think about it more. Then I keep feeling sicker. Okay? Just lay off with the mother-hen bullshit for a bit."

He raised his eyebrow in warning.

"You can stow that crap too. I'm really not in the mood right now."

My man came close like he was going to kiss me, but I knew this move too well by now. He was about to level some sexy threat in my ear that would have the opposite effect of straightening out my unpreferred behavior and bad attitude.

But he knew that too. When he rumbled low and dirty in my ear and breathed his warm breath up and down my neck while he told me exactly how and where he would teach me to mind my manners? It just made me burn hotter for the bastard. He really should change up his tactics once in a while, because it was all becoming too predictable.

I put my open palm across his face like an octopus with five tentacles and stopped him from advancing past my cheek.

In an equally low tone, I growled, "Don't."

"Put. Your. Hand. Down." Pause. Pause. "Immediately." Each word came out like a distant bolt of thunder. Each a commanding sentence on its own.

Shit.

Well, I might have just tested and found what *too far* looked like for my dominant man.

His eyes were like pinpoints in the middle of sage-green ice blocks. His brow furrowed between in a deep vee. That beautiful, chiseled jaw jumped with every beat of his heart, and his plush lips pressed together in a menacing slash.

He was utterly breathtaking.

"You have to the count of ten to be in that bathroom"—he thrust a straight arm in the direction of the plane's lavatory—"at the back of the plane. Don't you dare lock the door, because I'm coming in right behind you. Don't you dare defy me like that again. Go now. One."

Immediately I stood but tried to repent. I reached for his arm. "Elijah," I whispered for privacy.

"Two," he growled. "Just go, beauty."

"But..."

"Three." One brow up. "Four. Five."

"Too fast!" I protested. We were both using regular conversational volume and attracting unwanted attention.

"Go!"

That time, he barked, and I jumped.

Grant looked up and widened his eyes but quickly looked down again.

When I passed by, I heard the tall bastard snicker, so I doubled back to ask exactly what was so funny. But I barreled right into Elijah's chest instead.

"No," he said calmly, like he was scolding a puppy. "Six."

I looked up and defiantly said, "You're really being an asshole right now."

"Not soap anymore, remember? Keep it up. Seven."

By that point, three more faces turned to see what was going on, and I pictured kicking my "fiancé" in the balls the minute we got into that tiny restroom. How dare he embarrass me in front of my friends and family?

I opened the slim door so hard I figured it would bounce off the opposite wall and slam shut on the rebound. But true to his word, Mr. Banks was hot on my heels, so he stopped the flying panel from hitting the bulkhead. We filed into the small enclosure, and he flipped the lock into place and crossed his arms over his toned chest. I mirrored his pose while we stared at each other.

He tilted his head until his hair fell to the side, so I did the same. But because mine was in a high ponytail, the entire mane dropped over my shoulder.

Elijah's nostrils widened like an angry bull as he watched my blond waves tumble over my breast.

Well, well. Turnabout is fair play, isn't it?

"Talk to me, beautiful."

"Regarding?"

"This." He waved his hand up and down my torso like he was showing a prized heifer at the state fair.

"Explain," I said simply, using the exact tone I heard every other person in this posse take when using the expression.

He grinned for a long moment at my remark but then got serious when he saw I wasn't going for levity.

"The attitude. The bite. The tone." He moved to touch me, and I turned slightly out of his reach. Not like there was far to go in the cramped toilet room, though.

"Did I do something that pissed you off and you just haven't told me yet? Because if that's the case, will you please tell me so we can talk about it? I don't like thinking I've hurt you in any way. I don't like the way you're treating me right now, and I definitely don't like the way you're treating me in front of our friends, who all know how crazy I am about you."

He paused there, maybe hoping he had struck the nail on the head with his first assertion. I continued my wordless, angry stare because I was scanning my mind and couldn't put a finger on the right place to start. This entire impromptu shotgun wedding had me raw, even though I'd agreed to it. Now that the plan was in motion, I wanted to press *pause* and give the whole idea better consideration. The term *cold feet* was getting a new definition.

Apparently my silence gave my man the green light to plow on to other things that might be wrong between us, and shit, did he go for it.

"You're making an ass out of me, and frankly, it doesn't feel good, beautiful. I've been in this position once before, and I don't want to play the humiliated jackass role in a relationship again."

"Elijah, no—" I tried to make him stop.

But this one seemed to really make sense to him, so he went for broke.

"It seems like right when I get really serious about a

woman, she wants to treat me like a dumbass and lead me around by my balls in front of everyone to make an ass out of me. I'm having déjà vu, you know?"

"That's not fair, and you know it," I said, my alto voice gaining volume.

He stabbed his finger into the countertop with each statement. "No." Stab. "I know how I feel." Stab. "And I'm being honest with you here." Stab. "That's how I feel." Stab.

I stared at him for a long moment because things were about to be said that couldn't be recalled. But we never talked about his past, and if he wanted to dig up these skeletons right here, right now, fine by me. I'd hand him a fucking shovel and keep one for myself.

"Okay, fair enough. However, that wasn't my intention." I sucked in a deep breath through my nose in an effort to calm down. "But your history with your ex, or two thousand exes"—I angrily thumbed back into my sternum. So much for calming down—"is not my cross to bear. You shouldn't throw that bag of shit on me or our relationship." This time, when I drew in a breath, it was solely to put more power behind my already thunderous-when-angry voice. "Ever! And I resent the fact that you just did! On the night of our fucking wedding!"

Yes, I was bellowing now. In an airplane lavatory. And there was no doubt that everyone out in the cabin could hear me because I was well aware how loud my voice could be when I put effort behind it. But there was no way he should've just brought that shit up.

No way in hell.

Anger quickly turned to raw emotion, and hot stinging tears burned down my cheeks, around my clenched jaw, and down my neck. They poured out in racking sobs, and I couldn't remember the last time I'd cried so hard. I faltered physically, and my ass hit the closed toilet seat, but I continued to crumple forward until I was hugging my knees.

Sensing his motion as Elijah reached for me, I quickly sat up and glared at him through the torrents of tears.

The stubborn man still looked like he considered comforting me somehow, so I found enough voice to seethe, "Just get away from me."

Fine, it was shaky and feeble as far as commands went, but he took the words for their weight and dropped his outstretched hand.

He left the small bathroom after that and closed the door behind him. The quiet snick of the lever sounded like a gunshot in the small space when I moved it into the locked position. I flopped down on the only available seat again and cradled my face in my palms.

How had this all gone so sideways? There was no way I was in the wrong, though. I shook my head for no one to see, but it still felt good to be sure of my words—my assertions. Elijah was the one who had unresolved demons, not me. Everyone knew it, but they all just tiptoed around it because they didn't want to deal with his broody, bossy bullshit.

Well, guess what? Neither do I.

Once on the ground in Las Vegas, a black Suburban met us on the tarmac. We all piled into the back and made our way down the strip to our hotel. So much had changed since the last time I had been in this city, I didn't recognize anything. I gaped out the window like a tourist, which was probably a good thing because it helped relax my nerves and I could try to forget about the drama of that miserable flight. If only my stomach would get the memo we were on solid ground now and stop tossing and turning at every mention of dinner ideas from the gang.

Each time Elijah tried touching me or casually putting his arm across the back of my seat, I would casually move out of his reach. We had a lot to talk about and to clear up before his hands were welcome on my body again.

The one thing that kept playing on a continuous loop in my mind was him accusing me of treating him the way that despicable woman, Hensley Pritchett, had. It got to the point I saw red all over again. I knew how he felt about her and how everyone else in this group—minus two members—felt about her, so how dare he use her name and mine in the same sentence? Ever?

Before that nightmare broke out on the airplane, Elijah had explained to me that we were staying at a newly erected property owned by Stone Global Corporation. Everyone knew of that famous family for one reason or another.

Typically, the females of the household were familiar with the cosmetics and beauty products the company produced. The health conscious knew of the vitamins and supplements division and home gym equipment line. There were traditional gas and alternative fuel stations and adjoining convenience markets across the nation, and since several of the family members had become parents, they branched out into baby products, too.

Talk about diversified!

But this was the company's first foray into luxury resort and entertainment properties. From the moment we crossed through the opulent gates at the entrance of the off-strip property, you could see no detail was forgotten.

I couldn't wait to be out of the stuffy vehicle and go

exploring on foot. I couldn't remember how many hundreds of acres he'd said this resort covered, but lush greenery was all around us from every window's view.

"When is your tee time in the morning?" Abbigail asked to no one specifically.

"Five thirty," Sebastian answered and pecked her lips when she smiled up at him.

Even sitting beside him, she was engulfed by his hulking frame. The way he looked at her made my heart hurt, so I quickly looked away. I'd watched them earlier on the plane too, and the man could not keep his hands off her, even if in the smallest way, at all times. It was like she was his life-force and he had to stay plugged into her to exist.

When I met my sister's eyes across the tight aisle of the SUV, she was watching me watch Abbi. Averting my eyes, I felt her nudge my foot. I didn't want to attract unwanted attention, so I ignored her. When she nudged me a second time, I met her gaze and gave my head an imperceptible shake. We'd have time to talk once we got to our rooms.

The group had reserved a large villa for three nights. There was one main living, dining, and entertainment space and an enormous gourmet kitchen. Branching off around the main house were separate cottages, where we would each sleep.

My sister had insisted on making the trip with us the moment she found out about the getaway from Elijah's personal assistant. Apparently that dude was in some hot water with his boss because he had sworn he wasn't going to say anything. However, the first chance he had, he'd spilled the beans to my sister.

She in turn threatened to tell our parents what was going

on if she and Carmen weren't allowed to come. My bossy man had no choice but to let them come because he didn't want to deal with my parents in the very little time we had before we left Los Angeles.

I grinned then, thinking about the fuss my sister had kicked up with my boyfriend and what a joy it was watching him back down to her. He thought I was stubborn? Ha! He had no idea who he was messing with when he got into it with Agatha Christine.

My grin slowly spread into a wide smile, and the devil man noticed. Of course he misunderstood its meaning, though, and presumed I'd decided to have an attitude adjustment or something equally asinine.

"Ahhh, that's much better. I'm so glad to see you've decided to have a good time," he said and slung his heavy arm across my shoulders and pulled me into his warm body with a squeeze. He bussed the top of my head like an obedient child, and I wanted to elbow him in the solar plexus.

Forcefully, I pulled out of his embrace and sat forward on the black leather seat.

Over my right shoulder, I glared at him and said, "What?"

His eyebrows hiked nearly into his hairline like they were attached to a little rope on a pulley, and somewhere out of sight, a little man was tasked with cranking those suckers up, up, up. This thought made me chuckle but only gave him more ammunition for his stupid idea.

"I said I'm glad it looks like your mood has changed. You look happy again. We're going to have such a good time. You'll see." He nodded once like his word was law and we could move on now.

"When was the last time you were in Vegas?" he asked.

"I don't think you answered me when I asked you that before. I'll bet a lot has changed." He rubbed his open palm down my back, and I dodged out of his reach just a bit too late.

This seemed to confuse him, because now the little person let up slack on the rope and his brows lowered down, down, down, over his icy green eyes.

After leaning in closer to him, I said, "I didn't answer you because I'm not speaking to you. And my mood hasn't changed. I was thinking about something else when I was smiling—not about being here with you." I said it all through gritted teeth, being very careful to modulate my seethe as to not cause a scene like I did in the plane's lavatory.

How would I ever look at these women again? How would I expect them to take me seriously in the kitchen or think me capable of handling their business if a crisis came up like I completely already had proven I could do?

I was going to have to resign.

I was trying so hard not to let my anxiety win this particular war while locked in this small space with this group of people because it would only serve to fortify what they must already be thinking.

The moment the car lurched to a complete stop and the resort's bellman opened the door, I was off like a shot. Elijah was hot in pursuit, but I couldn't stop to worry about it. I was about to be sick, and the farther I made it from watchful eyes, the better.

In the cover of a semiprivate hedge line, I bent at the waist and vomited for several minutes. Someone came to stand with Elijah, and this spectator was kind enough to bring a bottle of water and retreat. Because when I was done embarrassing myself and stood fully, only Elijah approached slowly.

The dumbass looked like he'd both seen a ghost and won the lottery. What the hell could've been going through his mind was anyone's guess. Clearly I didn't know him half as well as I thought, so I wasn't about to even stab at an idea.

He handed me the water bottle with a fully outstretched arm, as if I had the plague and he was in danger of catching it if he got too close. I leaned out past his wider frame and realized everyone had disappeared. It was just the two of us standing there. Not even a staff member to be seen.

"Are you okay?" he asked in the quietest voice I ever heard from him. He looked scared, and I knew the way I had been treating him for the past few hours was probably to blame.

I just shrugged, then took a gulp of water. "I don't know. My stomach's been bothering me all day. First I thought it was nerves. Then I thought it was that small plane, you know?" Tears started at some point between that comment and my next. "Then maybe the fight we had." I took another gulp of water.

He reached for the bottle, but I glared at him through my blurry tears, and he pulled his hand back. Maybe he finally clued in he was about to lose the appendage if he didn't back off.

"And then the SUV, and there were so many of us in there, and it was hot and stuffy, and I couldn't breathe, and then we got here, and I just—" I sucked up the watery snot running from my nose in the most unladylike nasal sound ever. "Yeah, that was it for me. My anxiety..." I waved my hand wildly. "Well, you know how my anxiety is, and I've been so nervous and worked up, and I don't know." I clutched my belly. "Oh God, I'm..." Shaking my head, I said, "I'm going to be sick again. I'm going to be sick." I thrust the water bottle into his chest and ran past him, back to the hedge, and threw up every bit of water I'd just drunk.

This time, when I was done, I backed up a few feet and dropped to my knees. I felt so weak, I couldn't even stand. It was hot in the desert, and I just didn't feel well. Elijah dropped down beside me and pulled me into his lap. I was too weak to fight him off anymore, so I just let him do it. And honestly, it felt good in his strong arms. He always felt so good around me.

My man rocked me gently in his arms for a few minutes, whispering that he loved me and he would take care of me. I finally looked up to him and croaked a miserable sound. I needed water so badly.

"I'm so thirsty. Please, I need some water."

"Your sister's on her way out. I texted her to bring some water a few minutes ago. I'm sure she'll be here soon." Elijah pressed his cheek to my forehead. "You're not warm, beauty. I don't think you're sick. After we get some water in you, we should get you to bed, though."

I didn't have the energy to argue with him, so I remained quiet and enjoyed the comfort of his arms. He could carry me back to California in a few days if he felt like it, and I would let him. My sister must have come and gone without me knowing, because a fresh bottle of water was placed in my hand. Maybe I'd drifted off?

"Go easy this time so it stays down, beautiful. Small sips." He sat me upright a bit more.

While I sipped water, he took advantage of my busy mouth and got some things off his chest. Maybe he'd been rehearsing a speech while waiting for Dah and while I slept for a few minutes.

"Hannah, please hear me. I know I have serious

apologizing to do. I know I fucked up on the plane. I know that. But first we need to make sure you're okay and that the baby is okay. Please stay with me tonight and let me take care of you. I promise I'll be on my best behavior."

I pulled back in his arms, pushing his chest for leverage. "Pardon? The baby? What the fuck are you talking about, the baby?" Oh, I was back to red alert in less than fifteen seconds. I stood up so fast, the world spun like a merry-go-round. I reached to grab something to steady me, and luckily, he was on his feet just as fast to hold me once more.

But then the bastard had the nerve to give me the head tilt and paused a moment to let me download what he'd just unboxed for me. I just continued to glare at him—or at least what I thought was him—because I was seeing about four or five versions of someone, so I focused on the middle one and figured that was probably the actual person.

Finally, he said, "Are you going to tell me you're not late?"

"Elijah!" I shrieked. "We use a condom...like...every time! Did one break? Did one break and you didn't tell me?" I accused and threw my hand on my hip for extra effect. Oh, Christ, could the world stop spinning for just one minute here?

Just do a girl a small solid?

He tilted his head to the other side, and his fucking hair flopped that way too. I heard the growl rumbling up from my throat and tried to stifle it, but it came out anyway. His slow grin told me he heard it too, goddammit.

No. God damn him!

"Baby," he said so matter-of-factly I wanted to kick him in the balls. "We haven't used a condom since right around Bas and Abbi's wedding. That was like five weeks ago. We've probably fucked three hundred times since then." He ended the comment with a careless shrug.

A fucking shrug.

"Have you had your period since then?" he asked boldly.

"You seem to know everything else. You tell me," I shot back and knew I wasn't being fair. I was as responsible for all of this as he was. Every single time this man came inside me, I knew we were rolling the dice. It just started to become the norm, and then we started talking about the future and eventually getting married. I just didn't realize he was on some hellbent path to make it happen this month.

"No, my beautiful queen. You haven't," he said, trying to hold back his lazy grin.

Fuck this gorgeous man. Why was he so stiflingly handsome? My God, if I was pregnant, my parents were going to kill me. Just thinking the word *pregnant*, my stomach flipped over on itself.

Like a lightning strike off in the distance, something cracked in my memory, and my now-teary eyes focused on Elijah.

"Oh my God," I barely breathed. "You knew," I accused the man. "You fucking knew this on my birthday." I reached up to place my hand on the necklace he gave me, and the reason behind the emeralds came crashing in.

I pressed my forehead into his chest and tried to breathe. If there was a poor little baby inside me right now, I wasn't being very kind to the sweet, innocent angel so far. Way too much turmoil and emotional upheaval for one so new. I needed to settle down and find a pregnancy test. Immediately.

After a solid moment of calming breaths, I said, "Well, let's go get this over with."

Elijah was visibly confused. "What?"

"First, we need to get our hands on a pregnancy test. And if it's positive, we have a group wedding to be part of. Because I'm not joking, dude. My dad will cut you up into tiny pieces and use you for bait at the end of the Venice Pier."

CHAPTER ELEVEN

ELIJAH

I'd bet my bank balance that she was knocked up. I'd known it for the past week, and so far, she was handling it pretty well, all things considered.

I had a pregnancy test packed in my bag because I knew this was going to come up and we would need to use it. I actually had two of them because you could never trust one. It would probably piss her off that I was prepared, but at least we would save a trip to a drugstore out on the strip.

"Do you think you can walk?" I asked quietly. "I can call the desk and get a golf cart out here to drive us to the villa."

My queen was like a bomb waiting to detonate. One wrong move or question and she'd go off.

"No, I'm fine. It will do me some good to move. Get my blood circulating properly. I'm so dizzy from vomiting, though. The thought of eating makes me want to do it all over again," she said while holding her stomach.

"All right, I think if we take this path, it will lead us in the right direction. That's the way your sister went after she brought the water. Our villa must be that way. I'll text Carmen and find out the exact number."

I waited a minute and made sure she was still with me. I wasn't used to her being so quiet, and I felt like I was the one babbling nervously for a change. I felt lucky she was even talking to me at this point.

"This place is something, huh?" I said, looking across the vast property.

You really couldn't help appreciating the landscape. And right now, talking about anything besides the baby-shaped elephant between us seemed like a good idea.

"This is so unlike you," she said, looking at me while we walked.

I wanted so badly to touch her. Touch her in any way. Hold her hand, wrap an arm around her shoulder and pull her against me. Hold her around her tiny waist that wouldn't be tiny for much longer. Anything, just to feel her, be reassured by that contact. Know that everything would be okay.

I finally spoke again. "What do you mean?" I asked quietly.

With a small smile, she said, "I don't think I've ever heard you small talk this much in the entire time I've known you. It's almost charming."

I stopped walking, and when she realized I had stopped, she doubled back. "What's wrong? Are we going the wrong way?"

"No, I think this is the right way. Can I ask you something?"

I kept my gaze fixed to hers and waited for her permission to go on. God, this was ridiculous. I felt like a schoolboy. No. Fuck that. I didn't even go through this shit in school. I was so out of my wheelhouse with this woman, and I had a feeling life with Miss Hannah Farsey would always be like that. And I couldn't wait to find out.

"What is it?"

"Will you let me hold your hand? Please?" I offered her

my hand, palm up. It was the first step in reconciling with my beautiful woman, and I needed it more than she knew.

I wouldn't force her into marrying me if she didn't want to. Earlier today, when we started on this journey, my mindset on the matter was completely different. But seeing the way it ramped up her anxiety and affected her body physically, I changed my mind.

I felt terrible that my behavior could cause that. And now the baby too. Knowing that there was a baby inside her shifted everything for me. I would do everything in my power to protect them. And that included tamping down my own naturally dominant behavior.

Now that behavior shifted from having my needs met and meeting Hannah's needs to my family. This woman had no idea how fiercely protective I would be.

And it all started right here, when she placed her hand in mine willingly. My heart swelled in my chest, and I exhaled tension I had been holding inside. I felt hopeful again for the first time since that horrible fight in the airplane restroom. Hope that we would find our way back to each other and to our easy, carefree, loving relationship.

"Thank you."

Hannah turned and looked at me but didn't let go of my hand. "Why are you thanking me?"

"For honoring me with your body. Even in this very small way. I'm telling you; I know how badly I fucked up today. I know it will take you some time to completely forgive me for that, and I don't blame you. I was so out of line saying the things I said. I don't know…"

I scrubbed my free hand down my face. Fuck, I didn't want to get into this again, but we were going to have to eventually. It was the only way it was going to get out of the way.

"I don't know," I said again.

"Let's not worry about all of that right now. We can talk about it tomorrow or whenever." Hannah waved her hand through the air like she was batting at dust motes.

"Whatever you want," I agreed.

She just studied me with a wry smile as we reached the door to our cottage.

"What is that look?" I asked, and I could feel my face mirroring her expression.

"I'm trying to figure out what happened to the bossy, dominant guy who knocked me up. Have you seen him around?" she asked with a glimmer of mischief in those ocean-blue eyes.

A lazy grin, familiar and effective, slid into place, and I heard Hannah suck in her breath. "I'll look around when we get inside. I'm sure he hasn't gotten too far."

My beauty wrapped both arms around my neck and pressed her lips to mine for a chaste kiss, but I stole her breath by sealing my mouth completely around hers instead. When I released her from the deeper kiss, she looked flushed and a little dazed—and this time, in all the right ways.

With her plush mouth still against mine, she said, "Good. I didn't sign up for this pussy shit." With that, she disengaged from my body and walked ahead of me into our room, adding a little extra sway to that sexy ass I loved so much.

I stood there gaping like an idiot because her mood shifts were completely tossing me about, but I wasn't going to question anything at the moment. I would take this version of her over the airplane and car version any day.

From deep in the bedroom, Hannah called, "Hey! Check

it out. Our bags are here. That's super convenient. Do you know what room my sister's in, though? I'm going to have to find a drugstore somewhere. Maybe she'll go with me. I'm sure we can get an Uber out front, right?"

I rounded the corner into the bedroom right as she was coming out, and we nearly collided. I caught her around the waist and held on. There was a good chance she was going to be pissed off when I told her this next bit of news.

I leaned back a little so I could look her right in the eye when I spoke. "I want to tell you something, but I don't want you to get angry with me again. Okay?"

"You know how I love these setups of yours." She winced and patted my chest. "Let's have it."

Taking it as a good sign that she didn't pull out of my embrace, I forged ahead. "I brought something along for you. Wait here and I'll go get it out of my luggage."

It all but killed me to extract myself from her embrace, but we needed to find out for certain if she was pregnant. I rolled my eyes, knowing damn well she was. I already knew it last week when I told the guys on the roof and they gave me so much shit about it. But this would be the proof she needed to see.

Everything was about to change. Her life. My life. Our life together. That was the best part. Our life that was just about to start. I thought I had more butterflies than she did.

Holding it behind my back, I found Hannah in the sitting room in our villa. She was kicked back on the sofa but sat forward when I entered the room. The place had a bedroom, bathroom, and this living space with a sofa, chair, and television.

I sat across from her and put the small box behind me. I reached for her hands, and she gave them to me willingly, making my heart swell like it did before when she let me hold her hand for the first time after our fight.

Man, I hope I'm getting this timing right.

"Hannah, I love you more than I thought it possible to love someone. I want to start every day seeing your face and end every night worshiping your body. I will do everything in my power to make you happy, keep you healthy, and support you while you chase your dreams. Whatever those may be, from this day until the day I no longer walk this earth. Will you do me the greatest honor and live the rest of your life as my wife? I will honor you always."

I dropped to my knees in front of her, took the ring out of my shirt pocket, and slid it onto her left ring finger, never taking my eyes off hers.

Tears tracked down her cheeks, one after another, after another. I didn't know if they were happy tears or sad tears, because she wasn't saying a word. She just kept darting her gaze from the ring to me, then back.

Finally, I couldn't stand the suspense and asked, "Beauty?"

She jumped a little, like she'd forgotten I was in the room with her, and a radiant smile broke out across her lips.

Unexpectedly, she flung her entire body into my arms and said, "Yes! Yes, I will marry you. Thank you, my beautiful, bossy, breathtaking man. That was so beautiful. Thank you."

She peppered my face with tear-wet kisses, and I couldn't hold her close enough. I wanted to squeeze her until her body became part of mine and we would never be apart for a single moment. I would protect her from every danger and celebrate every milestone with her.

But really, wasn't that what a marriage was? Fuck me, I

was the happiest man alive.

Finally, Hannah sat back on the sofa, and I moved back to the chair. She took a deep breath and said, "Let's do it tonight. With Grant and Rio."

"Baby, we really don't have to. I don't want you to feel rushed, and I don't want you to feel like you missed out on a big wedding with your family here to witness it. Especially your parents. You'll never forgive me, and consequently, I won't forgive myself. If I took that away from you, you would grow to resent me for it. If girls dream of the perfect proposal their whole life, they must dream of the perfect wedding too."

"Of course they do. But Elijah, if I'm pregnant, it would be even worse if I'm not married. I'm telling you; I know my parents. Plus, I want to marry you. I want to do it tonight."

I took her hands again and waited until she settled, because she had been getting more and more agitated as we sat there.

"Beautiful, listen to me. It was very important that I asked you to be my wife before we found out if we're also about to be parents. I never wanted you to think that the only reason I proposed was because of the possibility of a baby. I love you. A standalone declaration—I love you. I want to be with you. With a baby, without a baby, with twelve babies. I want to be with you."

"Whooaaa now, let's not get carried away. A dozen babies is a pretty tall order. Even for a man with your reset time." She winced and held her stomach. "Christ, that actually made my uterus hurt just saying that."

And then she shot to her feet and clapped her hands like we just came up with a plan to rob the property's casino.

"Okay, I need to call my sister," she declared as step one

of the plan but searched the room with a bewildered look. "Oh, dude, do you know where my handbag is? Oh no, I may have left it where I was puking." She sank dramatically back onto the sofa and smacked her forehead. "We have to go back and trace our steps because I really don't recall picking it up." She finally focused her darting gaze on me.

"Settle down, love. Agatha took it when she brought the water. Text her, and I can either run across to their villa or she can bring it over here."

Her shoulders instantly dropped back down to their normal position. "Oh, thank God. That would've been the worst, you know? And I'm already convinced I'm going to have to resign from my job."

Wait. What?

Where the hell did that come from? Oh, but she was off and running now, and I'd seen these anxiety dust devils spin up before.

"I must have looked so irresponsible and unprofessional, and let's be honest, immature, yelling the way I was in that damn bathroom. How am I going to face my employers ever again?"

She shot to her feet again and started frantically pacing back and forth, back and forth. Christ, I was surprised there wasn't smoke coming from her heels, because she was quickly wearing a path in the tightly woven area rug.

Finally, I caught her around the waist and pulled her between my legs. "Please settle down." Softly, I kissed her belly. "If my baby is in here, you need to relax. That little one feels every bit of stress you feel, okay?"

Fortunately, she didn't pull away or get angry. The exact opposite, actually, and I was so thankful. Hannah wrapped her arms around my neck and sank down onto my knee.

"I know you're right. My mind is spinning in fifteen different directions at the moment. Can you ask my sister to bring my bag over here? And then I can see if she will go to the drugstore with me. I really want to just know once and for all."

"I can definitely do that, but I think I can do one better," I said with my brows raised in hope that she would take the next gesture as positively as it was meant.

Christ, but then I had a lightning bolt of a memory strike in my mind of the day I gave Abbigail that pregnancy test in Twenty-Nine Palms. The scorched earth of where that memory was burned still smelled of her angry fire and brimstone and how well that gesture went over.

This woman of mine had a way of making me question myself like I'd never done before.

Live without apology. Live without apology.

I chanted it to myself while she looked on, probably thinking I was taking leave of my faculties.

"Elijah? You okay?"

"Hmm? Yeah, great," I rushed out like the crackpot I felt like. "Why?"

"You were muttering something I didn't quite catch. What is it, baby? Are you nervous? I thought you wanted me to be pregnant. Are you having second thoughts now?"

Her frantic energy morphed into fear and concern before my eyes. I needed to reassure her. Immediately.

"No. No way. I really do want it," I insisted. "More than anything, actually." I chuckled then but quickly got serious. "I can't wait to see your beautiful body grow and change with another life inside. A life we made from our love."

"My goodness, you're full of so many romantic words

tonight. Okay, well, text Dah. Let's pull the trigger already."

"I have a pregnancy test here," I rushed out with no preamble. I pulled the purple box out from behind my ass on the chair. How she hadn't seen it by then was anyone's guess. Normally, the woman didn't miss a trick. She'd have to take her eyes off her engagement ring for more than a minute at a time to notice, I guessed. Something that gave me a burst of male pride.

Shit, at least I knew I got something right.

And judging by the look on her face, that was where that bit of luck ran out.

"Where did you get this?" She shook the box once with each word of her question like she was keeping time with a maraca. The pieces inside rattled about with her question.

"I brought it with me from home," I replied directly.

"Oh. You just had this lying around? You just keep a stash of pregnancy tests lying around for the occasional slipup with your subs?"

"Don't," I said simply. I knew if I didn't stop her early on, she'd take my silence as acquiescence and become a runaway train.

"Don't what?" she defied with a tilt of her chin.

I saw the gesture as an offer and gripped her there firmly with my thumb and forefinger. "This mouth is about to earn you a really red ass if you don't stop with the sassy disrespect. Is that what you were going for? I know you like a bit of pain, beauty, but there are much more fun ways to go about it."

My guess was she was dealing with hormonal surges similar to the premenstrual type, because the hot and cold flashes of her mood were almost hard to track, they were swinging back and forth so wildly. It was also possible they were fucking with her mental health challenges, and she was trying to figure out which end was up herself.

A third and very real possibility was that she was scared. And if that were the case, I needed to be more supportive. But she also needed to let me be. I knew this woman well enough by now to know that oftentimes, when her anxiety was getting the best of her, she needed to be grounded before she could be rational.

With a deep inhale, I let go of her chin and stroked my hand all the way down her arm until I clasped her hand in mine. I brought it to my lips and kissed her softly on the ring I just placed there while keeping my eyes fixed on hers.

"I love you. I know this is probably really scary right now, so let's go see what we're dealing with. I'll wait outside the bathroom, and then we can wait for the results together. I will always stand by your side, Hannah. You'll never have to go through scary stuff alone again. Okay?"

Those expressive blue eyes filled with tears while I spoke my truth to her, and by the time I finished, wet tracks streaked down her flushed cheeks. Without saying another word, I wrapped her into my arms and held her while she silently shook in my hold. She needed to just let it all go, so I didn't say anything more. I stroked her silky ponytail and rubbed her back until she finally went still again.

"Better?" Leaning back to see her face, I waited for her to level her gaze to mine.

After a very big inhale, she said, "Yes. Thank you for being so patient. You are the most wonderful man who ever walked this earth, and I'm sorry I've been so difficult. I can't really explain what keeps coming over me." She shook her head in bewilderment and rubbed at her furrowed forehead.

"Hey," I said, pulling her hand down. Placing a kiss on the tense spot instead, I went on. "Don't stress about it, beautiful. You have a lot of extra hormones flooding your body right now. Things are going to be a little wonky for a while."

"Wonky?" she laughed, repeating the unusual word I just used. "And why are you such an expert in all these womanly things? I thought you didn't have younger siblings?"

"Ready to take that test?" I started walking toward the bedroom's en suite bathroom, and it was such a jarring subject shift, it felt like being in a six-car pileup in a morning rush hour intersection.

True to form, my girl was hot on my heels into the bathroom, so at least we were moving closer to the goal.

"Why did you just do that?" she sniper-fired at my back.

"Do what, love? I thought you wanted to take the pregnancy test and know for sure if you're carrying our baby?" Intentionally, I slid the grin I knew she couldn't resist into place before rounding back on her and reaching for her waist.

"No." She tried to push my hands away, but I was done letting her sassy side run amuck. Deftly, I grabbed her by her jean's belt loops and yanked her so fiercely she *thunked* into my body.

"Pardon me?" I said against her lips. "We're right back to this? Already, baby?"

Her pupils looked like ink blots in the dimly lit bathroom, filling her sapphire irises almost completely. My little doll. I wanted to dress her up in frilly panties, knee socks, and patent leather shoes and make her kneel in the corner with her nose pressed to the wall. Maybe then this bad attitude would either correct itself or she could do something else while there on her knees to take both our minds off all the negativity.

A dark growl came from low in my throat after painting that damn daydream for myself, and I dropped my head back on my shoulders and stared at the ceiling. A fresco mural was painted there that I hadn't noticed before, and I studied the scene, trying to make sense of it, and willed my erection to settle the fuck down.

"Oh, my. What's going on here, Mr. Banks?" Hannah slid her hand to the front of my slacks, and I immediately stopped her progress by cuffing her wrist.

Bringing my head level again, I narrowed my eyes. "You're a real handful today, aren't you?"

"I'd say you're way more than a handful—every day." She gave me a cheeky wink, and I burst out laughing.

"Get your ass in there and piss on that stick. Now, woman," I instructed in my most dominant tone. "Leave it on the counter when you're done and come find me in the bedroom. We'll see if we can find something to do to pass the time while we wait." I reached down the front of my slacks to readjust myself, and her eyes followed my movement.

I turned her by the shoulders and shoved her toward the toilet. "Go."

It seemed like it took her thirty minutes to finally join me in the bedroom. I watched her nervously sit on the end of the bed, wringing her hands in her lap.

"What the hell took so long?" I questioned from where I was propped against the upholstered headboard and a pile of thick pillows, laptop balanced on my thighs.

"Well, first I had to read the directions. And I read them like four times to make sure I was doing it right because I don't want to get a false positive or false negative. I don't know... Is that a thing? A false negative, I mean. And then I was so nervous I couldn't go, and I was sitting there, waiting and waiting. It's stressful, you know?"

My smile just grew and grew with every adorable thing she said. Who had to read directions to pee? Only this woman. I really couldn't love her more than I did in that moment. Although in about five minutes, I'd probably be eating those words with a little tiny baby spoon and spork if every hunch I had was right.

I closed my computer and went to stand in front of where she sat nervously on the edge of the bed. One shove pushed her back, and I crawled on top of her. It had been way too long since I'd felt her beneath me, and I was done waiting. I'd already set the timer on my phone for five minutes and had hit start the moment I heard her come out of the bathroom, so I needed to make every second count here.

"Elijah, I—"

"Quiet, now," I whispered and moved her legs apart with my knee. I didn't want to crush her with my full weight, but I wanted her to feel secure beneath me. A lot of times her anxiety settled with my body on top of hers like this, so I'd do everything in my power to calm her through these next few minutes while we waited.

"Do you mind if I take your hair down?" I asked beside her ear before kissing my way down her neck.

"No. I think that would feel amazing, actually. But I can do it."

She tried to sit up, but I stopped her with a stern look.

"Oh, bossy man is here, I see." She looked up with glittering eyes.

"He's always here. But there's a sassy girl who is about to get in so much trouble if she doesn't take it down a few pegs.

I can't warn you seriously enough." I sank my teeth into her shoulder to punctuate the caution.

"Hmmm." She gave a mixed hum and groan and then added in a husky tone, "I'm not super threatened by your warnings." Hannah shrugged. "You know?"

I hung my head until my chin tucked into my chest. This woman still had no idea how dark I liked to play. Pregnant or not, there were so many things I could do to make her ache, in all the right—and wrong—ways. She was lighting matches near an open fuel line and didn't even know it.

"Hannah…" was all I could manage. My voice sounded like I'd just had a shot of tequila with a gasoline chaser.

"Yes, Daddy?" She stared up at me but squirmed against my cock.

"Oh, is this the game you want to play? Funny, because I had a similar fantasy going before of punishing you with your nose to that corner." I motioned across the room with my chin and circled my hips into her harder, making her hiss.

She just stared up at me with those wide blue pools that I wanted to dive into. Slowly, she shook her head.

"No to which part?" I pressed for clarification, because now that the image from before was back in my mind, I was really struggling to let it go. Fuck, what I wouldn't give to stripe her ass with a cane right now.

I groaned.

She grinned.

We were definitely thinking of different things.

"Come closer to me. I want to kiss you," Hannah said through her wide smile.

It was an opportunity I would never pass up—to feel her satiny lips with my own—but all I got was a peck and she was right back to that infectious, enormous grin.

Pulling way back so I could take her in fully, I accused playfully, "All right. What's going on with you? You've got something going on in this beautiful brain." I used the chance to kiss her forehead, each eyelid, the tip of her nose, and finally her mouth. But this time, I deepened the kiss until she moaned so low in that alto, husky way she did sometimes, my cock pulsed with a need so primal, I wanted to pull her pants down and fuck her right then and there.

"Mmm, Daddy, when you kiss me like that, I want to spend the rest of the night in bed with you," she whimpered between kisses. "With you so deep inside me I can't remember my own name."

"Not gonna lie, baby, this daddy talk is making me so hard. Can you feel what you're doing to my cock? Is this your new thing?"

And there went that wide smile again. Like the cat that swallowed the canary ... And it hit me like twenty open-palm backhanders, and I popped all the way off the mattress and stood beside the bed with my hands on my hips.

"You little shit."

"What?" she said, scampering to sit up.

"You already know. That's why you were in there so long." I stabbed my finger in her direction and then toward the water closet. My own grin mirrored hers, and I narrowed my eyes playfully.

She bit her lip, trying to stifle her giggle, but it wasn't enough to hold back her wide smile again. She was off the bed too then, and we were pushing each other to get to that little white stick on the bathroom counter.

My size and speed meant I reached the thing first, and

I swept it up in my grasp and held it high above my head so she couldn't snatch it out of my hand. I looked up at the damn thing, and sure enough, clear as day and as bright blue as my woman's eyes staring up at me, two lines appeared in the little window.

Hannah wrapped her arms around my waist and studied me with enormous eyes. They filled with tears while I watched.

"Congratulations, Daddy," she whispered.

"Congratulations to you, Mamma. Are you happy?"

She nodded continuously while tears rolled over her cheeks and down around her jaw. "More than I ever dreamed possible. And it's all because of you, Elijah Banks. Thank you for coming into my life like you knew you belonged there the whole time. Like you knew we were meant to be together. Like you'd stop at nothing to make it all happen. I love you so much."

CHAPTER TWELVE

HANNAH

While getting ready this morning, my soon-to-be husband had regaled me with all sorts of details about the charming wedding chapel where our ceremony would be held, including the fact that it had been part of this colorful city's landscape for more than eighty years.

"How incredible is that?" Elijah had asked excitedly from the shower, but I'd barely been able to take my eyes off his naked body long enough to register a word he'd been saying. He'd finally noticed my gawking and stopped with the Sin City history lesson long enough to clear his throat to catch my attention.

"My eyes are up here, young lady."

"And your point is?" I had asked, tilting my head to see his firm ass when he'd turned to rinse the suds from his hair.

Doing my own hair had been tricky. Because at that point, I'd had no idea what my dress would look like or what style it would be. Elijah had chosen my dress, and Grant had chosen Rio's.

How many women let their men choose their wedding dresses for them?

Now, moments from walking down the aisle at the Graceland Wedding Chapel on Las Vegas Boulevard, Rio and

I stood side by side in the dresses that had been waiting for our arrival, staring at our reflections in the bridal suite's full-length mirror.

And honestly, our men had nailed our style. We suspected they must have had help, either from Abbi or Agatha, and possibly even Carmen, because that man had more style in his pinky than most men did in their entire being.

Rio's dress was ideally suited for her tiny frame and fit her personality perfectly too. It reminded me of something from the 1960s, and if it weren't a wedding dress, she could've pulled it off with a pair of knee-high go-go boots and hit one of the hotels that housed a high-end night club. It was a slim trapeze-style dress with one inverted box pleat up the center in the front and finished with a huge bow at the neck in the back. The hem was just above the knee, giving the tiny bride some added visual height. Overall, the details were few but dramatic and completely fit the woman's personality. We both loved everything about it.

Since it was a second marriage for her, Grant chose a custard color rather than pure white, and a little pillbox hat and birdcage veil that matched perfectly. With her pixie haircut, it was a stunning look.

Of course, all these men were cut from the same cloth, so both our grooms included lingerie and shoes to their exacting standards. Rio and I rolled our eyes and then giggled madly as we unpacked our treasures. I couldn't speak for her, but I truly felt like a queen being treated so caringly and lovingly with every detail handled for me.

I gasped when I pulled my dress from its nesting. And then promptly burst into tears.

"Oh no, you don't," Rio said and began urgently fanning

my face. "You're going to have to fix your makeup, and we don't have time for all that. Seriously, stop," she gently instructed and then got a bit more aggressive when it didn't look like I was heeding her advice quickly enough.

"You're going to look like you're doing the walk of shame instead of walking down the aisle. Come on, now, pull it together," she said more forcefully.

"I know, I know," I said. "These fucking hormones are already running me up and down the flagpole."

My dear friend did her best impression of my soon-to-be husband and let her head fall to one side. She studied me through squinted eyes and said, "Hormones? Already? Hannah Farsey, what haven't you told me, you little cow?"

Biting my lip only worked for a nanosecond to stifle my grin. The damn thing quickly split my face, and her expression soon mirrored mine. For as much as Grant had done to help her learn healthier ways to deal with her emotions, the woman still wasn't a hugger the way I naturally was, so I was completely taken off guard when her spindly but surprisingly strong arms all but strangled me in a joyous hug.

"Oh my God, Hannah Banana! I'm going to be an auntie? When did you find out? How far along are you? It can't be that far. I mean, I just saw you put on that sexy-as-hell lingerie, and your body is totally kickin'."

My sputtered answer came between laughing at her comment and giggling from being so overjoyed. It felt so amazing to share the news and not worry about being judged or fear letting anyone down.

"I just took the test last night. I haven't been feeling well for a few days." I waved my hand through the air. "Well, since my birthday, really, but I brushed it off, thinking maybe I'd partied too hard or stayed up too late."

"But you barely drank that night, from what I remember, right? I mean, I know it was only a couple of days ago, but shit, the way things have been going lately ..." She cradled her face beneath her sweet little veil and shook her head. "Jesus, it seems like three weeks."

We both got lost for a moment, thinking about the crazy pace we'd been keeping, and for me, the whirlwind my life had become since moving in with Elijah.

A knock at the door made us both refocus with a start.

"Yeah?" Rio shouted manically.

"It's Abbigail," my other boss and friend answered softly.

Quickly, Rio whispered, "Is this public knowledge? Are you guys going to wait to tell people until the second trimester?"

"Oh, I doubt it. My guess is that bossy man of mine is out on the strip right now, passing out flyers alongside the porn distributors and panhandlers."

Rio spurted a laugh, and while the comment was meant to be a joke, Elijah was so excited about the news, I wouldn't play the odds against it happening.

Abbi gasped and instantly fluttered hands to her mouth when she saw the two brides before her.

"Look at the two of you. Oh, wow. Just ... wow, you guys. These dresses are stunning and so perfect on. I'm so glad they fit. What do you think? Do you like them?"

Her enormous green eyes were welling with tears, and Rio and I beamed at her.

I rushed to her and wrapped her in a warm hug, and she rocked me gently in the embrace. Fortunately, I kept the waterworks in check by thinking unpleasant thoughts instead of soaking in the abundance of love rolling off the fellow mama in my arms. We were a hot hormonal mess between the two of us, and it dawned on me that Abbi would be so helpful as a mentor as I went on this journey as a first timer.

"Guess whaa-aat?" Rio sing-songed the inquiry like a bratty little sister. I had so many of them, I recognized the sound of a troublemaker when I heard one.

I spun around and widened my eyes at the little menace, and she widened hers right back along with a sly grin.

Sheesh, wouldn't I get to be the one to spread my own good news?

There was no way I said that last question out loud, but after Abbigail took the bait, Rio followed up with the most random factoid about the chapel we were about to be married in.

"Did you know Elvis really came to this place one time? I think Grant said in the sixties or something." She rolled her eyes dramatically and continued, "Oh my God, last night he was reading off the website like it was the most exciting thing he'd read in years. I think I dozed off somewhere in the middle of it, though."

Abbi and I both giggled while she told her tale, and then I added, "Elijah was much the same. They're like big kids, those two."

"I have to admit, I'm a bit jealous." Abbi lowered into one of the stuffed comfy chairs while woefully letting that admission escape.

Rio and I looked at each other before focusing on her.

My two employers' reconciliation was still pretty fresh. Especially in proportion to the relationship their emotional explosion upended in the first place. Every controversial conversation felt like playing Russian roulette—even to bystanders. On numerous occasions, I caught myself holding my breath when I overheard them talking, just praying the discussion wouldn't escalate into a full-blown battle.

But like I was experiencing with my beautiful husband-to-be, when two strong personalities came to the table, milk was sometimes spilled.

Once again recentering on the conversation in the room instead of my own thoughts, I quickly picked up on my friends' conversation.

Abbigail sat forward on the white upholstered chair and straightened the hem of her flowy dress. "I'm sure I'm worrying over nothing. You know how I can get up in my own head."

Rio made a soft splutter and sympathized, "Something I can completely relate to. But think about it. You've seen him interact and play with Vela as long as you've known him. I'm sure they laugh and have fun, right?"

Okay, so I had missed a key detail while I was strolling through their history. Did the great Sebastian Shark have a flaw after all? And was his woman committing the ultimate betrayal by spilling all the tea about it?

There was another knock on the door, and we turned our heads to see the chapel's ceremony coordinator, Lynn, poke her head inside.

"Are we ready? Just five minutes." She smiled sweetly. "You girls look breathtaking." Panic changed her facial features first, but then she rushed inside and closed the door and leaned against it. She whipped through her paperwork while muttering sentiments I couldn't hear, being the farthest away.

"I only have two weddings scheduled for this group. Is

that still correct? Is there a commitment ceremony along with one?" She scanned the three of us, and Rio was the first to understand what she was asking.

"No," she answered with a grin. "It's just us." She pointed between us and then thumbed over to Abbigail. "She's already hitched, and her husband wouldn't share his ballpoint pen, let alone his wife." Playfully, Rio gave her former sister-in-law an exaggerated wink so a tense standoff didn't ensue from her jab.

"I'm going to go get your handsome men in position and then come back for you. If you have to pee one last time, fix your lipstick"—she waved her hand through the air—"or whatever...now's the time. Okay?" She bounced her gaze from my pixie-sized boss to me before giving a reassuring nod. The woman darted from the room as quickly as she had arrived, humming "Viva Las Vegas" as she went.

Great balls of fire, this is really happening.

And yes, I knew that was Jerry Lee Lewis, not Elvis, but it was the same era at least. Both songs were well before my time, so I had to get credit for even knowing them in the first place, let alone working them into a joke to calm my nerves. Even if I were the only one privy to the funny comment.

I checked my reflection one last time. The dress Elijah chose for me was an exquisite A-line style that hit just above the knee. Simple flowers cut from the same stiff material as the dress were sewn in a cascade from the high band collar down the full length of the dress until there were just a few scattered around the hem. Like in nature, each flower was unique in size and shape, and more than one layer had small pearls sewn in the center to hold the pieces together as well as secure the entire flower to the dress.

Turning, I found two sets of tearful eyes studying me.

I realized I was subconsciously caressing my flat belly and quickly moved to wring my hands instead, like I often did when I was nervous.

Both women were openly smiling at that point, and Abbigail was the first one to break the silence. "So, he was right?"

Rio elbowed her in the ribs, and together, Mrs. Shark and I both said, "What?"

I guessed Abbi's was the one-word stand-in for *What was that for?* based on the look she was spearing Rio with. Whereas mine was shorthand for *What are you talking about?* No doubt they could discern that by my screwed-up face of confusion.

"Ladies." Lynn ducked her head in after a fast knock on the door and saved my friends from having to explain why they both looked so guilty.

Hmmm. Definitely coming back to that one.

The woman did a visual lap around our group and plowed ahead. Probably thinking one of us was getting jitters and not about to play into it.

"It's time. You both look beautiful. Sweetie, do you have a veil?"

I looked left and then right, as if I had been holding it and set it down. A nervous giggle bubbled out, and I just shook my head. But really, I couldn't remember if I had seen one in the garment bag, either. Regardless, it was too late because I didn't want to be the one to hold up the process. My hair was in a half-up, half-down style and curled into full waves, so there was already enough going on between that and the detail on the dress.

"Let's just do this. I don't want to forever be known as the girl who was late for her own wedding," I said through tight lips, trying to force a smile now that my anxiety was really kicking in.

Abbigail gave us both one last squeeze and hurried out to join Sebastian. Since Rio and I both suffered from anxiety, we couldn't decide who should walk down the aisle first. So, this morning at breakfast, the boys had arm-wrestled for the right to pick for us. At the last minute, someone threw in the caveat that the brides had to straddle their groom's lap to distract them during the match. The whole thing had been quite entertaining.

Every member of that posse should have known, however, just how focused my man could be when determined. After he'd pinned Grant's hand to the poolside table, he stood with me still in his arms, strode across the deck, and jumped into the deep end of the private pool we were all sharing. He took those few seconds to confirm his hunch that I'd like to go second and shouted that declaration before we hit the water.

This man. My man. Life would never be dull. I knew that with every beat of my heart.

Now, I was being corralled into a holding room off the main hall. There, I caught most of the service on closed-circuit television in between rehearsing the short vows I wanted to say to Elijah.

Since Rio didn't have a close relationship with her parents, she hadn't even called them to tell them she was getting remarried. She'd said she'd touch base with them sometime next week.

I couldn't imagine being that removed from my family, but I knew not all were as close as the Farsey crew.

My beautiful bestie walked herself down the aisle and into the arms of the man who adored her. Their ceremony went quick, and within fifteen minutes, they were sharing their first kiss as husband and wife. Elvis escorted them back down the aisle, singing one of the King of Rock's best-known songs.

With a knock on the door, Lynn was back to usher me to my starting point for the short walk down the aisle. But when we rounded the corner into the reception area, I heard a familiar gasp and then a throat being cleared.

I shot my stare from the ground where I was carefully mapping each step so as to not face-plant in the impossibly high heels my groom had picked for me to wear. When I focused on the stoic man dressed so handsomely in the same dark-gray tuxedo Grant, Elijah, and their best man Sebastian were wearing, I was certain my mind and heart were playing a cruel trick on me.

"Daddy?" I looked around the empty lobby. Was this another look-alike actor? Was I set up by this trick-playing crew I traveled across state lines with?

"Hannah, you look so beautiful." He beamed with fatherly pride.

"What . . . How . . . When did you get here?"

We hugged after I finally settled on one full question. For a long moment, I just soaked up the love and calm reassurance that came with being in his arms. When we parted, I pressed beneath my eyes to hold back the tears.

"Is Mom here too?"

His broad smile continued to calm me. "Of course she is. And all your sisters, too. We wouldn't have missed it for the world. Elijah called last night and insisted on sending a plane. We all flew out this morning."

"He did what?"

"He called to ask for my blessing, then asked if we could

make it for the ceremony. Although this isn't what we would've preferred for your special day..." He looked around the worn-out facility with a bit of a frown but quickly let go of the judgment.

"You know we wouldn't be anywhere else. But right now"—my dad gestured toward the closed chapel doors with his chin—"everyone's probably thinking I'm trying to talk some sense into you back here." His sly grin couldn't be contained, and he peeked out from beneath hopefully raised brows. "Any chance of that?"

"Dad!" I smacked his arm playfully but got serious with my next comment. "I love him more than I thought it possible to love someone. I want to marry him."

"Fair enough. Let's get you up there, then. What do you say?" He made a pointed show of looking around the back side of my body. "No veil?"

"Elijah picked everything out since this was all a bit of a surprise," I said and got away with that short explanation because Lynn reappeared to confirm we were ready.

I whispered one last time, "You're really okay with this?"

"If it's what you want, baby, then yes. He's a good man, and he loves you. That's all your mother and I could ever want for our girls."

"He is a good man, Dad. The best, actually." I smiled up at the original man of my dreams and gave a solid nod. "Let's do this!"

The first few notes of "Love Me Tender" played, and I took a deep breath.

This was one moment of so many from this day that I wanted to file away for safekeeping. When we got back to California, I'd pull them out like treasured souvenirs while I told friends and family about how incredible the whole surprise was. I'd show pictures and undoubtedly cry and recount every detail I could remember.

Years down the road, when my husband and I talked about the day we got married, our children would giggle when we told them that Mommy was already pregnant with one of them on our special day but we kept the secret just between us. They would love that one of them was our very special little wedding guest and that it wasn't until months later when my belly started getting round that we spilled the beans.

My heart quickened when I saw him standing at the low altar. But that wasn't unique to the occasion. It was the man who affected me that way. Elijah was breathtaking in his tuxedo, and his potent sage stare was filled with adoration. I floated down the short aisle to him, thankful to have my father's arm as an anchor. Otherwise, I might have drifted off into the clouds, my heart and soul were so buoyantly happy.

This whole trip had started out as one big shit show, but my soon-to-be husband really did everything he could to ensure it was the wedding of my dreams. I still wondered how I captured this incredible man's attention in the first place.

In front of our family—both the people who were blood related and those we chose to love through friendship and circumstance—Elijah and I vowed to love each other unconditionally and completely, regardless of the obstacles life put in our path.

We acknowledged there would be good times and bad times, too. No matter what the case, we'd show up for it, and we'd put in the work necessary to keep our home a happy, safe place and always full of love.

After we exchanged rings, Elijah bent me back over his

arm and sealed the deal with an extremely inappropriate kiss—especially given my parents were seated in the very first pew watching the whole thing.

The endorphin rush from that one kiss was enough to have me considering running back to Malibu on foot right then and getting our life started as man and wife. I mean, why wait?

The stifling heat still baking right outside the building's old wooden doors was a fast reminder why. The temperature variance between outside and inside was enough to shock my system back to reality.

Four of our hotel's town cars waited for our party in the venue's parking lot. The lead vehicle was designated for the newly married couples with a large *Just Married* sign, streamers, and empty tin cans tied securely to the back bumper. Elijah filed in right behind me, followed by the Twombleys. Sebastian and Abbigail rode with us as well so the three guys could share the special day.

My red-haired boss already had a round swell to her abdomen, and her new husband couldn't keep his hands off her belly. Honestly, no one would've noticed the way her body was changing, but his constant stroking and petting her was calling more attention to it. It was adorable to see the bossy man reduced to such a pile of gooey protectiveness, and the infant wasn't even the size of an avocado yet.

I had a feeling I was getting a preview of what I was in for myself. And I totally couldn't wait.

Elijah pulled me closer with an arm around my shoulders, and I smiled up at him. He leaned closer to my ear, and his warm breath skittered over the sensitive skin there.

"I love you, wife."

My smile grew wider just hearing him call me that. It

reminded me that I had a question for Rio, but with Abbi in the car too, I decided to wait.

I was curious if she was taking Grant's last name. My friend had a strong, fierce, and independent side, but she also completely relied on her new husband for so many things to survive this sometimes fucked-up thing called life. I wasn't sure which side of the betting line she'd come down on. Elijah might already have insight on the topic, as he so often did where his best friends were concerned, so I'd have to get his input when we were alone.

"What are you thinking about so intensely, beautiful?" he asked, looking like he already knew it had something to do with him.

"Quantum physics," I said through a grin, and as my playful man dug his fingers into my side, I squealed.

"Christ, not you too." Grant laughed and poked his index finger into his ear. "I just regained my hearing after this one blew out my ear drum with a similar screech."

"You bring it on yourself when you dig those long twig fingers into my ribs." Rio smacked lovingly at his chest.

"Woman, what have I told you about hitting me?" Grant asked in a serious voice.

"That you love when I rough you up a bit?" Mischief sparkled in her caramel irises.

Abbi snickered behind her hand.

Bas raised one brow in her direction, and she immediately went serious again.

Grant and Elijah both pointed at her at the exact same time and then looked at Rio and me. Only Elijah was foolish enough to comment, though.

"You see that? The pair of you could learn a thing or two."

As if we were a well-rehearsed female chorus of incredulity, the three of us hitched up our replies, "Pardon me?"

Bas came to his defense. "Okay, no killing the man on his wedding night. There must be a law against that."

Our shared villa came into view through the car's tinted windows. We had a few hours here before we were all meeting for our reception dinner in one of the award-winning restaurants in the main casino. The men were also looking forward to a few hands of poker after the meal.

"Perfect timing," I said a bit gleefully when the car came to a stop. For one thing, I was ready to share some alone time with my new husband. For another, if he made one more comment like the one he just had, it wouldn't be me defending him from the indefensible.

CHAPTER THIRTEEN

ELIJAH

She really was the most beautiful bride I'd ever seen. I tried to commit every moment to my memory so later I could spend some time writing it all down while she was getting ready for the rest of the evening.

Another dress waited for Hannah in the bathroom. Matching shoes and the jewelry I'd given her for her birthday completed the outfit for the dinner reception. As a second part of that surprise, I'd asked her sisters to come over and help her get ready. I thought she would enjoy spending time with them since they weren't able to be together for the first part of the day.

Although, now I was questioning my judgment on all the planning ahead. Because I didn't miss the hungry look she was giving me when we just walked in the door, and I was seconds from texting Agatha and delaying the sister squad by thirty minutes. That was all it would take to get my mouth on my new Mrs. to relieve some of the pent-up need I saw burning in her fiery stare.

"You keep looking at me like that, Mrs. Banks, and I'm going to bend you over this sofa and see how sexy that lingerie looks under this pretty dress," I warned her with a growl.

"You don't see me stopping you, do you? Here, I'll even

get you started," she said with a cheeky wink over her shoulder and began inching up her perfect wedding dress so I could see the tops of her thigh-high stockings and the straps of the garters holding them in place.

One purposeful stride and I was right behind her, yanking her dress up around her waist so I could see the whole ensemble at once. A masculine groan came all the way up from my balls as I greedily groped her ass and thighs.

"Jesus Christ, Hannah." With my flat palm on her shoulder blade, I bent her farther over the sofa. Instead of her usual protest, she quietly complied.

"Good. Such a good girl," I praised and dropped to a squat behind her. "Open more for me here." I tapped the inside of her ankle, and she widened her stance.

Smart girl finally figured out there were times to argue and there were times to just do what you were told.

Knowing I was on a time crunch, I pulled her lacy panties to the side and got right to work licking and nibbling her sweet pink folds.

"How's that, beautiful? Feel good?" I taunted. I knew damn well it felt good. I could hear her panting from my position on the floor. I needed to ramp her up fast and get her off quick, though.

"Yes, God, yes. So good, Elijah. Please don't stop."

"Will you come for me, baby, or will I have to spank it out of you?"

"No. No, I'll come. Please, just do what you're doing. Harder. More. Please."

"Harder?" Interesting request, and I wasn't quite sure what she meant, so I'd leave it to my own interpretation. I bit into her entire clit and held it gently between my teeth while fluttering over the whole bundle of flesh with my tongue.

"Oohh, my wife likes that," I took a moment to husk. "A lot, I'd say, if all this wetness is any indication," I commented to the open room like I was giving a demonstration to a lecture hall. I swept up the dew with two fingers and used it to plunge right into her pussy.

"Fuck!" Hannah cried out. "Christ, Elijah."

"Fuck *yes* or fuck *no*, baby? Tell me what you want. Let's get you off, beautiful. Give it to me, Hannah." While I was encouraging her, she thrust her hips back farther and swayed back and forth, taking her own pleasure on my hand. I was going to explode in my tuxedo pants if she kept it up.

I needed to have my mouth on her somewhere, and all the milky skin of her ass and thighs were right there in my face. While I continued to fuck her with my hand, I licked and bit her ass cheek, teasing a path along the white garter. Every time I got near her pussy, she inched her legs open wider, shamelessly inviting me to enjoy more of her.

In that husky, deep tone she took on when aroused, she moaned my name one last time and breathlessly stuttered she was about to climax.

"You're the sexiest fucking woman I've ever known, Hannah Banks," I praised and pulled her down to sit in my lap while she came down from her release. "You're gorgeous all flushed and satisfied." I brushed her hair back from her face and kissed her lips.

"Mmmm, thank you for that. You taste like me right now," she said and wrinkled her nose.

"And aren't you the most delicious thing you've ever tasted?" I said and kissed her again, this time really deepening the kiss.

She looked at me with sleepy eyes. "I want to take a nap, right here in your arms."

With perfect timing, what sounded like a football team knocked on our front door. Hannah shot up from my lap in a comical flurry of panic and began straightening her panties and garters, then looked to me for help.

"Just go into the bedroom. I'll see who it is."

"It's my sisters. I can already tell by that insane knocking," she said with a big smile.

"Go. Just holler when it's safe for them to come in."

She gave me a quick peck and wrinkled her nose again. "You better brush your teeth or something. You smell like sex."

She quickly turned and hustled toward the bedroom, but not before I pinched her sexy ass that was showing beneath the hiked up hem of her dress.

The girls banged on the door again, and I shouted, "Coming. Settle down." When I opened the door, four versions of my wife stood there grinning back at me, and it was almost eerie how much they all looked alike.

"Did we interrupt?" Agatha elbowed my stomach as she walked by, and I grinned.

"You've been hanging around the wrong guys. A gentleman doesn't kiss and tell," I teased back. "And watch the flying elbows, or I'll have Carmen take you in hand."

I couldn't see Carmen doing any such thing, and I think we both knew it. Judging by her next comment, I hit that nail on the head.

"Dude. Be serious." But she gave a quick glace around to her other sisters, and I picked up the subtle hint. Not here, not with the present company.

From back in the bedroom, Hannah called to her sisters,

and they all filed down the hall to the suite. Clemson hung back from the gaggle for a moment and scuffed at the floor a few times until she was sure the room was clear of her sisters.

"Hey, Clemson. Enjoying your trip so far?"

"Oh, yeah, it's great. This place is really something," she said, looking around awkwardly.

"Have you been to Vegas before?" I asked the youngest Farsey girl.

"Uhh, yeah. Once or twice for swimming. But that was an entirely different experience than this has been, you know?" She gave a shy smile, and I was pretty sure I'd never seen the expression on this sister's face before.

"What's going on, Clemson? You seem uneasy about something. I realize we don't know each other very well—yet." I slid a hopeful grin into place and immediately worried it could be misconstrued as flirtatious.

"It's probably dumb, but it's been bothering me since the day Dah—sorry, Agatha—and I came over to swim."

"Right, I remember that day. I'm so glad you guys came over. I think Hannah misses you guys more than she lets on to me." I thought about that for a few beats but realized Clemson was waiting to continue with what she wanted to discuss.

"Sorry. Please continue."

"Okay, so this woman showed up at your front door when it was just Hannah and me there. Dah hadn't arrived from work yet. Hannah checked a camera or something you have mounted at your front door." She shrugged. "I don't know, maybe it's all part of a more complicated security system you have?"

The girl was starting to look a little pale, and I wondered if I should go get Hannah. But Clemson was very careful to wait for her sisters to be out of earshot before she started telling me all of this.

"Like I said, I don't know, but I saw Hannah use an iPad in your kitchen to see who was at the door, and then she tapped out a few messages on the same device before she called me in from outside. She explained to me that it was an ex of yours and the woman had been causing trouble but not to worry about it—that your security team would be right around to take care of her."

I nodded along while Clemson told the tale. "I'm sorry you had to cross paths with that woman in any way, shape, or form."

"Well, you're really not going to like this, then. I haven't told anyone—not even Hannah or our parents."

"Let's hear it, Clemson. I don't want anything about that woman to ruin your sister's wedding day. Whatever you know about Hensley Pritchett, just tell me now and do it quickly before one of your other sisters comes out here looking for you."

The younger girl didn't flinch at my dominant mannerisms or find me too forceful or overbearing. If she did, she certainly had a great poker face.

"Our dad always says there are no coincidences in life. Before that day, I'd never seen that woman around anywhere. Since that day, I've probably seen her five times. Random places, but places it's odd someone I don't know from any other place keeps turning up, you know?"

"I don't think I'm following you one hundred percent, but it could be an age gap thing, admittedly." Usually, Hannah would be here to bridge the divide on things like this because I didn't always speak fluent teenager.

Clemson rolled her eyes and sat on the edge of the sofa cushion. The kid looked like she would spring up at the slightest sound from the back bedroom.

"So, this woman was at one of my swim meets. Why? It's not like she'd ever been to one before, and of course I've been swimming with the same girls for years, so I know whose family is whose. Also, I saw her walking a dog on our street. The woman looked so uncomfortable with the animal, it was almost comical. More like the dog was taking her for a walk, you know? I've never seen her on our block or any of the surrounding blocks. When I'm not swimming, part of my training is running. So I'm out on our neighborhood streets. I would've seen her before."

"Thank you for telling me this, Clemson. And I appreciate you telling me and not your parents. They wouldn't even know who the woman is, so telling them wouldn't make much sense."

"I've seen your security guys in the neighborhood, you know, following the family around," Hannah's youngest sister remarked. "Even though I'm sure they think they're doing a really great job staying in the shadows, I always know right where they are. None of my sisters have ever said anything to me, though, so I don't think they know they're being followed."

The young lady intrigued me more and more with each additional comment she made.

"Do you mind me asking you something personal, Clemson?"

I wanted to retract the question the moment it came out because I felt the air between us shift from casual and confident to guarded and awkward.

"How is it you've already become so aware and so vigilant at your age?" Hopefully she heard the admiration in my question.

"I'm not sure I know what you mean."

"Hannah's told me about the attempted abduction when she was a child—do you feel like that shaped your habits now too?"

Maybe I was stretching too far to connect things that weren't connected. The investigator portion of my mind wanted things to be linear.

"I guess I never gave it much thought, but yeah, probably. We've been reminded of that nightmare in one way or another every day of our lives. I wasn't even alive when it happened, and I feel like I lived through the incident so many times I've lost count..." She drifted off and thought for a minute or two.

Finally, in the most solemn tone I'd ever heard from this particular Farsey woman, she said, "So I think it's shaped all of us, whether we like to think it has or not."

The young girl stood up and gestured dusting her hands off by rubbing them together briskly. "Well, my work here is done. I'm not sure what you want to do with that information, but I felt like you were the guy who should have it. I don't want to see my sister in danger any more than you do. Don't be a stranger, brother." She gave me what I was mentally branding as her trademark saucy wink and headed toward the bedroom to join the rest of the sister squad.

Shit, if my life weren't exciting before, adding these five bombshells to the mix certainly would ensure it was about to be.

Our impromptu reception was set up in one of the casino's fine dining restaurants, where we had a private room reserved for the evening. After we enjoyed an extraordinary meal, the newlyweds took turns feeding their spouses cake for the photographer before the masterpiece was whisked away to be carved into pieces for everyone to enjoy.

Eventually, the tables were cleared and moved out of the room. In no time, our private dining room became a private poker room instead, and two dealers made their way into position. Most of the men quickly selected their positions, along with Hannah, Rio, Agatha, Clemson, and the Farsey matriarch, Lisa.

Bas leaned in and asked the men within earshot, "Why am I not surprised these are the poker-playing women?"

"They can't all be professional shoppers, Shark." Dave Farsey laughed into his drink, and the rest of the men joined in.

It was so refreshing to see a man not naturally cower to Sebastian. And sure, he might have heard of Bas—most people in the business world had. But the man was an accountant. He probably wasn't interested in the drama behind the lifelong rivalry with Viktor Blake or who was dumping dead bodies off the coast of Malaysia. As far as that second dumpster fire—that wasn't even public knowledge yet.

Grant extracted his face from his bride's neck long enough to make an offer to the table. "Who wants to get in on a little side action? Place your bet on the next baby Shark, boy or girl, and tie breaker will be guessing birthdate. When is she due, Bas?"

Sebastian's wide grin spoke a thousand words. "She's due February tenth."

Rio sat up suddenly, looking like she just thought of something. Grant noticed right away and asked her to discuss it with the group.

"I remember when Abbi was pregnant with Kaisan, she had such a strong intuition that he was a boy. Has she had that with this little one yet?"

Everyone's stare bounced from Rio back to Sebastian, and that proud smile split his face again. "She definitely has. But"—he held up his hand to stop the rising commotion—"she swore me to secrecy."

I did an intentionally terrible fake cough and said, "Pussy whipped."

He laughed fully then. "Damn straight I am. You'll see in no time. What do you think you're having?"

Fucking Sebastian. I heard the words coming out of his mouth, but similar to that old hag nightmare, I was paralyzed to do anything. I couldn't move to physically shut him up with, say, my fist, or talk over him so his words couldn't be heard by the people in the room who weren't in the know. I couldn't even breathe deep enough to just yell gibberish so all eyes would focus on me and his words would be forgotten.

Nope. Just froze. Froze and stared.

Thank God for Rio. There were words I never thought I'd say—or think. The little mischief-maker caught on to the situation faster than anyone else and tried to mop up Sebastian's spilled milk.

"When you guys have a baby. I'm sure that's what he meant. You know we've all been teasing so much that it's going to happen before you get home with the heat between the two of you!" Rio rambled in her nervous chirpy tone.

"Yeah—sorry, man. I guess that could be pretty awkward. Especially with Mom and Dad sitting right here," Bas said and thumped me on the back—really hard—to snap me out of the panic-induced trance I had sunken into.

That definitely did it, and I snapped my glare in his direction.

Sorry, he mouthed and winced. Well, shit. I couldn't

remember the man apologizing to me for anything. Ever.

"Oh, cut the shit, gentlemen." Lisa Farsey stood and spoke above the din. Everyone fell silent and looked in her direction. Talk about a queen holding court. It was almost comical the way she got the room to fall silent with one comment.

"We already know she's pregnant. Congratulations, by the way, you two. We can talk more about it when we get back to California. Right now, somebody deal me some cards!"

In my periphery, I saw Hannah leaning across to the other table and grabbing Agatha's hand. Yep...she was my first guess too, but I watched my wife kindly accuse her sister of spilling the baby beans and Agatha laughing while shaking her head no.

At least it was a friendly back-and-forth and no one was truly pissed off. I knew Hannah had really wanted to wait to tell everyone the news. Firstly, we were still adjusting to everything that was changing in our lives, and secondly, it was very early in the pregnancy and there was always a nagging feeling in the back of your mind and heart to not get too attached in case something went wrong.

Thoughts for a later time. Like my new mother-in-law so wisely stated, somebody deal me some cards. I had a poker game or five to win.

★ ★ ★

We tumbled into bed around two in the morning, both more exhausted than we could remember being. The day was filled with so many emotions—thankfully, all amazing ones—but now I felt like I'd been run over by a convoy of semis and just wanted to go to sleep.

By the time I came out from a quick shower, Hannah was already peacefully sleeping on her side of the bed.

The family was scheduled to fly home in the morning, and both newlywed couples and the Sharks the following day. This had been the longest period of time Grant, Bas, and I had all been away from the office at the same time, and we were sure we'd be coming back to more fires than could be put out with a few emails and conference calls.

The impromptu trip was worth every second I'd spend clearing the piles off my desk. Also, that was what I paid Carmen for.

But the next morning, as we assembled in the lobby to say goodbye to the Farsey clan, Carmen and Agatha were missing.

"When's the last time anyone saw them?" Lisa asked the group.

"We all went to the casino after you guys finished playing poker," Maye offered. "When was that?"

"That had to be around twelve thirty," Hannah supplied. "We stopped at that little café and had some tea before bed. My stomach hasn't been the best, so I thought it might help me sleep."

I pulled her closer and kissed her temple. "Boy did it. I think that's the best you've slept in weeks."

"Mmm, me too. I've been missing the waves, though." She smiled up at me.

"Do you want to go today?" I asked my bride. Anything to keep her happy. "I'm sure the pilot can make a quick turnaround. It's such a short flight."

"Let's find our missing sister first," Clemson reminded us with an annoyed glance my way. "I don't like the feeling I'm getting about this."

"Has anyone checked the cottages?" Shep asked, finally looking up from her phone. It might have been the third time the young woman spoke the entire trip.

"Sheppard, can you go do that, please?" Lisa asked. To her husband, she said, "Why don't you and I take a lap around the casino? If anyone finds them, text the group chat please."

"Elijah and I will wait here. Maybe they went to grab a bite to eat and lost track of time. That would totally be like her."

I waited until everyone split up to add my two cents. "But it's not like Carmen at all. That man is more punctual than I am. He's the one who keeps me on time. And why are both their phones ringing straight through to voicemail?"

My gut was starting to feel more and more like Clemson's. Especially every time I thought of how often she said she had seen my ex pop up around this family.

"I'm going to call Lorenzo and Marc to see if they can get a track on her from Malibu. I'm not sure how long range their systems are, but I think it should work." I gave Hannah a lingering kiss and said close to her ear, "Please stay right here with your sisters. Don't wander away unless you tell me. I'm going right outside that door so I can hear." I leaned back to make sure she was listening. "Okay, beautiful?"

"Yes, okay." She pecked my lips again and went to stand by her family.

Outside, I connected quickly to my team and asked them to track Agatha. I gave them her last known location, but they found her before I could finish talking.

"She's on property, coming up from south of your location. Looks like in a vehicle by how fast the target is moving."

"Oh, it's probably this cab coming up the access road. All right, thanks, guys. Sorry for the panic call. These bombs are going to make me crazy."

"Bombs?"

"Bombshells? Blond bombshells..." I chuckled. "There are too many of them to keep track of. We just started calling them the bombs for short."

Lorenzo chuckled on the other end of the line. "You just let me know if you need a hand with that, boss."

"Oh, for fuck's sake," I said and palmed my forehead when I saw Carmen and Agatha tumble out of the back of the cab.

"Everything okay?" Lorenzo asked.

"Uhh, no. Not even close. I have to go. Thanks again." I stabbed the *End* icon on the screen and shoved my phone in my back pocket while jogging across the porte cochere.

"What the fuck have you two done?" I asked with a mix of disbelief, horror, and humor whirling through my exhausted brain. Maybe I should hustle them off to their cottages and say they came back too drunk to make the flight.

"Look!" Agatha shouted while pointing in my direction.

Okay, so the drunk part wouldn't be a lie.

I reared back from the smell of her breath. "Jesus, girl. You smell like the worm at the bottom of a bottle of tequila."

"Oooh noooo, señor. *No digas la palabra tequila, por favor,*" she said without skipping a beat.

Baffled, I looked at Carmen—who was also very drunk—and he shrugged. "She speaks Spanish?"

I had my phone back in my hand and connected to my wife. She picked up after one ring.

"Hello, dear. Can you please come out front? Alone. Please come alone. I love you." I cut the call. She'd ask a million questions, and this picture really spoke for itself. I almost wanted to capture her reaction on video, but her emotions were still pretty volatile, so I decided against that.

The next time those automatic doors slid open, my gorgeous wife strode out into the desert heat like she was Isis herself. Just as I imagined it, the first eyeful she got was of her very drunk sister, propped up by her very drunk, brand-new brother-in-law.

"Agatha Christine! What have you done?" Hands flew up to her mouth, and her eyes immediately searched for me.

Well, that made me feel like the goddamn king of the world. Not going to lie about that.

"What have they done? My parents are going to freak out. Elijah! Fix this!"

I hopped back a little in surprise. "What do you mean *fix this*?"

"Do something. Make them get unmarried. They can't be like this in front of my parents. My dad will have another heart attack!" She was ramping up with every word, and her deep voice was doing unfair things to my body.

Always at the wrong time, man...

"Okay, first of all, you need to calm down for our baby inside your body. When you're stressed, our baby feels stressed. Come over here and sit down, and I'll go drag those two dipshits over here so we can figure out the details of their big day."

"You're right." She took an exaggerated calming breath. "Okay, you're right."

I doubled back the few steps I'd taken to warn Hannah about her sister's new bilingual status. "Also, apparently Agatha is flawlessly bilingual." I raised my eyebrows, expecting to be dropping a bomb on one of the bombs, and she just cradled her face in her palms again.

"She must really be shitfaced. That only comes out when she's hammered."

"Why am I just hearing about this now?"

"About what? That she's an irresponsible drunk?" Hannah laughed. "I have to tell the family we found them."

"No, that she's bilingual."

"I don't know. It never came up, I guess? Oh, shit, another car is coming. Go get them out of the road. They're actually sitting down."

As I hustled across the driveway to get the two lovebirds out of the way, I shouted to Hannah, "Text your family that we found them but are taking them back to their rooms since they are too drunk to make the flight. They will come back with us tomorrow."

Laughing at the sight of the couple, I helped them to their feet. Agatha had a cheap veil hanging from the side of her head by a few loose bobby pins, and the edge of the tulle was torn and had a lipstick stain.

"Let's try to get this off so you can save it in your memory box," I offered and motioned toward the headpiece. It was the most conspicuous part of their wedding attire, so I thought getting it off should be priority one.

"Oww! *Dios mio,* Elijah. *Me estas hacienda daño.*"

"Stop hurting my wife," Carmen mumbled from beside me.

"I'm not hurting her, dipshit. Why don't you help me, then? Get this thing off her head so you two aren't attracting so much attention. Although the T-shirts . . ."

They both looked down at their cheap Strip-souvenir-shop shirts and beamed with pride. His said *Groom* in bold black block letters, and hers said *Bride.* When they looked back to me, still sporting their big, cheesy grins, I just burst out laughing.

Holy shit. I could not wait for them to sober up, because the ribbing related to this fuckup was going to be endless.

"Okay, babe, you stay here and say goodbye to your family," I said to Hannah, "and I'm going to get Ricky and Lucy here to their cottages. Shit, I hope the keys still work. If not, I'll put them into ours until we can straighten everything out with the front desk. Please come straight back to the room, okay? No, you know what, I'm going to send Grant down to meet you. I don't want you wandering around alone."

"Elijah, stop with the mother-hen routine. My God. There are so many people here. Nothing's going to happen to me. Please just get them out of here."

"All right. I'm sure you're right. Please thank your parents for coming, and tell them we'll see them back in SoCal."

"Go," she ordered through a smile and one more kiss, and then we went our separate ways—Hannah to load her family into the waiting SUVs and me to get the newly married Carmen and Agatha behind closed doors to sleep off what was sure to be one hell of a hangover.

CHAPTER FOURTEEN

ELIJAH

When was the last time I started a workweek on a Wednesday? It was surreal logging into my desktop computer for the first time midweek, and maybe I'd already given that same fact a few laps around the track, but it was that rare of an occurrence, I couldn't stop marveling at how different it felt.

Just a few minutes before we were meeting on the roof, I heard a commotion out by Carmen's desk. I put my computer to sleep with the intention of going straight to our gathering once I settled the problem outside my door.

Like a bad penny that kept turning up, there stood Hensley Pritchett arguing with my assistant.

"No, Ms. Pritchett, he does not want to see you. In fact, I'm under strict instruction to call security if you show up in this building. It baffles me how you keep getting up to this floor." Carmen was on his feet with his desk phone in one hand and dialing with the other.

Since I'd yet to be discovered, I leaned back against my doorframe and watched the drama unfold.

"Carmen. It's Carmen, right? Why don't you just let me inside Mr. Banks's office, and I'll wait for him quietly in there? No one has to know." The little tramp leaned over his desk so her cleavage was right in his face and purred, "It can be our little secret."

I'd already seen more than I could stomach.

"First of all, I don't think his wife would appreciate your tits in his face the way they are, so back up. Secondly, he told you I don't want to see you, and he's correct. Third, you have a restraining order, and you're violating it. Again. I hope you go to jail this time. No, wait." I held up my index finger as though I'd been struck with the best idea all week.

"I'm going to have my attorney *ensure* that you go to jail this time. Also, if I hear that you are lurking around my wife's family, their neighborhood, her sister's high school, places they eat regularly, or anything similar? I'm going to press stalking charges. I don't know what's going on with you, but you need to get a grip. Get a life. I'm a married man with a child on the way. You and I are over. We've been over for a long time. You made sure of that. Now run along. Oh, look! Here's security to see to it. Bye now."

Without looking back, I made my way to the elevator to go to the roof and unwind with my two best friends. It took several attempts to get the card reader to recognize my identification, though, because I was trembling so badly. Starting out the day with Scotch instead of coffee was probably a bad habit to get into, but damn it, if ever there was a morning where it sounded justifiable, this was it.

Bas and Grant weren't on the roof yet, so I took a lap around the perimeter and enjoyed the fresh air. This was a much better way to calm down than throwing back shots anyway. Lots of deep breaths, pleasant thoughts, and positive affirmations set my mind back on the right trajectory. On the second lap, I heard the stainless-steel elevator doors slide open, and the tall guy with the big grin and the serious guy with the permanently stern expression stepped off the lift.

"Good morning, gentlemen," I said to my buddies. "How is the first day back looking for you two so far?"

Predictably, Grant went to make himself a cup of coffee, and Sebastian strolled to the refrigerator beneath the island and grabbed two bottles of water.

He stood up tall and looked to Grant. "Do you want water, big boy?"

"Nah, I'm just going to stick with the jet fuel this morning. Had a shitty night's sleep."

"Nightmares?" I asked and watched Grant carefully. I noticed in the past, he had been tempted to not be honest—or at least sugarcoat the answer.

"Yeah. I hate them. That's just the bottom line. I hate them. I hate having them. I hate how I feel right after having them. I even hate this bullshit the next day, you know? Dragging my ass all day and constantly having to think of why. And yes, before you ask," he said, holding up his hand to stop me even though I hadn't said a word, "I have an appointment with my therapist. But that was already on the books."

"Can you pinpoint anything that triggers it? Are you still keeping a dream journal?"

"Do you hear this fucking conversation we're having right now?" He looked at me and grinned. "We used to reminisce about the chick we fucked the night before. Now we're talking about dream journals, for Christ's sake."

Grant sat down with a heavy sigh, but it was Bas who reminded him, "You didn't answer the question. Can you pinpoint a common factor that's setting them off?"

Before answering, Grant slowly turned in Shark's direction to level him with a dirty look. Not that it even fazed Sebastian, so he went on. "The only thing I've noticed is when my sleeping location is interrupted. And isn't that ironic? I used to move around from property to property and it was no big deal. I preferred it that way." Grant laughed. "Obviously this bullshit wasn't a part of my life back then, but since we were away for a few nights in Las Vegas and then came back home... That changeup—maybe it had something to do with it. I don't fucking know."

"Well, it's worth mentioning to the doctor, right?" Bas asked.

"Doc says everything is worth mentioning to him. I shouldn't edit details out. Just because I think they aren't important doesn't mean they aren't. So I've been trying to get better at that. And as much as I joke about it, writing stuff down as soon as I wake up and calm down, I write down what I can remember."

"Is it always the same stuff?"

"Yeah, mostly. Or one or two odd details change. But I keep hoping that one day, one of those things is going to be the thing that blows this wide open for me."

"What do you mean?" Bas asked.

"Like I'm going to realize I've seen one of these morons somewhere else before, or they said something in a conversation I overheard and forgot. I know I've told you before they were barely drugging me enough, so they talked freely around me, thinking I was wasted, but I wasn't."

We were all thoughtful for a minute or two. I wished I could take my friend's pain away. If there was a way, I would do it in a heartbeat.

Grant sat up taller. "Enough of that bullshit, though. Tell me something good. How is Abbi feeling? How's Hannah feeling? We've decided to try to join you guys in parenthood.

We're going to give it a few months of trying the regular way, and if I can't knock her up, we're going to see a fertility doctor."

I sprang to my feet, and so did Grant. He and I were the huggers of the trio, so I gave my best friend a solid hug and clapped him on the back a few times.

"Dude! Congratulations! That's awesome to hear! Can I share that with Han? Oh my God, she's going to be over the moon."

I stepped aside so Bas could congratulate Grant too. They did the handshake-shoulder-smack combo that non-hugging men did, and Sebastian commented, "Great news, man. Abbi is going to be thrilled for you both. And once she figures out that all three of us can have children of the same age, she will be so excited. Having come from a large family, she loves that shit."

Grant addressed my earlier question. "I think Rio will probably tell Hannah at the kitchen, but if she hasn't by the time you see her after work, I'm sure she wouldn't mind if Hannah knew. She's pretty excited. Without prying, because honestly, I just don't want to talk or know about her dead husband's junk, you know? I'm not sure if it was his issue or hers, or if they ever knew what the problem was. I think it was the former, but like I'm saying, I just don't want to pry or really know unless it ends up I have to."

"Makes sense to me." I nodded along while he explained.

Bas did much the same.

"So, guys, I got a big problem with Hensley Pritchett."

"Yeah, we tried telling you that eight years ago," Bas said in a dull tone.

"No, I'm serious. When we were in Vegas, I had a very interesting conversation with Clemson. Maybe not interesting as much as enlightening or informative? I don't know—

disturbing probably covers the whole discussion best." I massaged the sore muscles in my forehead. So much tension had gathered there from scowling.

"Remind me again," Grant started, "Clemson is—"

"The baby bomb," I said matter-of-factly.

He nodded at once, and I went on with recounting what she had told me.

"This morning, just before I came up here, Hensley was trying to get into my office again. I don't know how she keeps getting past security, and I hate to fire good men over that she-devil, but I think examples have to be made this time."

"Plus, don't you have a restraining order? What good are those things if the person just comes near you anyway?" Grant asked.

Shark laughed. "This city's police department has been a joke when it comes to protecting its citizens. Look at all the shit I've been through, and where have they been? But boy, give them an opportunity to point the finger when the media is looking, and they're right there, posing for the cameras."

I winced because I hated discrediting law enforcement in any way. It was a difficult job, and there were so many politics at play behind the scenes. Granted, Bas seemed to have landed on somebody's naughty list down at headquarters. That skeleton had yet to fall out of the closet, but one day it would, surely at the most inconvenient time, too.

"So, I'm just trying to figure out what to do. Maybe I should just meet with her once and for all. Find out what the fuck she wants so she goes away. Why is she being so persistent? This can't be a torch she's carrying for me. You've seen the woman. She can't be having problems picking up a man. That's not what this is."

"I'll tell you what this is," Grant said without missing a fraction of a beat. "For once, you are not pining for her. You've moved on, and she can't stand it. She's the kind of woman who collects men like trophies. It's a control thing. She wants to control when it ends. And not just when but also how it ends—and where. When she lets you go completely. Until then, she likes to keep you squirming on her hook. But you cut bait, and she doesn't like it one bit. The more uninterested you seem... it's my guess"—he finally paused for a breath and a shrug—"the more desperate her attempts at earning an audience with you will become."

Sebastian and I just stared at Grant until he grinned and said, "What?" But even though he looked boyish and innocent while asking it, he knew damn well why we both eyed him so curiously. He just wanted one or both of us to stroke his ego a bit.

Fine. I'd give him the credit he deserved on this one. "When did you get so wise in the ways of womankind?"

"Shit! Speaking of womankind," Bas fretted and jammed his phone back into his pocket. "Pia is going to be here for a meeting with Jacob Cole in about ten minutes. I need to get my ass downstairs. I don't need a dressing down in front of junior." He snatched up the empty water bottles and threw them in the recycling bin so we left our meeting space as tidy as we found it.

"No kidding," I said.

"She wouldn't hold back, either," Bas added about the sibling he adored.

In the elevator, I agreed to keep them posted about whatever security plan I decided on regarding Hensley. I didn't think she was much of a threat, necessarily, but with everything else that had gone on recently, we didn't need additional problems.

Grant and I didn't need to sit in on the meeting with Jacob and Pia but privately agreed it would be fun to see the two finally meet in person. They'd been working together for a while, but schedule conflicts had kept them from a face-to-face meeting up to this point. Now, we were like a bunch of nosy big brothers on her first date, hoping there might be some sort of spark between the two.

Pia was already waiting for Sebastian in his office and had a bunch of sketches laid out on the conference room table. We all got a pint-sized surprise when we came through the door, though, when our favorite little lady was along with her mom for the meeting.

"Uncles!" Vela shouted and bounded up from where she'd been working on schoolwork at the table, where we all usually sat for morning coffee. Well, before we started meeting on the roof. Now, those old favorite black leather sofas barely saw any action.

"Hey, pretty lady!" I said and swept her up into my arms for a hello hug. "My goodness, you're almost too big for me to lift anymore. What will I do then?"

"You're going to have to start swimming harder, Uncle Lijah, if you can't lift me anymore." She narrowed her eyes and poked my chest with her little finger. "You still feel hard everywhere. Are you teasing me again?"

"Yes, darling, I'm teasing you. But you're definitely getting bigger."

"Let me be the judge," Grant said and held his arms open for her to climb into.

"Oh my God, you boys spoil this girl something terrible.

She climbs all over your good clothes like a monkey."

"Oh, Dub, just let them get their practice in now. They're going to need it." The bastard couldn't wipe the grin off his face if someone paid him.

"Wait. What's this?" Pia's grin lifted with her tone as she volleyed her gaze between the three of us.

"Well, shit, Bas. Why not just tell her all my news?" I laughed but realized I just swore in front of Vela. "Sorry, baby." I kissed the back of her head since Grant was still being a niece hog and wouldn't give her back.

"Uncle Lijah, is Miss Hannah having a baby?"

My God, this child had melted my heart from the day she was born. All our hearts. She was the only human gifted with the privilege of calling me anything other than my God-given name, and when she stared at me with those enormous and innocent blue eyes, I thought this was what fatherhood would be like. Only fifty million times better.

"Well, guess what?" Now I rounded my tall buddy and took our little one from his embrace whether he liked it or not.

"What?" Vela asked excitedly.

"Hannah and I got married this past weekend, so you can call her Auntie If that's okay with Mama?"

Pia rushed over and gave Vela and me a big group hug. "I'm so happy for you, Elijah. Finally, someone captured that generous, beautiful heart. You make sure she treats you like the treasure you are, or she'll have me to answer to."

"And me!" Vela interjected with her little hands balled on her hips.

"But what's this about a baby?" Pia asked, eyes dancing with joy like her brother's when he was truly happy.

"Hannah's pregnant. Very early days. We have our first appointment on Friday."

"Double great news!" Pia exclaimed and hugged me, holding her daughter again.

"Another new cousin, Mama?" the young girl asked to be sure.

"Yes! Isn't this a great day?" Pia focused on her daughter for a moment.

"But wait, there's more ..." I said and motioned to Grant with my chin since he had very patiently waited his turn.

"Rio and I also got married this weekend," he said proudly.

"Oh my God! You guys!! I'm so happy for you. But I'm a little pissed now. Because you robbed me of all this amazing wedding planning!" She laughed and blotted the corners of her eyes after stretching up to hug Grant and hold his face between her palms. "I'm over the moon happy for you."

Pia took both our hands. "I've loved you both like you were my own brothers for our entire lives. You've helped me raise this little miracle when it was just the five of us. There were more times than I can count that I wouldn't have survived without you in my life. I wish all the happiness in the world for each of you. I love you both."

"Thanks, Pia. I love you too," Grant said and beamed at her through shining eyes.

"Thank you, sweetheart. I love you." I gave her another squeeze and saw Craig open the door for Jacob Cole over her shoulder.

Ooohh, way to ruin a moment, office worker.

"Hey, Jacob, how's it going?" Bas greeted the architect. "Sorry about all this. Grant and Elijah were just sharing some great news with my sister and niece."

Our emotional circle opened up to become a receiving line of sorts so Bas could finally properly introduce Jacob and

Pia. I let Vela slide to her own feet, and she went to stand by her mother.

But something was terribly wrong. All the color had drained from Cassiopeia's face in those twenty seconds, and the air in the room was so still, a cricket could hear a silk thread drop. Even the eight-year-old—or hell, was she nine now?—who normally couldn't sit still to save her life, didn't move an eyelash.

Finally—thank God—finally, Pia tilted her head a bit. Maybe she wasn't understanding... or believing what she was seeing.

"Jack?"

Jacob had a similar reaction, but he sneaked a quick peek to Bas too before rounding back to Pia.

"Cass?"

Moving out from behind her mother, Vela took a few confident steps forward and studied the man before pointing right at him. In an unwavering voice—and likely the only steady one in the room at the moment—the little girl stated plainly, "You're my daddy."

ALSO BY VICTORIA BLUE

Shark's Edge Series:
(with Angel Payne)
Shark's Edge
Shark's Pride
Shark's Rise
Grant's Heat
Grant's Flame
Grant's Blaze

★

Elijah's Whim
Elijah's Want
Elijah's Need
Jacob's Star

Misadventures:
Misadventures with a Book Boyfriend
Misadventures at City Hall

Secrets of Stone Series:
(with Angel Payne)
No Prince Charming
No More Masquerade
No Perfect Princess
No Magic Moment
No Lucky Number
No Simple Sacrifice
No Broken Bond
No White Knight
No Longer Lost

**For a full list of Victoria's other titles,
visit her at VictoriaBlue.com**

ACKNOWLEDGMENTS

Big, enthusiastic thanks to all the amazing readers who continue to support this series. Every member of my online group, Victoria's Book Secrets, is so special and important to my heart and my drive to continue hitting the keyboard. Very special thanks to Megan and Amy for keeping all the wheels turning, and to Faith for all the amazing pictures and design prowess. As always, thank you to Scott Saunders, the absolute best editor on the planet, and to all the members of the Waterhouse Press team for the continual support of this project. I'm beyond grateful. Last but not least, thank you, Ms. Angel Payne, for the countless sprinting hours and for your enduring friendship.

 XOXO VB

ABOUT VICTORIA BLUE

International bestselling author Victoria Blue lives in her own portion of the galaxy known as Southern California. There, she finds the love and life-sustaining power of one amazing sun, two unique and awe-inspiring planets, and four indifferent yet comforting moons. Life is fantastic and challenging and every day brings new adventures to be discovered. She looks forward to seeing what's next!

Visit her at VictoriaBlue.com